CACTIZONIANS' TREASURE

A Novel by:

BART AMBROSE

CACTIZONIANS'

TREASURE

BART AMBROSE

Aim-Hi Publishing, LLC
1542 Lakeside Dr. W.
Canyon Lake, Tx 78133

Aim-Hi Publishing
1542 Lakeside Dr. West
Canyon Lake, Texas 78133

Publisher's Catalog-in-Publication Data
Names: Ambrose, Bart, 1946 - ;
Title: Cactizonians' Treasure / by Bart Ambrose
Description: Aim-Hi Publishing LLC, 2021. | Summary: Two friends working for the CCC in 1934 discover a stash of gold in a cave from an old train robbery. They devise a plan to recover the gold and keep if for themselves.
Identifiers:
Library of Congress Control Number: 2021924317

ISBN 978-1-7321131-2-3 (Mass Market Paperback)

Subjects: Mystery – Fiction. | Treasure hunting – Fiction. | Old West – Fiction. | Train robbers– Action – Adventure – Arizona – Fiction:.Caves

First Printing: December 2021

PROLOGUE

ARIZONA, 1887

"Kid" Smith was fed up. Fed up with the gloom and oppressive blackness of the cave, the constant pungent odor of bat crap, and being stuck there with the other members of "Doc" Smart's gang. It was nothing like what he had always dreamed his life as an outlaw would be.

The gang teased him relentlessly about his age. He sulked and went off by himself when one of the older men asked him if his mother had actually weaned him. Severe acne continued to plague him and, along with his babyface, made him an easy target for their teasing.

At nearly eighteen years old, he considered himself as much or more of a man than any of them. He dreamed of being a rich and famous outlaw, feared and admired by lesser folk. His outfit looked the part with a black shirt and a black felt cowboy hat. He topped off his outlaw look with a fancy tooled leather gun belt with a Colt .45 in the holster; he was anxious to use it if given an opportunity. Smart's gang out of El Paso gave him what he hoped would be a quick route to the wealth he thought he deserved.

Doc Smart was a wily, wiry man with leathery skin deeply tanned from a lifetime in the desert sun. He was a man of few words with piercing grey eyes that could pin a man like a bug on cardboard. Doc managed to avoid all but a few short stints in jail through most of his forty-five years. He expected the men in his gang to follow his orders without question; those that didn't weren't around long.

They had robbed the Southern Pacific's Sunset Express near Pantano, Arizona, for the second time in four months. The outlaws fired numerous shots after they stopped and boarded the train's engine. Amazingly, no one was hurt in either hold-up. The Wells Fargo Company used the trains' express cars to transport gold, silver, and other valuables; it made the shipments tempting targets. The only security for the rich cargo was a Wells Fargo 'messenger' or agent, who rode along inside the train car. The robbers had no difficulty convincing the agent to cooperate—they threatened to blow up the car with him in it if he didn't,

The cave had been their hideout after both robberies. It was about twenty miles east of Tucson in the foothills of the Rincon Mountains. Doc chose the cave to hide from the posse he knew would be in pursuit, and it had served them well after the first holdup. He expected it would do so again. It was an ideal hideout, a perfect place to stash their loot until the heat from the law cooled. The cave's passages were mainly unexplored.

There were many places among the dark stalagmites and crevices to hide their plunder.

The outlaws used emptied US mailbags from the train to carry their looted gold and silver. Doc placed them on a ledge inside a little crevice behind an outcropping of stalagmites. The deep shadow hid the spot from their lanterns' light. He marked the location with a small circle of rocks a few feet away so he could find it again. "Nobody's gonna find that," he growled to himself.

He told the gang they would split up the loot when they were no longer being pursued. They had already spent the cash from the first robbery in Tucson and El Paso and planned to do the same with the second haul.

But the Kid was worried. He didn't trust Doc, much less the other men in the gang. There were five of them to split the loot. He wondered if there was a plan afoot to reduce their numbers and increase each individual's take. He was the youngest and newest member; he figured he might be top of the list in such a plan. A deeper worry was that Doc would simply find a way to return without any of them and take all of the riches for himself. The Kid knew he had to find a way to protect himself and protect his share. It was his ticket to the future of his dreams.

He had ventured a ways from their camp area to relieve himself on the second night of this stay. On his way back, he was carefully picking his way along in lantern light, with one hand on the rock wall beside him for balance. Without warning, the rock seemed to disappear. He fell to the side, catching himself on another rock wall about three feet away. Confused, he stepped back and shone his lantern onto the spot. He squinted at where his hand had gone, pulled it back, and the opening seemed to vanish. It was some weird, almost magical illusion of light and shadow in the cave, like nothing he had seen. He slipped through the invisible gap into a cramped space some five feet wide and ten feet long with the lantern to light his way. It was flat and entirely hidden by the strange illusion of the rock face.

Maybe he could use this discovery to his advantage, he thought. An idea for a plan took shape in his mind; he would have to move quickly to make it work.

The next night he slipped away after dinner. The others were deep into the grunting and snoring of sleep after drinking copious amounts of whiskey. The campfire died down to embers, and he waited until he was well away from the area to light his lantern. He removed the bags containing their loot from the crevice Doc had chosen. Then, moving as carefully and quietly as possible, he stashed them in his new hiding place. It was a hundred feet or so further into the pitch-black darkness of the cave. He placed some large rocks on and around the bags to shield them from discovery, should someone else happen onto the spot. The Kid checked every sight angle and was satisfied no one would ever find his hiding spot. Nearing their camp, he doused his lantern and stealthily rejoined the others. He had insured his future as best he could.

***

The cave entrance gave an unobstructed view of the narrow desert valley below it. The men rotated through the day, keeping a lookout. The lookout shouted an alarm on the afternoon of the fourth day of their hiding: Riders were coming up the valley toward them! He said it looked like about a dozen men.

An Arizona monsoon thunderstorm, pregnant with ominous bruised clouds, was approaching. Rain quickly obscured the posse. Doc shouted at the men to grab their gear and follow him. He led them further into the cave to a second, smaller entrance he had found. They slipped out into the driving rain as the first posse members arrived at the main cave entrance.

The gang kept their horses tethered down the hill from where they emerged from the cave. They quickly saddled up and headed out in the pelting rain. "It's our lucky day, boys!" Doc shouted. "Them lawmen wouldn't see us if we rode right over 'em! This rain will wash out our tracks. Move quick now, and we'll give 'em the slip for sure!"

Doc's gang was well away by the time the posse discovered the second cave opening. They found where the men camped and searched the area around it. But there was no sign of the

5

loot they had taken in the robberies. "Looks like they give us the slip out this other hole. They got that gold hid in here, somewhere," Marshall Virgil Earp said. "I've heard this called the "Five Mile Cave" because it supposedly wanders into the mountainside for five miles. We don't have the gear or time to look for it. We'll come back and do a proper search in a couple of days." They spent the rest of that day fruitlessly looking for the robbers' tracks.

Doc figured they were safe when there had been no sign of the posse in pursuit. The gang made their way through the desert eastward to New Mexico and on to El Paso. They gave all the small towns along the way a wide berth. Doc was familiar with out-of-the-way ranches where they could rest for a night and get water for their horses and themselves before continuing.

They holed up in some caves in the mountains near El Paso for a few days before venturing into town. Kid Smith was depressed to find himself hiding in another dark cave. It wasn't his idea of the exciting life of a successful outlaw.

Some of the men thought they should rob the train one more time. It had been easy pickings, they said, and it would make up for the gold the Wells Fargo agent had fooled them out of on the first robbery. That agent had hidden part of the gold shipment in the pot-bellied stove used to heat the express car. His trick made him a hero and local celebrity.

Doc said, "Much as I'd like to get even with Wells Fargo for that, this ain't the time to do it. We need to lie low for a while and let the heat die down." There was some grumbling from a couple of men, and he continued, "They've got Marshall Earp and Constable Dodge out of Tombstone leading the posse looking for us. Those men don't give up easy, and I figure they ain't quit lookin'. We don't want to do anything to bring them here."

***

The Kid was ambitious and impatient; he saw an opportunity to get ahead. Maybe, he thought, he could also make a reputation for himself. He convinced Dick Meyers, another of Doc's gang, that they could pull off a robbery on their own. A few nights later, they piled some railroad ties on the tracks and stopped the Sunset Express train a few miles outside El Paso.

They forced open the Express car door, but the Wells Fargo Messenger inside was ready for them. He snuffed out the light in the car, placed his pistol on the floor by the door, and jumped to the ground. When the robbers told him to relight the lantern, he reached in and grabbed his revolver. He quickly spun around and opened fire on the men at close range. Meyers was shot through the heart and died on the spot, but the Kid ran off down the track, wounded. The agent took careful aim and shot him in the back.

He fell beside the tracks with his life oozing out over the gravel of the rail bed. The agent stood over him with his pistol covering him, just in case. The Kid's eyes fluttered as he drifted away. His final thoughts were that he was dying a rich man, and he would take the secret of the gold and silver he had hidden in the cave with him.

CHAPTER 1
JIMMY

Jimmy awoke to someone poking him in the side and a loud voice saying, "Hey sleepin' beauty! Time to change buses!" He opened his eyes to see Reuben Haynes standing over him. His booming, obnoxious laugh reverberated through the now nearly empty bus. Reuben was one of three other men from Colorado who, along with Jimmy, had joined the Civilian Conservation Corps, known as the CCC.

They had each been given five dollars by their recruiter for travel expenses before boarding the bus for a trip to Arizona. Their job would be helping to develop a cave near Tucson for public use. Their bus stopped in Albuquerque, New Mexico, and the recruits changed to a bus headed to Las Cruces, New Mexico. They were scheduled to take a train from there to Tucson. Jimmy had slept most of the way from Santa Fe. He grabbed his bag and joined the others exiting the bus in Albuquerque and boarding the next one.

He and his fellow recruits settled in on the bus for the next leg of their trip. He was stiff from his long nap on the last bus; the design of Greyhound seats didn't accommodate Jimmy's lanky, six-foot three-inch frame very well. He was thankful the bus wasn't packed, allowing him to stretch out over two seats.

He remained a little fuzzy from the dream on the previous bus. He could still taste the sweetness of the last kiss he dreamed of sharing with Kathleen the night before he left Denver. She had promised to wait for him and write him every day of his six months working for the CCC. Jimmy hoped to one day save enough money to buy her a ring and ask her to marry him.

He settled in for the ride, watching the high desert landscape slide by the window. He hoped he was doing the right thing. It had been a last resort to try to save his family from becoming homeless and joining the endless soup lines of people devastated by the Depression. His mind drifted back to that fateful day that had set the stage for his family's troubles.

***

He trudged home after a long day stacking boxes and sweeping up at the department store where he worked. He bent into the wind with his coat's collar pulled around his neck—the blowing snow bit at his face like a thousand pinpricks. The February storm blew into Denver off the Rockies' front range, creating instant whiteout conditions. The buildings around the downtown area where he worked were ghostly giants, barely glimpsed through the blowing snow.

His neighborhood seemed otherworldly, its familiar trees and houses almost invisible in the storm. He neared the front of his home and saw a strange car parked in front. He couldn't make

10

out the details in the snow, but as he got closer, he saw it was a Denver police car. Fearing the worst, he ran to the house and burst through the front door, nearly knocking over one of the police officers standing there.

His mother sat on the couch in their living room, head in her hands, sobbing uncontrollably. Jimmy looked from her then back to the two police officers. The officers stood with somber faces and their hats in their hands. One of them asked, "Are you her son?" Jimmy nodded numbly. "What's going on? Why are you here?" He asked.

The officer continued, "We are sorry to say your father was killed in a car accident. He hit a patch of black ice near the Rocky Mountain Lumbermill, and his car spun into an oncoming log truck. It appears he died instantly."

Jimmy was speechless. His mother cried, "Oh, Jimmy!" and it was all she could get out. He sat down by her and held her as she wept into his shoulder. He didn't know anything else to do.

An officer gave him a card with their contact information, offered their condolences again, and left. Jimmy's mother's loud sobs filled the room; a ticking clock kept an ominous drumbeat.

His father's death was a terrible blow to Jimmy's family. He couldn't imagine how they could get along without him. His job had kept the family from the awful hardships that so many people endured during this seemingly endless Depression. Like many in those difficult times, Jimmy's father had no life insurance. Now Jimmy had unexpectedly become the man of the family. He had to be strong for his mother and younger brother, and sister.

The owner of the store where Jimmy worked pulled him aside two months later. "Jimmy, you're like a son to me. But our business is dying, and I can't afford to keep you on any longer." He looked down and scuffed his shoe on the floor, reluctant to go on. "I know you need this job, but I'm struggling day to day to keep our doors open." Jimmy could see the pain in his eyes and knew it wasn't easy for him.

The next few days were spent beating the streets and asking for any kind of work in every shop and business. Each day ended with him coming home exhausted long after dark. Most days yielded only a few cents to show for his efforts. He found occasional odd jobs: unloading a truckload of produce, sweeping up in one of the few remaining drug stores, filling in for a bricklayer's sick helper for a day. None of them paid much, but he was always hopeful he would make enough to buy a few staple groceries and help pay rent at the end of the month.

One day he was robbed by a group of men, and the dollar and change he had in his pocket were gone. He had tried to resist and received a black eye and several bruises for his efforts. Things were getting worse on the streets by the day.

He talked with his mother after dinner that evening about what to do. She said, "Jimmy, you can't keep on the way you are. It's going to ruin your health—or worse. I've been thinking more and more about what we heard President Roosevelt say on the radio a few months back." He could see worry lines on her face, grey hairs that weren't there a few weeks ago, and deep sadness in her eyes. She had always been a proud, strong-boned, erect woman but lately had developed a slight stoop. "Maybe that program he talked about is a way out for us," she said. She couldn't hold back tears, looking at her beautiful son, whose face was beginning to show the strain.

Jimmy said, "Yeah, I've been thinking some about that too. It's a way I could earn enough money to support the family and maybe learn a new trade. I worry about leaving you and Mikey and Sarah, but I can't keep doing what I'm doing. There are way more people out there looking for any work every day, and there's none. Soon I won't be able to make enough for us to get by."

"It's not your fault, son—you are doing everything you can." She laid her hand on his arm and said, "But I can't let you destroy your health the way you are going. Maybe this program the President spoke of is the godsend we need right now. They say it pays thirty dollars a month, and the government will send twenty-five dollars of that home to us. We can get by on that along with the state welfare I'm getting." She wiped more tears from her eyes. "I hate the thought of you leaving us; it tears me up inside. But this may be the way for us to get through these awful times."

She was right, Jimmy thought. It was the only way he could see to head off the nightmare of uncertainty and hardship for his family that kept him awake every night. He had spent all of April and half of May trying to find a way out, but each week seemed to be worse than the last.

He sat with Kathleen in the front room at her house the following morning and told her his plans. She sat bundled up against the cold; her family couldn't afford much heating oil. Jimmy thought she was the prettiest girl he had ever seen—the blanket she was wrapped in didn't conceal her full figure, and her long blonde hair spilled over her back. "I know you are doing the right thing, Jimmy," she said, dabbing at the tears welling in her blue eyes. She ran her fingers through his wavy brown hair and said, "I will be here when you return, and hopefully, things will be better then." They sat and held each other for a few minutes and shared one long, last kiss before Jimmy left.

He went to the recruitment office and signed the papers to join the Civilian Conservation Corps. They had already filled the Colorado openings, but they said they could send him to Arizona. Jimmy thought a minute and agreed. How bad could it be? A doctor examined him, pronounced him fit, and told him they would contact him soon with details on his assignment. He walked home, his stomach churning with the conflict between the sadness of leaving his home, his love for Kathleen, and the excitement of a new adventure.

His mother, brother, and sister walked with him to the bus depot on the morning he left. It was the first of June, a clear and warm day with the promise of summer. His mother held him, kissed him, told him to take care of himself and write when he could. His brother and sister both cried; it pained him to leave the family on their own. But he knew he was doing the right thing. It was the best he could for them.

***

Reuben's annoyingly loud voice intruded on Jimmy's memory. He was telling some crude joke that he seemed to think was hilarious. The other passengers simply smiled politely and looked away. Reuben's face turned red, and he turned toward the window and sulked.

Jimmy's attention came back to the present.

Arizona! Jimmy barely knew where it was. It was supposed to be a hot, dry, and desolate desert, nothing like Colorado. But if that's where the job was, he would make the best of it. He had never been more than a few miles out of Denver when the family would go up in the woods for a picnic. It was hard for him to imagine living and working anywhere else, much less off in some desert wasteland.

Jimmy was sitting across from a fellow recruit named William. "What do you think Arizona is like?" Jimmy asked him. "Suppose there are still Indians there?"

William laughed and said, "I don't know about Indians. Maybe we'll be close to the Grand Canyon. I'd sure like to see that!" They considered that possibility, then William continued, "I've read that it's hot in the desert, and not much grows there but cactus."

Jimmy nodded in agreement. "I heard this place called Tucson they're sending us is like the wild west; there's still outlaws and stuff. It's supposed to be close to Mexico, where Pancho Villa invaded the country. I hope we don't have to fight off any Mexicans or Indians either, for that matter."

A loud guffawing from the seat behind them interrupted their conversation. "You dimwits are even dumber than you look!"

Reuben Haynes boomed. All the passengers on the bus looked at him. "There ain't been no Indians there since the US Cavalry killed Geronimo and cleared out his bunch! And the Mexicans went back to Mexico after they chased out ol' Pancho Villa. Where'd you go to school, anyway? "

Haynes was a strapping loud-mouthed man who quickly established himself among the recruits as the resident bully. He was around six feet tall, three inches shorter than Jimmy, but he outweighed Jimmy by twenty or thirty pounds. An unruly mop of curly black hair topped a face with a bulbous nose so large it was almost comical. Jimmy figured that was part of what made him a bully. The men soon learned he would go out of his way to poke fun at anyone he considered less worldly than himself.

Reuben was quick to proclaim that he knew more than anyone else about Arizona. Jimmy asked when he had been there but got only a glare in return. Reuben's face reddened at Jimmy's mild rebuff. His ruddy complexion belied whatever emotions he experienced. From then on, Jimmy was on his list of people to get even with.

The towns they passed through in New Mexico were like being in a foreign country to the Colorado men. Most of the buildings were of Spanish-influenced architecture and made of adobe. Many of the places and street signs had Spanish names the men could not pronounce. As they traveled south, the landscape became more desolate. There were high mountains in the distance, but the desert floor was flat with spotty, scruffy-looking brush and a few cactuses. Jimmy was struck by how different it was to Denver and its surrounding countryside.

They were famished when they arrived in Las Cruces. Jimmy asked their bus driver if he knew an inexpensive place to get something decent to eat. He told him there was a *taqueria* near the train depot that was excellent and cheap. Reuben made a scene when they got there, saying," I ain't eatin none of that Mexican crap. I'm gonna find me a good ol' American hamburger." Then he stomped off down the street by himself.

Jimmy and the other two recruits were not familiar with Mexican food, but they decided to give it a try. Jimmy didn't recognize anything on the simple menu board and asked the owner/cook for a recommendation. They wound up with huge plates of beef tacos, green chili-filled burros, and refried beans. Jimmy was surprised at how tasty and filling it was. The fiery green chili was delicious despite causing his eyes to water and his nose to run.

The recruits waited at the Southern Pacific train depot. They were amazed and excited as the Sunset Limited pulled into the Las Cruces station. Jimmy had ridden trolleys in Denver and seen locomotives from a distance. Being close to the imposing steam locomotive was a new experience. The black behemoth was belching black smoke and billowing huge clouds of white steam. It pulled a dozen cars, each painted dark olive-green with black roofs. The cars rode on massive 6-wheel trucks. She was the oldest and longest-running passenger train in the US. Originally known as the Sunset Express, it ran the Southern Pacific's route from Florida to California. It ran three times weekly, serving large cities and many modest towns along its way. Many small-town stops in the west were not much more than stagecoach stations when the railroad was built.

The recruits boarded the train, and it moved out across western New Mexico. There were nine windows on each side of the cars, and each one was open to a searing blast of hot air. Jimmy said it was like standing in front of his mother's hot oven with the door open. It was early June, and the temperature was well over 100 degrees. He wondered how the rest of the summer might feel. The combination of the train's rocking motion with the heat made Jimmy groggy, and he drifted off into an uneasy sleep.

He woke a few hours later when the conductor announced they were nearing Tucson and would soon arrive. Jimmy first noticed the mountains—they were much larger than he had expected. They were not as high as the Rockies, but they were striking as they rose abruptly from the valley floor. The city seemed to be encircled by them. Clouds hung down over the highest peaks— and it was raining! Jimmy had heard it never rained in Arizona, yet here it was. A light steady rain, giving the town a fresh, clean appearance. Someone from Tucson said it looked like the rainy season was starting early.

The train came into the station near the downtown area of Tucson. The city wasn't nearly as large as Denver, but it was bigger than Jimmy expected. He had seen a couple of western movies with John Wayne and Gary Cooper. His notion of the west was of dusty cow towns with unpaved streets where people got around on horseback. He was surprised to see a modern city's trappings with sidewalks and cars plying the streets.

He noted the depot had the now-familiar Spanish architectural influence with a tiled roof, arched windows, and several arches and pillared entrances facing the street. A newsstand paper's headline caught Jimmy's eye when they left the train. It displayed a newspaper with a bold story. "Look at this, guys," he said, pointing at the paper. "They captured John Dillinger and his whole gang, right here in Tucson! I told you there'd be outlaws! And it says they caught 'em without a fight. Dillinger! Can you imagine?"

The news spread like a brushfire through the group. The recruits speculated excitedly about other outlaws that they might run into hanging around town. It was a young man's wild west dreams come true.

A man in a crisp, freshly pressed Army uniform approached them. His military, no-nonsense manner had the air of authority, and he was clearly in charge. "Listen up, CCC enrollees," he said. "I'm Lieutenant Godwin, the assistant commander of the camp where you will be living and working. Today you'll be meeting up with some other enrollees for a short trip to the Army's Fort Huachuca for your two-week training and orientation. Gather your gear and follow me."

He led them the short distance outside the train station to an open-sided Army truck with a canvas covering. It already held 16 other young men. They boarded and found seats among the group. The truck lurched forward and headed out of the city. Most of the men were from Tucson or nearby areas; Jimmy's group appeared to be the only group from out of state.

They reached Fort Huachuca, two hours southeast of Tucson. The fort was named for the massive Huachuca Mountain range. They loomed over the old army fort's buildings and grounds like hulking giants. The base was a few miles north of the Mexican border. It was spread over the foothills on the north side of the mountains and provided a commanding view of a broad valley formed by the San Pedro River. The town of Tombstone lay in the distant foothills on the other side of the valley.

A soldier from the base told them the Fort had a long history of fighting Indian wars with Geronimo and others. He said that the Fort had been home to the "Buffalo Soldiers," an all-black cavalry regiment, until the previous year. Someone asked why they were called Buffalo Soldiers. The soldier replied, "The story I heard is that it came from the Comanche Indian word for buffalo because the soldiers had curly black hair like the buffalo." One of the Colorado recruits asked if they were still fighting Indians, which raised a loud chorus of laughter. The soldier said, with a grin, "I haven't seen any hostile Indians in these parts, but you boys keep a sharp eye out—some of Geronimo's bunch might be holing up in the mountains!"

***

"This seems a lot like what I've heard about boot camp in the Army," Jimmy said to a new friend named Harry Taylor on their first day at the Fort.

"Yeah, me too. I guess they're gonna poke and prod us for a while. If we measure up, they'll put us to work on some project. But at least the food is okay!"

Jimmy made friends with several men during their stay at the Army base, but Harry quickly became his best friend. He was an outgoing man with a quick smile who came from a place called Ajo, Arizona. His striking red hair and a freckled face gave him a perpetually cheerful look. He was a high school wrestling champion, stocky and muscular, about 5 inches shorter than Jimmy. He turned out to be a practical joker, keeping everyone on their toes. His first joke was short-sheeting Reuben's bed on the second night. Reuben was furious, but the other recruits had a good laugh.

The men's rigorous schedule started with exercise and running in the morning before breakfast. Various tests and interviews, which included IQ and mechanical aptitude tests and psychological evaluations, followed breakfast. Afterward, they were assigned to police the Fort's grounds and do basic maintenance chores. The men weren't always aware the military supervisors were continually appraising them for their fitness and ability to perform assigned tasks, follow orders, and get along with others.

Reuben, true to form, had gotten into several arguments with other recruits. The group commander gave him low marks but allowed him to continue after some forceful counseling. Jimmy suspected it would take more than counseling to make much improvement in Reuben's personality.

The days passed quickly, and the men finished their training. They were loaded up in Army trucks to transport them to their work assignment. Jimmy's group went to a camp that was working on developing a large cave outside of Tucson. It sounded like an intriguing adventure to Jimmy. He and Harry speculated the whole trip about what it might be like to work in a cave.

CHAPTER 3
CACTIZONIANS

Jimmy jumped down from the truck and stood for a minute, rubbing his backside. "Damn, Harry! Sitting on that truck's hard benches and riding over that washboard road is like being kicked around by a gang of thugs."

Harry laughed and agreed, rubbing his butt, too. Looking around, he said, "This is just like where I grew up. Nothin but rocks and cactus. But the mountains are bigger!"

Jimmy took a pack of Camels from his shirt pocket and lit one. His father had left a whole pack in the house, and Jimmy took up the habit as a way to relieve his stress after his father died. His mother considered it a crutch, much to her distaste. They cost too much for him to buy more, and when that pack was gone, he would have none. He purchased this pack with his CCC advance money before he left Denver. He inhaled the harsh, unfiltered smoke and surveyed the scene.

Their new home lay in front of them. Green army tents, arranged in orderly rows, appeared to be where they would live for the next six months. The tents were on level ground next to the ranch's headquarters. It included the owner's home, a bunkhouse, some outbuildings, and corrals.

According to one of the men who spoke Spanish, the ranch was called *La Posta Quemada* Ranch, which meant "the burnt post ranch."

The camp nestled in a narrow valley at the base of the Rincon Mountains' foothills. Spreading sycamore and cottonwood trees lined a rocky, meandering creek. The mountain range's rugged, rocky high peaks loomed in the distance. Tall, many armed cactuses Jimmy learned were called saguaros, dominated the surrounding hills. They reminded him of mute sentinels watching over the valley. Some of them were thirty or forty feet tall with rows of sharp spines covering their trunks and arms. Bonnets of waxy white flowers that blossomed on their crowns stood out against the dark green of their trunks and arms. Ripening red fruits formed where the earliest blooms had started. They were unlike anything in Jimmy's experience. He was amazed to learn some of them were a hundred and fifty years old or more.

Jimmy would become acquainted with many other unusual desert plants, including the prolific and notoriously named "jumping cactus." The plants were also called teddy bear chollas, covered with what appeared to be soft bristles which were, in reality, sharp thorns. Their tips were so fine as to be nearly translucent, almost invisible, but if you touched one would be quickly and painfully impaled. It almost seemed the buds 'jumped' off as they easily clung to a victim. The only way to remove it without getting another hand stuck was to knock it off using a twig, knife blade, or comb. It was an efficient way for the cactus to propagate; the buds would take root and grow into a mature plant.

There were many other types of cactuses, along with creosote, mesquite, and palo verde trees. Tall galleta, grama, and other grasses grew on the flats, providing feed for the ranch's cattle.

Lieutenant Godwin assembled the newcomers in front of a large tent with a US flag flying in front. A man dressed in a flawless Army officer's uniform stepped out of the tent and introduced himself as Captain Yoder, the camp commander. He said, "Welcome to the Colossal Cave Camp. Our job here is to help you in any way we can to learn a new trade, provide educational opportunities, and better prepare you to return home when your service ends. Our responsibility is to develop an amazing cave as a park. It is a short distance away in the hills, and you'll learn more about it soon. Lieutenant Godwin will now give you your living assignments and instructions."

Godwin pulled a list from his pocket and called out names and a number for tent assignments. He said, "You will get your work assignments tomorrow. The dinner bell will ring at 5:30, and I suggest you be there on time". The men filed off to find their new home.

Jimmy and Harry were happy to be assigned to the same tent with six other enrollees. They were not so pleased to see that it included Reuben Haynes. He was always trouble; they hoped the camp life might settle him down some.

Payday, the camp's dog and mascot, immediately came into their tent to greet them. He was a feisty Jack Russel terrier with bright eyes framed by a brown mask. The camp's cook had named him Payday because he was born on the camp's payday. He was a friend to everyone in camp. The dog never missed an opportunity for a snack; he could stand, spin around, and do other tricks if he thought one of the men might share. He was a helpful sentry, always on the lookout for rattlesnakes around camp. The terrier had learned to keep his distance from them and would set up a ruckus until someone came to see what he had found. Jimmy tossed him a piece of jerky and made a friend for life.

They were not thrilled to find themselves quartered in old, green Army canvas tents. Jimmy had counted twenty-five tents, each housing eight men. "There must be about two hundred men here," Jimmy said. "I didn't think there would be this many." It was sweltering in the heat of the day— not much breeze found its way into the tent. The air inside had a lingering, stale, musty odor, despite having the front and back flaps open and the side coverings rolled up. The sunlight inside the tent was filtered by the heavy canvas, giving it a rather gloomy atmosphere on the brightest days. Payday gave all their belongings a good sniffing and, finding everything in order, curled up beside Jimmy's cot to gnaw the piece of jerky.

"I bet this tent's gonna get real smelly, too, with our sweaty bodies in 'em night after night," Harry said.

Jimmy laughed but wondered what he had gotten himself into. He held up some of the two new sets of clothing they were issued. "I guess this is what we'll be wearing from now on." One was a blue denim work suit and the other was a renovated olive drab Army uniform for dress purposes. "I doubt we'll be impressing any girls with these duds!"

Harry said, "Hey, Jimmy! Look at this. It says we're called "Cactizonians! I never heard of that!" He had found a camp newsletter from the previous month, which bore the strange name as its title. One of the other men who had been there a while said, "Forget that fancy name. Nobody can spell it, much less pronounce it. We're called the 'CCC Cavemen' by everybody except the guy who writes that rag. In Tucson, if you tell people you're a 'Caveman, they'll know exactly who you are." That brought a good laugh from the other men in their tent who were veterans of several weeks in camp.

Jimmy kind of liked that name, Cactizonians, because it was so distinctive and unusual. He decided he would share it with his mother and Kathleen when he wrote to them; tell them it was his favorite nickname for the camp.

They settled into the routine of camp life: Reveille at 6 a.m.,
washed and dressed in their work clothes by 6:30 a.m., then
physical training. After training, they headed for the mess tent
for a hearty breakfast. They soon learned that camp food would
likely be the highlight of their stay. It was plain, nourishing, and
served in large quantities. A typical breakfast consisted of
stewed prunes, cereal, ham and eggs, toast or biscuits, coffee,
and milk. Some enrollees were undernourished when they
arrived and soon began to gain weight.

After breakfast, the men policed the grounds, cleaned their
living quarters, and assembled in a rough military order for roll
call and announcements. Afterward, they loaded up in camp
trucks for transport to their assigned work sites.

Lieutenant Godwin assigned Jimmy to a group called the
"Wire Skinners." They installed electrical wiring and lighting
in the cavern for the crews to come later. They were often the
first to work in new areas. The Lieutenant selected him not
because of any particular experience but because he was taller
than the average enrollee and could reach the higher spaces.

Other teams improved access to the cave by enlarging the
cave's entrance, building rock structures to serve as
headquarters and facilities for the planned park, building trails,
and other projects. Several teams worked inside the cave after
the Wire Skinners installed the lights, building pathways,

stairways, and handrails for the tourists to come later. Two groups were working on the entrance road and parking areas.

Their workday lasted until 4 p.m. with an hour lunch break. Camp rules required them to wear their dress uniforms to dinner, another nod to military discipline. The men were encouraged to take classes and learn new skills or enhance ones they already had. The camp had a library and some educational facilities. Some of them were unable to read well, and the lessons helped them learn. Jimmy took a class to learn more about electrical work. He thought it would be a valuable skill to have when he went home.

On weekends a few men rotated with camp maintenance and other assignments. The rest were free to pursue any recreations they wished. A regular shuttle ran back and forth to Tucson, and many opted to go to town for a day or the whole weekend. Many of them were from the city, and the weekend allowed them to spend time at home with their families.

Jimmy and Harry's first trip to town to see a movie was on the Fourth of July. There were flags and red, white, and blue bunting on some of the downtown buildings. They could hear the popping of firecrackers occasionally as they made their way to the Fox Theatre downtown. The theatre had an impressive, towering, and brightly lit sign over its marquee. It had only been open a few years, showing first-run movies and occasional stage productions.

Jimmy said, "I thought Denver had it the worst from this Depression. But Tucson has similar problems. I saw soup lines and boarded-up businesses as we came into town. People we see here have the same sad looks on their faces; it's like the light has gone out of their eyes. I guess the main difference here is the heat."

Harry nodded and said, "We're lucky we have a few coins in our pocket so that we can do stuff like this once in a while. Most folks here and in the town I'm from don't have that luxury." They bought their tickets and bags of popcorn and settled in to watch John Wayne in "Blue Steel."

CHAPTER 4
LIGHTS IN THE DARKNESS

"Wow! It's like walking into the icebox at Miller's grocery store in Denver! Who would've believed it!" Jimmy couldn't contain his excitement when he entered the cave for the first time. It was like stepping into another world.

The temperature inside the cave was a cool 70 degrees. It was an abrupt, almost shocking change from the 100-degree plus temperatures outside. "I think I'll sleep in here from now on," Jimmy joked. "They say it's like this year-round!"

Big Al, Jimmy's team leader, chuckled. "You might be changing your tune, Jimmy, when you learn what kinds of critters you might be bunkin' with. There are things in here your momma never told you about!"

Jimmy noticed a pungent odor that made his eyes water. "What's that awful smell? It's worse than the open privy at Granma's house!" Al pointed out the piles of dung, pushed off to the sides.

"There are about a million bats that live in this cave, and they add to this collection every night. About 30 years ago, someone dug a tunnel to mine the stuff for fertilizer and cleaned most of it out. Supposedly it filled up seven train cars. Musta been pretty deep back then. Who woulda thought bat droppings was valuable?"

Jimmy's eyes slowly adjusted to the dimness inside the cave opening. "How far does this cave go?" he asked." I can't see anything past the first lights."

Big Al said, "Nobody knows. Some old-timers call it "Five Mile Cave" because someone thought it went that far. No one's ever thoroughly explored it. Might be five miles, might be more. I figger it would take years to trace out all the side tunnels, nooks, and crannies. We ain't got time for none of that. We got to keep up with the crews, getting lights in place so's they can see what they're doin'."

Big Al was a heavy but muscularly built man with powerful arms ending in ham-sized hands. He had a kindly appearance despite his size. He was quick to flash a broad smile with an easy laugh. Jimmy was immediately at ease with him.

Big Al was what the CCC called a "Locally Employed Man" or a LEM.' They were part of the CCC strategy of employing skilled men to help lead the work and contribute to their local economies. He had been an electrician in a Tucson shop that was closed by the Depression. The job was a godsend for him and his family, and he took his responsibilities seriously. He was now the team leader for the Wire Skinners electrical crew.

Jimmy walked a ways further with Big Al to the edge of where the lights reached. "You got to watch your step in here. The trails are barely roughed in," Big Al said. "You can easy break a leg or fall down one of these deep cracks. Some are so deep our lights can't find the bottom. Fall into one of those, and I'd have to write a tear-stained letter to your momma, tellin' her that we lost her little boy forever. I don't want to have to do that!" Jimmy wasn't sure if he was serious, but he didn't want to find out.

Al bit off a quid from a black plug of chewing tobacco, worked it around into his cheek, and continued, "This is a dry cave. Apparently, the water that carved these formations has long since dried up. The ones on the floor are stalagmites; the ones hanging from the ceiling are called stalactites. No tellin' how old they are. Some of 'em are brittle and break off easily. You have to be careful one of 'em doesn't get knocked loose on the ceiling and fall on your head! Our job is staying ahead of the trail crew, puttin' up lights so's they can see what they're doin'. It's dangerous and tricky work, and I want you to take your time, do as I tell you, and watch where you put your feet."

They had joined the others in Jimmy's work team, who were busy stringing electrical wire. One of them looked Jimmy up and down and said, "We need a tall man with a long reach to get this wire up high out of the way. You look like just the ticket to get it done!"

That became Jimmy's primary job with his crew. He worked ahead of the crews as they moved into new areas. He learned how to wire lights to provide the best illumination for the crews coming along behind him. Placing the wire high so it would stay in place was a valuable skill in their work.

***

The camp generally had a mail call twice a week. Jimmy was surprised to receive a relatively large bundle of letters from Kathleen, and he hurried to his tent to read them. True to her word, she had written to him nearly every day he had been gone. It took a while for her letters to catch up with him.

He read them hungrily, swept by a wave of homesickness. She said how much she loved and missed him and couldn't wait until he could return to her. He was glad to hear she visited his mother several times a week, who was doing well.

The first letters closed with a perfect lipstick kiss at the bottom. Jimmy noticed something curious, however, as he read the letters. Kathleen's expressions of undying love seemed to taper off as time passed. They became less romantic; there were no lipstick kisses on the bottom of the last two. He wondered what that could mean.

He sat down to compose his first letter back to her:

July 6, 1934

My Dearest Kathleen,

It was a thrill to receive all your letters. They arrived at my permanent camp today. It has been a busy three weeks, but we are now getting settled. We live in Army tents here. I have a new best friend named Harry, and we share the same tent with six other men.

We are working in a huge cave, trying to fix it up so tourists can visit it. It's hard work, but it is interesting. I'm with a group doing the electric work for lights. We're called Wire Skinners. It is very hot outside but nice and cool inside the cave, and that's a relief from the heat of the desert.

I do miss you so. You are on my mind all the time. I miss you the most at night when I lie on my cot staring into the darkness of the tent. This will be a long six months without you. But I hope that we can continue the life we always talked about when it's over.

I'll look forward every day to your next letter.

Love,

Jimmy

***

The weather had cooled off in the time they had been there, with what the locals called the "summer monsoon" starting in July. Billowing thunderheads began to develop in the afternoons, mainly over the mountains.

They frequently hit the valley floor with strong winds and often heavy rain and hail. Occasionally it rained so hard the rainwater would creep into their tents and make a mess of

36

everything. One storm blew down several of the camp's tents, then dumped what some old-timers called a "frog choker" rain. It turned the soil into a muddy mess, and the accompanying hail damaged many of the tents.

The ordinarily dry washes around the camp could turn into rushing rivers in an instant. Crossing them was dangerous until the flood went down. Even when no rain had fallen below them, storms over the steep, the Rocky Mountains could cause rapid runoff, quickly flooding the washes.

In August, a particularly heavy storm turned the camp's creek into a swollen torrent and flooded all the washes in the area. One of the men was a recruit who had recently moved from Chicago to Phoenix and had no experience with the desert. He was unaware of the danger a flooding wash presented. He had gone to Tucson in a camp pickup and, upon returning, tried to drive the pickup truck through a wash the main road crossed. Searchers later found the pickup about a quarter-mile downstream, half-covered in mud, rocks, and limbs. The man's lifeless body was covered in mud and debris inside the truck's cab.

The captain conducted a memorial service for the drowned man. He cautioned the men to be aware of the desert's dangers and not take unnecessary chances. "Remember, men," he said, "it only takes a few inches of running water to float a car or truck and carry it downstream. Do not cross a flooding wash;

wait for the water to go down." The flood-ravaged wreck of the pickup sat at the edge of the camp, a stark reminder of the captain's words.

***

The desert greened up quickly from the monsoon rains, and the hillsides took on a verdant look. New grasses and other plants seemed to sprout overnight, transforming the dry landscape. And, best of all, the nighttime temperatures had become much more bearable.

Their dinner fare was every bit as filling as their breakfasts, and there was plenty of it. Meat and potatoes, macaroni and cheese, various canned vegetables, and plenty of bread and butter were a typical menu, along with a cobbler or pudding for dessert. They ate far better than any of them had before they left home.

The main mess tent cook was another LEM named Charlie. The men called him "Old One-eyed Charlie" because he had lost sight in his left eye. He said his eye was damaged long ago during a gunfight with some cattle rustlers on a nearby ranch. A rock fragment from a ricocheting bullet had pierced it. Most of the men took the story with a grain of salt, like many other stories the man told. The enrollees soon learned he didn't appreciate the nickname, and they didn't use it in his presence. But everyone knew who "Old One-eye" was.

Charlie was otherwise good-natured. He had lived and worked most of his life on local ranches, served as a ranch and camp cook, and knew how to feed many hungry men. A skinny, stringy, weather-worn man, Charlie looked like he had spent his life in the desert sun. He had an ageless face, could have been fifty, could have been seventy. But he had bright, piercing blue eyes that never missed anything going on around him.

He loved to tell stories and tall tales, and one night, when everyone was served, he launched into one of his favorite stories about the cave. The newer recruits perked up while the others grinned knowingly and shook their heads.

"There's a hidden treasure in that cave," he began. "Been there since 1887 when outlaws robbed the Southern Pacific's Sunset Express. Twice! Them robbers used this cave as their hideout and stashed their loot someplace deep inside. They was all caught eventually, some of 'em killed, but none ever revealed the location of the loots hiding place." He had the whole group's attention, even those who had heard some version of the story before. "Nobody knows how much they got. Wells Fargo would never say how much they lost. Some say thirty thousand in gold and silver. Others say as much as seventy. Coulda been more. But the gang's leader, who supposedly was the only one who knew where it was hid, went to prison. Wells Fargo watched every move he made when he got out. So far's anybody knows he never went back for the loot. And that loot is still hid somewhere in that black hole today."

"Aw Charlie, yer as full a beans as yesterday's chili," another one of the LEMs laughed. "I been hearin' that story my whole life, and ain't nobody yet got a whiff of that gold. You know well as me dozens of folks scoured that cave from one end to the other. We'd a heard about it if it was found!"

Charlie replied, "Well, you believe what you want, and I'll believe what I want. I think it was so well hid that it ain't never been found, and maybe ain't likely to be." He went back to cleaning up and getting ready for tomorrow's breakfast.

The men laughed but stopped when there was a loud commotion outside the mess tent. Charlie said, "Somebody see what that dog's kyoodlin' about out there!" A couple of the men stepped outside, and there was Payday, bristled up, barking continuously, lunging back and forth at a rattlesnake coiled beside the tent. The dog would tease the snake into striking and then jump back. It was a dangerous game he had learned to play. One of the men found a shovel nearby, killed the snake, and went inside to find a tasty morsel of roast beef to reward Payday. He had likely prevented one of them from being bitten when they stepped out after dinner. Each man took time to pat his head or scratch his ears and tell him what a good dog he was.

"This cave reminds me of goin' into my dad's old silver mine," Harry said after his first day in the cave. He was relaxing with Jimmy and their tent mates after dinner. "My Dad's partners with my uncle, and I'd go with them to work it on weekends and holidays when I was out of school. It was cool inside, like our cave, too. Maybe cooler!" The men perked up, anxious to hear another story. Stories of any kind were the lifeblood of the camp. They were something to take the edge off the boredom of being in a hot, smelly tent with nothing else to do.

"Wow! A silver mine! What are you doin' here? Are your dad and uncle rich?" one of the men asked.

Harry said, "Nah, most of the silver played out years ago. They got the mine's rights real cheap and kept workin' the silver and gold that was still there. It was mostly one tiny vein, and it took a lot of work to get a little bit of silver ore. Seemed like more work than it was worth to me."

"It's an old Spanish mine and still has some of the old timber works they built," he continued. "We went down the shaft in an ore car on a winch that ran off an old gas engine. I always worried about it dyin' and leavin' us stuck down there. My uncle said not to worry 'cause there were ladders. But they were as old and rickety as the rest of the works. At first, I didn't trust them, either." He chuckled as he thought about it and said, "But I'm still here; stuff's stouter than it looks!"

One of the men asked where the mine is, and Harry replied, "It's way out in the desert south of Ajo near the Mexican border. It was mostly a hobby for my dad and uncle, an excuse to go out in the desert and drink beer. They'd load up the ore they stockpiled on a rented truck and take it down to Mexico about once a year; there's a smelter there where they could sell it. I think it mostly paid for their beer for the next few months." The men laughed and agreed that it was worth it if it paid for their beer.

Everyone but Reuben. He snorted derisively and said, "That's the dumbest thing I ever heard. All that work for a little beer? I wouldn't work for that. I figure to have my own business when I'm done with this CCC stuff. A car dealer. Sell Cadillacs to rich people."

"Aw, go on, Reuben," one of the other men in the tent jeered. "You're just like the rest of us. You ain't got a pot to piss in. Nobody's gonna loan you money to start a car dealer business." That brought loud laughter from the group. "Besides that," another man added, "with your personality, you couldn't sell heaters to Eskimos!" Reuben's face turned red; he glowered at them and stomped out of the tent.

One of the new men asked Harry about the town of Ajo. He said it was about 130 miles west of Tucson. "The name is spelled A- J-O, and we make fun of newcomers who call it A-Joe. It's "Ah Ho," like in Spanish. Another joke we play on newcomers is tellin' them the Spanish word means garlic, which is true. Then we tell 'em all they have to do is go outside of town, and they can find as much fresh garlic as they could ever want. It's always a good laugh when they come back and tell us they couldn't find any—'cause there ain't none around." Harry chuckled at the thought. "They say the old Indian word for the place was really for the reddish color of the hills. But it sounded kind of like the Spanish word for garlic, and that's what stuck as the name."

The men had a good laugh about the Ajo garlic gag. Harry continued, "My Dad and uncle, and pretty much everyone I knew, worked in the open-pit copper mine or the smelter in Ajo. They're the only jobs there. I figured I'd end up workin' there, too. My dad thought he could get me on full-time. Then the price of copper fell through the floor when the Depression started. They shut down the minin' operations, and the jobs disappeared. There was nothin' else there. So, here I am, with you and the rest of these grunts, muckin' around in bat crap in a cave." More laughter and nods of approval.

Harry was quiet for a minute before continuing. "The Phelps Dodge company owns the mine, and the company housing is where most folks I know live. There's even a company store," he said, "and pretty much everybody shops there 'cause they can buy on credit between paychecks. And that's what I hate about the place." The abrupt change of tone caught Jimmy and the others by surprise. "It's like livin' in a goldfish bowl, waitin' for your master to feed you, and controllin' your life. If you don't want to be a miner, then tough. If you want to go shoppin' someplace else, good luck. It's a long way to Tucson or Phoenix. Phelps Dodge keeps a thumb on everything in the place. I felt like it was crushin' the life out of me."

Jimmy and the others sat in silence. They had come from Tucson, Phoenix, and Denver, grand cities with every convenience. They couldn't conceive of a company town with only one store for everything.

Harry continued, "This CCC job is the best thing that could've happened for my family and me. The Depression put my dad out of work with no prospects to find anything else when the mine shut down. My father is a proud man, and he hated applyin' for welfare. But, like most of the other people in town, it was the best they could do. When the CCC sent a recruiter to town, I was first in line to sign. The money I make here keeps my family afloat. But I hope to God it's my ticket outta that hole and a better life. Maybe the Depression will end by the time I'm done here, jobs will come back, and my dad will be able to support his family again."

His story about working in the old silver mine got around. The Lieutenant assigned him to one of the crews working to clear the trail inside the cave. He figured he had some experience working around the rock in confined spaces and would fit that job. The prospect didn't excite Harry, but at least it was cooler than working outside.

* * *

Harry and Jimmy talked endlessly in their off-times about how they could better themselves after their time in the CCC ended. They sat on a bench under a shady ramada near the camp one evening. It was one of the few places around the campground where they could have a little privacy most of the time. Harry said he dreamed of opening a bar in Tucson. "Jimmy, now that prohibition's over, there's gonna be huge opportunities to open a legal bar and have entertainment and everythin'. It would be a real gold mine when this Depression finally ends— not like that hole in the ground of my father's. I'd make it a class place, with cocktails and such. Maybe a fancy restaurant, too."

Jimmy nodded and said, "That sounds great! But where will you get the money to do it? We won't save much on the five dollars a month we keep from our pay here—not if we keep spending it on movies and cheeseburgers!"

"I don't know. But I'm gonna find a way. I'm never goin' back to Ajo to work for Phelps Dodge." Harry picked at his fingernails, lost in his grandiose dream.

45

"I don't know what I'm going to do, either," Jimmy said. "I used to think I would go to college, study business. I could have; I had good grades in high school. But the Depression wrecked everything. Now I have to look out for my mother, brother, and sister. There's no work for me back in Denver. I worry about the family, and I miss my girl. But who's going to hire somebody trained to string electric wire? I'd be back to pounding the streets for crumbs! That wouldn't be much good, particularly if I wanted to get married."

Jimmy was intrigued by the cattle ranches he had seen since he had arrived and the stories One-eyed Charlie told about the cowboys on the ranches where he had worked. He began to imagine himself owning a cattle ranch, riding his range, and looking after a fine herd of cattle. He had never been on a horse, but he would lie awake nights thinking about it.

He told Harry about his dream, and he shook his head, laughing. "Man, you got the same problem as me! How you gonna buy somethin' like that on a CCC salary? You got any idea how much buyin' somethin' like that would cost?"

Jimmy admitted he didn't, any more than Harry knew how much his dream bar would cost. But both men were ambitious and determined to make more of themselves than they had so far been able.

"Maybe we could rob a bank," Jimmy said in frustration. They both laughed nervously at that idea, and Harry said,

"Tucson was good enough for Dillinger. We wouldn't have to go far!"

"Yeah, but look how he ended up. We don't want to do that!"

"No, but maybe one would be enough if we're careful."

That set both of them off on a whole new line of daydreams: robbing banks, hiding out with beautiful women, making enough to buy their bar and cattle ranch, and living respectable lives. At times being a criminal sounded better than going back to the dead ends of their previous lives.

Jimmy told Kathleen about his dream of owning a cattle ranch in Arizona in a letter that night. He said they could ride the range on horseback over lands they would own far as the eye could see.

CHAPTER 6
HIDDEN WAYS

Jimmy and Harry grew accustomed to working in challenging and often dangerous spaces in the cave. There were steep drops, ending in sharp stalagmites protruding from the floor, unstable ceiling formations that could drop from a minor disturbance, and many other unseen hazards. They had to be careful of each step. They occasionally found old Indian drawings on rocks and walls and ancient campfire remains. It was apparent many people had used the cave since ancient times.

One night after dinner, Jimmy took Harry aside and said, "I think I might have found where One-eyed Charlie's train robbers camped." When he was sure no one else was in earshot, he continued, "An old tin cup and a box of matches are sitting off to the side of an old campfire ring. The area is really beat down. It looks like several people had been there for a while. There are different sets of boot prints in places where the dust on the floor ain't been disturbed. Ol' Charlie might not have been spoutin' hot air, after all."

Harry said, "Well, there's been a lot of people in there over the years. Don't you think somebody might've noticed that before you?"

"It's not easy to see—it's kind of hidden in a pocket off the main passage. I had to get back in there to run some wire over a ledge. It might be something, or it might be nothing. But I think we ought to poke around in there when the crews are gone. We'll never know if we don't try."

A buzz of excitement ran through the men. Even the remote prospects of finding the legendary stash of treasure was a thrill. They made plans to slip away on the weekend when most of the camp was off in town or doing chores. Hopefully, no one would notice them.

Jimmy burned with impatience. He wanted to get back there to explore; the hours seemed endless until their Friday shift was over. They gathered up some hand torches and rope after dinner and hid them behind a supply tent.

***

They waited until the shuttle trucks left for Tucson on Saturday morning after breakfast. Many of the men went to Tucson for a day in town. Those who were left were busy with chores on their weekend assignments. The budding treasure hunters gathered their supplies and slipped off to walk the mile or so to the cave.

Just before they entered the cave, Harry grabbed Jimmy's arm and jerked him violently back and to the side. A western diamondback rattler as big around as Jimmy's arm lay coiled under a hackberry bush not three feet away. It struck viciously

49

at Jimmy with no warning. It would surely have caught him in his calf if Harry hadn't reacted. Jimmy stood there, shaking, as the snake watched them warily. Its triangular-shaped head and beady eyes tracked their every move. Then its rattle started an insistent buzz, and they gingerly walked around it, hoping it would find a better hangout before they returned.

"I guess what some of the old-timers say is true," Jimmy said. "They don't always rattle to give you a warning!" Another worker had been bitten twice by a rattlesnake a couple of months prior. He nearly died. It cost him his leg from the knee down, and he was sent home.

It was dark inside the entrance, darker than either of them had seen it before. None of the work lights were on, and they were staring into a black void. Their flashlight beams were swallowed up in a few feet, giving the unseen space a mysterious, foreboding quality.

They hadn't gone far when a family of ring-tailed cats spooked them. Their proper name was coatimundis; they chittered, squawked, and skittered around them. Both men were slightly shaken. The animals were no danger to the men, and a couple of families were in the cave. But the men's nerves were already on edge. Jimmy had seen a couple of the creatures outside the cave in daylight, trotting along with their long-striped tails held high in the air. He thought they were funny looking.

Jimmy's heart was still racing from his close call with the snake. "Damn!" Jimmy said, "I thought some kind of cave critters had us for sure. Those ringtails are usually long gone when we show up to work. They got my heart pounding after meeting mister rattler outside!"

"I guess when we turn on the bright lights, they high tail it," Harry said with a nervous laugh. "We prob'ly scared them worse than they did us."

They were afraid to turn on the lights in case someone else might show up. So, they continued cautiously on using only their hand torches, with Jimmy in the lead. Jimmy had left an inconspicuous grouping of rocks by the trail to help him find the spot.

"This is the place," he said, shining his torch into the inky darkness behind the rock outcrop. "Follow me, and watch your step, 'cause it drops down slightly behind this rock." The opening continued a few feet before making a sharp turn to the left and opened up into a small, more or less flat area. Jimmy shined his light into the middle of it, pointing out the remains of the old campfire.

He showed Harry where he had found the cup and matches. They searched the area carefully but turned up no other artifacts. Then Jimmy said, "Look here!" He shined his light on a spot on the rock face a couple of feet off the floor. "Somebody carved their name! Look!" He could hardly contain his excitement.

Their torches' glow revealed the faint outline of the name "Kid" Smith carved into the rock. "I'd bet anything this was one of the robbers! Let's look around some more and see what else we can find."

They spent another hour or so poking in the nooks and crevices nearby but found nothing. Their torch lights were weakening, and they needed to get out to avoid being stranded in the dark. Jimmy took the tin cup and matches with him to stash with his things in the tent.

They carefully looked around the entrance for the rattlesnake, which had greeted them earlier, before stepping out of the cave. It had apparently moved to a more promising location. The men had learned early that rattlesnakes were common around the area and to be wary, even in camp.

On their way back to camp, Jimmy said, "I'm going to find out who Kid Smith was. If he was one of the robbers, it means we might be close to where they stashed the gold."

"Well, Jimmy, we might spend the rest of our lives poking around in that hole and never find anythin' more than your tin cup and old matches. But if either of us finds somethin' that looks promisin', we can keep lookin'." The two men made a pact to share any findings, and should one of them stumble onto the treasure, they would share in it equally.

 ***

Jimmy received three letters from Kathleen at mail call. He took them to a picnic table at a quiet shady spot under a ramada where he could read them in privacy. She had written the first two before she had received his last one, where he told her of his ranching dreams. The third letter had a much different tone, not nearly as romantic as her previous ones had been. She said the idea of a cattle ranch in the desert sounded interesting, but she wasn't sure she would be cut out for it. Besides, she had never been on a horse. And, perhaps more concerning, she said she didn't think she would be happy living that far away from her mother and the rest of her family, much less in the hot desert. No lipstick kisses graced the bottom of any of the letters.

Jimmy was taken aback by her reaction. He had thought she would be thrilled with the prospect of the life he described. He lay awake late into the night, concerned and confused about where her reluctance to start a new and exciting life would lead.

***

The next day, Sunday, Jimmy caught a ride to Tucson and found the downtown library. He asked the librarian if she could help him find information about the old train robberies. She chuckled and said, "I wish I had a quarter for all the people who've come in here and asked me that question. I could probably retire. Come with me, and I'll get you started on what we have."

It was the first time Jimmy had been in an extensive library. The librarian helped him find a book on the subject and some old newspaper clippings from that time. It didn't take Jimmy long to locate the information he sought. Kid Smith was indeed one of the notorious Doc Smart gang that had twice held up the Sunset Express. A Wells Fargo agent had killed him during a third attempt on the same train outside of El Paso. There was no mention of anything else about him. But Jimmy was more excited now; he had confirmed that his find was a real clue. He couldn't wait to get back to his exploration. The librarian gave him a big smile when he thanked her. Then went in search of his ride back to camp.

Conflicting emotions raced through Jimmy's mind. How could he, even in fun, have possibly contemplated a life of crime; robbing banks, hiding out with fast women, running from the law? That wasn't the way he had been taught to live. And Kathleen seemed quite cool to his dream of buying a cattle ranch and spending their days riding their spread. Now, with what he had recently learned, he was becoming obsessed with the notion of finding a hidden treasure that was probably just an old camp cook's fantasy.

He felt huge waves of guilt that he hadn't paid more attention to Kathleen. He thought she loved him, but now it seemed their relationship had taken on a worrisome tone. The newness of his life at the camp had kept his focus elsewhere. He tossed around on his cot that night, disturbed by thoughts he couldn't resolve. Did he truly love her? How had she so quickly passed from his awareness? He had to clear up his uncertainty and be honest with himself and with Kathleen.

His thoughts drifted to his mother, and he felt guilty about not writing to her more often. He had not been the best son, so he resolved to write to her more often. Reveille jolted him awake after a largely sleepless night. He had barely dozed off when the blaring bugle sounded.

CHAPTER 7

ILLUSION

Jimmy and Harry weren't the only men in camp who had taken an interest in One-eyed Charlie's tales of outlaws and hidden treasure. Several of them, including Reuben Haynes, had also launched weekend explorations to find the stash. Reuben's job was on one of the crews building the new headquarters and storage buildings outside the cave entrance; he knew little about the cave's interior. He and the other two Colorado men pretty much stuck together, and they tagged along with Reuben on his cave searches.

Reuben was constantly leering at Jimmy. He made no secret of being suspicious of Jimmy and Harry spending so much time together. They did their best to avoid him, but he seemed always to be lurking nearby, watching them.

At dinner one evening, Reuben was holding forth in his typical annoying and braggartly manner. "Me and my boys is gonna find that treasure, and then we're gonna leave you misfits behind rootin' around this hole in the desert. We're gonna live in style, maybe come visit you sometime in my fancy new Cadillac automobile." His cohorts nodded in agreement, but none of them could get a word in between Reuben's bluster. "I'll have enough gold to buy up half of Denver when I go back. I bet they'll even name the main street after me!" He went on until most of his audience had drifted away, most shaking their heads at his arrogant fantasies.

Jimmy and Harry discussed Reuben's chances on their way to their tent. "I don't think that blowhard could find his ass in the dark," Harry said. "He don't know anything about the cave. He's more likely to get lost, and we'll have to find and rescue him."

"Yep. His main job is hauling rocks for the new buildings. I figure that's about all he's good for, but I worry the idiot might stumble onto something fumbling around in the cave. We can't let him know what we have found or what we are doing cause he'll start spying on us—even more than he does already. He asked me the other day where I'd been spending my time. I told him I liked looking around in the desert for arrowheads and stuff, but I don't think he believed me."

Harry said, "There's somethin' that's been botherin' me if we ever did find that loot. I doubt Reuben and his bunch have thought about it either." He stopped to knock a jumping cactus bud off his boot with a dead mesquite branch. "Last year, my dad got upset because the President made it illegal to own more than a hundred-dollars-worth of gold. If you had more than that, which dad did, it had to be sold to the government at a set price. Dad had been hoardin' some of it for years. He took it out of the old Spanish mine; said it was retirement insurance."

"I didn't know about that. Only a hundred dollars? What did your dad do? Did he sell it?"

"Hell no. He said they'd have to take it over his dead body. Not only that, the price of gold went way up this year, like fifty percent more than the government was payin' before. I dunno what he's gonna do with it, but he ain't givin' it to the government."

Jimmy was quiet for a couple of minutes. "So, you mean if we ever found the treasure, we'd have to sell most of it to the government? That's not fair!"

"Nobody says the government is fair. But it's the law. And there's another wrinkle," Harry continued. "If word ever leaked out we found that gold and silver, there'd be people all over us wantin' a piece of it. There's lots of desperate people who would do about anything to get it. We gotta do everthin' we can to keep it secret."

"The CCC will let us sign up for another six months if we want. I've made up my mind to do that," Jimmy said. "It will provide six more months of income for my mother and family." He gazed off into space and said, "I think there's a chance of finding that robbery stash if I have more time to look. That would solve a lot of problems!"

"If you're in, I'm in too, Jimmy. I don't have anywhere else to be, anyway. Besides, I can't let you have all the fun," Harry laughed.

Robert Sims was a new recruit who had just been assigned to the Wire Cutters. It was his second day on the job. He stepped close to the edge of a crevice to better view a ledge he was preparing to string electric cable on. With no warning, the rock collapsed beneath him. He cartwheeled into the dark void, bouncing off the narrow rock walls on either side.

Jimmy, who was training the new man, instantly recognized the clattering rock's sound. A scream followed it, then silence. He picked his way carefully to where Robert had dropped the roll of wire he was using. Shining his light over the edge of the precipice, he could see the man lying unmoving in a crumpled heap. It looked to be maybe thirty feet down. It was sheer rock on both sides with no handholds.

He yelled for help, then called to the injured man. Robert didn't move or respond. The crews always kept a hundred-foot coil of good rope in the new areas where they worked. Jimmy grabbed it, tied one end securely around a large boulder near the crevice, and dropped the other end down to Robert. Then he lowered himself over the edge.

Several other men heard Jimmy's call for help and gathered around. Jimmy reached the bottom, where he found the trainee unconscious and bleeding from a head wound. The impact twisted his left leg at an unnatural angle, and his right forearm was bent, showing bone protruding through the skin.

Jimmy's training on dealing with such a situation kicked in. He trimmed the rope to a manageable length and used it for a makeshift sling around Robert's limp body. Then the men on top slowly pulled the unconscious man up and got him onto their emergency stretcher. Two men rushed him out toward the entrance while the others tossed the rope back down to Jimmy and hauled him back to the surface. The men were calling him a hero. But Jimmy felt that he had somehow failed in teaching the trainee about the cave's dangers

Big Al, Captain Yoder, Lieutenant Godwin, and Jimmy spent the rest of that morning going over the accident's circumstances. Robert was sent to a Tucson hospital to treat a scalp laceration and concussion and several broken bones.

Jimmy said, "I'm responsible for what happened to him. I warned him about the danger and showed him the kinds of things to avoid. I think he was in a hurry to show what he could do. I should have stayed closer to him. "

Big Al said he was there when Jimmy was teaching the trainee about safety, and he couldn't see that Jimmy could have done any better. The new man was simply not careful enough.

A lengthy discussion on whether any new safety precautions were needed ensued. The men finally agreed that all new trainees would receive several hours of safety training before setting foot in the cave. That would be followed by the same kind of on-site training that Jimmy gave Robert.

As they left the captain's tent, Big Al told Jimmy that he had done well and that his quick action probably saved the new man's life. Jimmy wasn't sure that made him feel any better.

***

The following day Jimmy was finishing up the last few feet for the day's wiring run. He reached out to balance himself on the rock and fell forward, banging his shoulder. At first, he was confused by it. That rock had looked close and stable enough, but when he reached out for it was more than an arm's length away. Jimmy had never seen anything like this in the cave. It was totally deceptive in the light of his miner's helmet.

He stepped into what appeared to be a shadow and shined his hand torch into the darkness. There was an opening about his body's width. He slipped through it into an open area about five feet wide and ten feet long. In his light's beam, barely visible at the far end of the space, he could see a corner of some kind of white fabric sticking out from behind a jumble of rocks.

His hand trembled with the light. He was almost afraid to look behind the rocks, fearing it would be a disappointment. He carefully moved some rocks to the side where he could get a look. There, covered in dust, was a large white bag. Two more were stuffed behind it. He brushed some of the dust off the first bag, revealing fading black letters. It spelled out

61

"US MAIL. PROPERTY OF THE US GOVERNMENT."

Jimmy dropped his hand torch and stood there in momentary disbelief. He had found it! He had actually found it! By sheer accident and dumb luck, he had stumbled into a fantastic hiding place. None of the dust on the floor had been disturbed; he was sure he was the first person to enter it in over forty years.

It was quitting time, and someone called his name outside in the cave. He quickly slipped back out into the open area. "I'm about done here," he called back. "I'll catch up in a few minutes." His mind was in a whirl as he used some stones to mark the spot discreetly. He could hardly think what to do next except to tell Harry.

It was a beautiful September evening when Jimmy came out of the cave. The summer rains had greened up the hillsides around the cave's entrance, and the breeze seemed to hold fresh promise.

CHAPTER 8
SECRET PLANS

Jimmy and Harry made plans to ride into Tucson the next day with some other men to take in the new John Wayne western, "The Man from Utah" It was always a treat to get away from the camp on the weekend for a few hours. What better way to spend time than watching John Wayne tame the west?

It was a perfect opportunity for Jimmy to share his news away from their tent mates' prying ears— Reuben, in particular. There weren't many secrets kept long among men sharing such close quarters.

As soon as they arrived at the theater, Jimmy pulled Harry aside. "I found it," he said in a whisper. "I found the treasure!"

Harry stared at him for a moment. "You're puttin' me on. C'mon, what're you up to?"

"I'm dead serious. I stumbled into the hiding place shortly before quitting time yesterday. It's there, I tell you! There were three canvas bags with US MAIL printed on them. Unfortunately, I didn't have time to look in them, but there's nothing else it could be!"

They paid twenty-five cents each for their tickets and moved on to their seats. There were few other customers in the theatre, mainly other men from the camp. Jimmy suspected it was difficult for most people to justify a movie's expense in such hard times. He wondered how the theatre continued to stay in business. Both of them bought a five-cent bag of popcorn, and Harry whispered, "What're you goin' to do?"

"You mean, what are *we* going to do," Jimmy continued in a whisper. "We swore to be partners if one of us found it. Far as I'm concerned, that's what we are."

The show was starting, and they had to be quiet. Both men were brimming with excitement, thinking to themselves what to do next. They paid little attention to John Wayne trying to solve a mystery of what was killing local rodeo riders. Neither of them could have described the movie had they been asked. After the movie, they had a few minutes of private time to discuss what to do next.

Harry said, "We're gonna have to be careful not to be seen together goin' and comin' from the cave now. Reuben and his bunch are already suspicious. I caught one of them watchin' me several times."

"Yeah, we have to find some way to deal with that bunch. They're a pain in the butt. How about this: let's leave separate times, a half hour or so apart, and go different directions. I could double back when I'm sure it's clear and meet you at the cave. I scouted the area after work last Friday, and I have a plan for how to handle the bags."

Neither of them slept that night: Visions of riches, cattle ranches, and fancy bars filled the hours until reveille.

Harry hatched a mischievous plan to divert Reuben's attention. He made sure he was in earshot of Reuben and his cronies at breakfast and said loudly to Jimmy, "I heard from one of the old LEMs that there's clues about the treasure hid somewhere around the *La Posta Quemada's* ranch house. He said the outlaws hid out there for a while when they left the cave. One of the men wrote down directions, hid the note in a tobacco tin, and then buried it somewhere near the house. I'm gonna check it out when I have time."

Sure enough, after breakfast, Reuben and his cohorts were off in a rush, carrying picks and shovels. Jimmy and Harry had a good laugh, and Harry said, "Guess we don't have to sneak around today!"

Jimmy slapped him on the back and said, "No, but we probably ought to leave separately anyway, so no word gets back to Reuben. Let's get started."

As usual, there was no one around the cave's entrance on a Sunday morning. Most of the enrollees had enough of it during the week. They each brought miner's caps with lights and hand torches, and Harry carried some large burlap potato sacks he had pilfered from the mess hall.

Jimmy led him to the spot and shined his light on the wall.

"There's nothin' there, Jimmy! You sure we're in the right spot?"

"Watch this!" Jimmy stepped into what appeared to be a solid rock wall and disappeared. "Come on in," he laughed. "It 's not magic!"

Harry felt along the wall. His hand seemed to disappear into what appeared to be a shadow on the rock's solid face. Amazed, he followed Jimmy around into the cramped space. Giggling like a young girl, Jimmy shined his light on the three bags hidden behind the rocks. Neither of them said anything for a while.

Finally, Harry broke the silence and said, "What the heck are we waitin' for? Let's see what's in them bags!"

Jimmy sliced one open with his knife. There were more, smaller bags inside. His blade split one of them and spilled its contents, a double handful of glistening American gold coins. "PROPERTY OF WELLS FARGO & CO." was printed on the smaller bag. The material of the cloth bags was starting to rot and come apart due to age.

Both men caught their breath. Gold! More gold than either could have imagined! The coins were bright in the light of their lanterns. They still looked brand new, even after over forty years in the dark. The robbers had filled each mailbag with more of those smaller bags, and they found two bars of solid gold at the bottom of the first one. "Oh, my God, Harry! Look at it! Oh, my

God!" He choked up and couldn't say anything else for a minute.

Harry said, "Let's get it into these new bags. We can worry about countin' it later, but we best get this done before anyone gets suspicious of where we might be."

The next bag was a mixture of gold and silver coins. They quickly put it into one of their burlap bags. The third bag was heavier, with mainly gold and some silver coins. But in the bottom were three more pure gold bars. They were stunned. Neither of them could wrap their brains around the value of what they had found. They transferred the old sacks' contents into their burlap bags. Then they set out on the second and most critical part of their plan.

Jimmy had earlier found the second entrance to the cave, hidden far back in its depths. He noted it showed signs of some use over the years. One of old Charlie's stories told how the robbers had escaped a posse by going out that hole during a heavy summer thunderstorm. He said they escaped capture, with no trace of how they had done it. It appeared feasible to Jimmy, and he had explored the area outside the hole.

And now, he planned to make great use of it again. They lugged the four heavy burlap bags the few hundred feet from the hiding place to the exit hole. Harry handed them out to Jimmy.

Jimmy had found an excellent hiding place down the slope, in a jumble of boulders with a hidden cavity. It was large enough

for their four bags and couldn't easily be seen. "Be careful going down the slope," he cautioned," we don't want to leave signs of our passing here. We'll erase our tracks and put back any rocks we kick loose." It was tricky footing carrying the bags' weight, and they had to move slowly to avoid slipping.

They finished that job and, satisfied there weren't any obvious signs of disturbance, went back into the cave. They carried a couple of mesquite branches with them and erased their boot prints in the dust of the cave's floor until they reached the treasure's previous hiding place.

Jimmy went back and double-checked that they didn't leave any coins lying around. Then he took the remnants of the original bags and buried them deep in the rock pile. He backed out, erasing his tracks as he went.

Satisfied they had accomplished their goal and covered their tracks, they headed back out of the cave's main entrance. They had used up a good part of the day and would have to make their way back to camp at different times to avoid any suspicion of their day's activities.

***

Reuben Haynes had watched with interest as Harry was sneaking through the tents. Reuben left his cronies to continue searching for the buried clue while he followed Harry. He saw Harry join up with Jimmy and enter the cave. An extremely odd activity to be doing on a Sunday, he thought. He stayed hidden a ways from the entrance and saw the men come out several hours later. It seemed even stranger that they separated before going back to the camp at different times. His suspicions were confirmed; they were up to something they needed to keep secret.

CHAPTER 9

A GATHERING OF WOLVES

Trouble came to circle the partners in the way the scent of blood on the wind will attract wolves. The smell of money was in the air, and money was an irresistible draw for certain hungry predators. The camp's rumors and speculations had spread the odor of potential riches to Tucson and beyond.

Reuben's loose lips were the primary source of rampant rumors, both in the camp and in the city. He was always bragging loudly in Tucson diners and bars about how he knew the treasure was there, and he would be the one to find it. People who didn't know him were starting to pay attention. The word was spreading.

The first sign of trouble came from the Pima County Sheriff and an agent for the US Treasury. A week after Jimmy and Harry had removed and re-hidden the money, Captain Yoder held the camp's enrollees after their usual morning muster. "Men, these two gentlemen have some important information you need to hear and heed. It could affect any one of you." With that, he introduced the two visitors.

The Sheriff spoke first. "You men have no doubt heard rumors and stories about train robberies that occurred near here in the late eighteen hundreds. The robberies were a fact. However, there is a lot of speculation about what may have become of the loot the robbers stole. Many people speculate it is hidden in the cave where you men are working." Jimmy and Harry cast furtive glances at each other. "I don't put much stock in those stories myself," the Sheriff continued, "and the fact is many men have combed the cave thoroughly with no results other than finding a few Indian artifacts. But I need to warn you: Times are desperate for many people, and desperate people do desperate acts. The thought they might find that stolen treasure could cause a rush of people looking for it. You could be in danger if someone thinks you have found it, or know where it is. You should be cautious of strangers approaching you about it." Then he turned to the Treasury agent. "This is Mr. Turner, who has additional information you need to know."

Jimmy hoped that no one noticed he had broken out in a sweat on a cool morning. It trickled down his shirt front, making him feel conspicuous. He could feel his grand dreams fading in the face of what he was hearing.

Turner was a young, no-nonsense type of man, dressed severely in an immaculate black suit. His cold, steel grey eyes peered out over a neatly trimmed black mustache, and long sideburns punctuated his stylish black fedora. Harry said later he looked "citified" and not much older than himself and Jimmy. "Kind of young to be a Treasury agent," he told Jimmy later.

Turner stood silent for a moment, fixing the men in front with a hard stare. "It is my duty to inform you that current law in the United States requires that any gold in excess of one hundred dollars in value must be turned over to the federal government. The government pays a fair price for anything over that amount. Should you find the stolen goods the Sheriff referred to, you are obligated to sell any amount valued over one hundred dollars to the US government."

The agent had an unnerving habit of picking out an individual and staring straight into his eyes as he spoke. He picked out Jimmy for the treatment as he continued, "That said, there is another consideration, should you find it. You are liable for income tax on any proceeds you realize."

A loud shuffling of feet ensued. The men looked around, wondering who or what had brought this on. So far as the camp knew, no one had ever found anything of particular value in the cave. They had heard One-eyed Charlie's tales, but no one truly believed them. But here was something new. These men must think that robbery loot is there, or they wouldn't be going to the trouble of warning them!

Agent Turner gave them a final warning. "There are severe penalties under the law for violating either the tax laws or the gold restrictions. You could be fined and or sent to prison if you do so. I will leave my card with Captain Yoder, and you may contact me with any questions."

With that, he stepped back, and Captain Yoder dismissed the men to their day's work. The camp was buzzing as they went about their duties. Many of them had heard Reuben's constant chatter and bravado in the mess hall, claiming he had clues and was going to find the treasure. Most of them dismissed him as a braggart and blowhard. But now, there was additional interest in what he had been saying. Maybe there was something to Old Charlie's tales, after all.

Other wolves were circling the scent, their presence not yet made known.

***

J.W. sat at the counter in a greasy spoon diner, drinking weak black coffee that tasted like yesterday's brew. He thought a nickel a cup was about five cents more than it was worth, but there were refills and free sugar. If he dumped enough sugar in his cup, it hid the stale taste of the brew. Besides, it was what he could afford. A sign in the window advertised pie and coffee, 15 cents. He figured the pie was likely as stale as the coffee.

He pushed his beat-up Stetson back on his head, giving him the look of a cowboy recently off the range, with old denim jeans, a faded chambray shirt, and a pair of heavily worn and cracked Justin boots. He wasn't a cowboy, though; he hated horses and had no interest in spending long days out riding the desert chasing cows. No, J.W. had a much different calling—he was a thief. And a burglar. And a mugger. Anything to put some money in his pockets without too much work.

His attention was focused on a loud-mouthed windbag sitting in a booth with a couple of other men. They were dressed alike in the uniforms from the C.C.C. camp. The blowhard was noisily bragging that he had the inside track on finding the robber's loot in the cave where they worked. He said it was merely a matter of time until he found it, cashed in the gold, and went back to Denver to start a Cadillac car dealership.

J.W. had more than a passing interest in what the man was saying. First, it represented a possible way to make some real money instead of the penny-ante crimes he existed on. Second, it was a matter of family pride. He was related to Doc Smart, the gang leader who robbed the trains and hid the treasure. The family legend was that he had been cheated out of the riches he had stolen. So it would be only fitting if he, J.W. Smart, were the one to bring it back into the family.

He had an old buddy who was one of the L.E.M's at the camp. J.W. knew he was home in Tucson on weekends and went to find him. His friend agreed to keep an ear to the ground and report any useful information he might learn. In return, J.W. offered him a reward of one hundred dollars if his help led to the treasure.

***

Simon Gregory was excited about a new opportunity. He had spent many long years working for the Wells Fargo Company as a mid-level accountant, but his true love was history— the Wells Fargo Company's history in particular. The company's records were extensive, but his interest focused on the unrecovered assets from various robberies in the past.

An article in the San Francisco Examiner piqued his interest. It highlighted the work of the C.C.C. and mentioned one of their projects to develop a cave near Tucson, Arizona. More research confirmed the cave was the one referenced in the company's records as the place suspected of being the place a band of robbers had hidden gold and silver after daring train robberies in 1887. Many searchers had failed to find it over the years since. Now there was much more activity in the cave, and the chance of someone finding the treasure was much greater.

The company's records indicated the gold and silver value to be much higher than had ever been disclosed to the public— well over one hundred thousand dollars in 1887. Far more now. That stash was something Gregory could use to pad his retirement from the company and live comfortably indeed—if he could find it. He picked up his phone and called his contact with the Western States Detective Agency.

***

The bright, sunny October Tucson day was a welcome change for Martin Hoag. It was nice to get out of the cold, foggy weather of San Francisco. He had worked a couple of other jobs in Tucson in the past and had some reliable connections there. He was the sole owner and employee of the Western States Detective Agency, a name he used to make himself appear more credible to his clients.

He thought he looked the part of a dashing private detective: bold striped three-piece single-breasted suit, cuffed pants, a bright mustard-colored shirt, a black tie, topped off with a white Panama hat. He switched from cigarettes to a pipe when he thought it made him look more authoritative. The warm days didn't discourage him from his idea of dressing for success. He strutted and stood out like a visiting celebrity on the streets of Tucson.

He took this job because of a possible large payout, though he was only being paid enough for necessary expenses if, and until, he was able to complete his task. At Wells Fargo, Simon Gregory anticipated the treasure's temptation and made it clear that they would need to work together to cash in on the gold. He, Gregory, as an employee of the company, was the only one who could do that.

The detective planned to do everything possible to find and take possession of the stolen Wells Fargo gold and silver. The reward Gregory promised him for success was exceptionally high.

Hoag immediately sought out some men from the camp who were in town for the weekend. He steered the conversation to the lost treasure after some friendly discussion in a diner. Hoag said he'd heard it was nothing but wishful thinking on the part of people who had looked for it. Reuben's name eventually came up in the conversation, and the detective decided he would be his starting point for information. He learned Reuben was currently in town, taking in the latest western movie. Hoag waited outside the Fox Theatre downtown with a description of him in hand.

When Reuben emerged, the detective approached him and offered him money to report any suspicious activity. The detective said the Wells Fargo Company hired him to find their stolen property, and he would reward Reuben generously if his help led to a successful recovery. Reuben was impressed with the smartly dressed man; he perfectly fit Reuben's notion of a big city Cadillac salesman. He didn't hesitate to accept the offer, and, besides, he thought, he would say nothing to the detective if he found the treasure first.

Reuben shared his suspicions about Jimmy and Harry and agreed to meet the detective outside the camp twice a week to pass on any information he picked up. The detective gave him ten dollars as payment for the information he provided that day.

$$***$$

Jimmy and Harry discussed the visit from the Sheriff and the Treasury agent. Harry said, "Damn! Now the whole camp's gonna be lookin' everywhere for that loot. It's gonna make it a lot harder for us to do anything with it without bein' seen."

"Yeah, but that's not the half of it," Jimmy said. "Now we have the law sniffing around, and that agent sounds like he means business. Maybe he's trying to make a name for himself. And that warning from the Sheriff about desperate people coming around is another worry. I think the stuff will be safe where we hid it, but we have to move fast to come up with a good plan for what to do next."

Jimmy thought for a minute. "I guess we're going to be criminals if we try to keep it. And we're going to have to watch our backs—no telling where trouble might spring up next. We need to think long and hard about all this." The dinner bell rang, and they went separately into the mess tent for the evening meal.

CHAPTER 10
CRIMINAL MINDS

Sleepless nights haunted both men. Their already tricky task had just become much more so and dangerous too. Their thoughts stalked them: Is it worth it? Should they give it up to the government? What if they didn't and were caught? There were many things that could happen. Were they willing to take that risk?

So far, they didn't have any plan for how to proceed. Jimmy had focused on simply getting the stash out of the cave to keep someone else from finding it. Neither he nor Harry had yet come up with a workable plan for moving it away from the camp or what they would do with it once they did. They only had their dreams of a fancy bar and a sprawling cattle ranch. They hadn't thought through how they could make any of that happen.

Jimmy wrestled with himself through the night about what to do. He had never thought of himself as a criminal. But that's what he would be if he didn't follow the government's rules. What would his mother think if he were arrested and put in jail? And how would she get by without the money he earned for her? It was almost too painful for words.

But, he thought, on the other hand, why shouldn't he get a break? After all, he didn't rob the trains. He rationalized that if any of the earlier searchers had found it, they wouldn't have been likely to turn it over to the government either. Why should he? Wasn't the government part of the problem that had brought on the Depression and put them in this situation? He didn't think what he had found would serve anyone who desperately needed it if it just disappeared into the US Treasury.

The reality that nagged at him was that he had absolutely nothing to look forward to as a career when his time with the CCC was up. The Depression had only gotten worse, and there were no prospects he could see. It was a terrible choice.

Was it a bad thing to be able to help his family through these challenging times? Or allow him and Kathleen to marry and live comfortably? How would he explain his newfound wealth to her, or to his family for that matter? The answers to his questions, like sleep, eluded him until reveille woke the rest of the camp.

Harry worried about the criminal risk too, but he had already thought a lot about what it meant. He knew that to make use of the gold, they would have to find a way around the government's restrictions on holding it. That alone would put them at risk of arrest. They had already taken the first step to being lawbreakers. As far as he was concerned, they might as well go all the way.

He had nothing to look forward to back in Ajo. He desperately wanted to find a way to avoid working in the mine or smelter, barely making a living. Their find would gain him that freedom. To him, helping his family far outweighed the risks. He thought of a way to get the bags of loot away from the camp as he tossed and turned in his sleepless hours before dawn.

The partners made plans to go into Tucson the following Saturday, where they could be free of prying eyes and ears to discuss what they would do. They found a sidewalk taqueria and ordered chili burros, tacos on the side, and bottles of Coca-Cola. A table with a faded umbrella for shade near Speedway Boulevard, away from other customers, further masked their discussion with traffic noise from the busy street.

Jimmy spoke first: "We have to decide how far to take this. Right now, we could forget it and go on as if nothing had happened. I don't think we broke any laws yet. But I've chewed on it for a week, and that's not what I want to do. I sure don't think the government needs that gold as much as you, me, and our families. I'm willing to take a chance to try and make this work like we discussed. Fifty-fifty partners."

Harry chewed on a taco and washed it down with a swallow of Coke. "I feel the same way. This is our one chance in life to make somethin' of ourselves. Sure, it's risky, but I think it's worth the risk. If we never take any risks, we'll never amount to anythin'. And I ain't goin back to the mine in Ajo. No way!"

"Well, I suppose it's settled then," Jimmy said. "After all, it's not like robbing a bank! But we have to figure out what to do with the stuff. You have any ideas about that?"

"We gotta figger out how to get it down the hill so we can get it away from the camp. That gold and silver must weigh close to two hundred pounds. I got an idea of what to do if we can bring it down and put it where we can get at it fast."

Jimmy said, "I have an idea, too. The whole camp knows your story about your family's silver mine and how you used to help work in it. So you would know something about the kind of rock that's valuable. We can use that to start a rumor we're looking around the hills for silver or gold."

Harry nodded in agreement. "Yeah, everybody knows there's old mine diggings scattered around here. We need to get a couple of those rock hammers next time we're in town and start pretendin' we're pokin' around some old prospector diggins' up in the hills.

They continued talking and planning for a while, then made their way to a movie theatre for a matinee where they knew some of the other men would be. It gave them a good cover for being in town, in case any suspicious minds wondered why they were there. This time the film was Cleopatra, starring Claudette Colbert. She wore lots of gold jewelry and a golden headpiece. All that glitter made it difficult for Jimmy to pay attention to the story. His mind kept wandering to the treasure he had found and what their next steps should be. They got back to camp in time for dinner, ready to start working on the next part of their plans.

***

The partners decided not to spend much time together the next day, Sunday, to avoid arousing suspicion about what they might be doing. Harry joined in on a camp football game while Jimmy stayed in their tent, composing a letter to Kathleen. They avoided each other except at mealtimes when the conversation was always about something far removed from the cave's treasure.

Jimmy was feeling guilty again for not writing to Kathleen more often. He had been so engrossed with finding the treasure and trying to figure out what to do with it that he had lost track of time. In the beginning, they wrote to each other every week. But as Jimmy had become more preoccupied, it tapered off to every two or three weeks. Now it had been about two months since he had written to her.

As he thought about it, it seemed strange he had received no letter from her recently. His last letter from his mother mentioned that she saw less of Kathleen and supposed she was busy with her own family. He began to wonder if that was a bad sign.

He sat and tried to clear the turmoil from his mind, then started to write in his scrawling hand:

October 17, 1934

My Dear Kathleen,

I'm sorry for not writing sooner. I have been so busy that time seems to pass by without noticing. It has been an exciting time with lots of activity in the cave.

I hope you and your family are doing okay in these difficult times. I expect you are busy too, and maybe find it hard for the time to write.

The CCC will let me sign up for another six months here. It looks like the best way for me to continue to make enough money to keep my mother and family in their home. I realize that's a long time to ask you to wait for me. And there's nothing for sure to look forward to after that with the Depression going on.

I want to stay in Arizona. There are friends here that I can depend on. And I want to try and get into the ranching business someday. I can tell you are not too excited about that idea, but I hope you will consider it. I truly hope you will join me. We could be very happy here. I will keep you in my thoughts,

Love, Jimmy

He sealed the letter in an envelope, took it to the mess tent where he could buy a postage stamp, and put it in the box for outgoing mail. He hoped Kathleen would come around to his thinking.

***

Harry pulled Jimmy aside after dinner the following Wednesday. "I think I may have a way to do what we need. But I'm gonna have to ask one of my cousins who lives in Tucson to help us. I think he can get a car and meet us out here someplace. We grew up together, I can trust him, and I don't think he'll have to know what we're doin'. But I will have to go into Tucson to talk to him."

"How can you keep him from knowing what we are doing? Won't he be suspicious of you not trusting him?"

"I'll tell him it's some secret Indian artifacts or somethin'. I think he would be happy if we buy his gas and pay him somethin' for his time. I can see how he acts when I ask him. If I don't think it will work, we can find another way."

Jimmy thought about it and said, "It's worth a try. How about this? Let's scout around some of the old prospector diggings and see if we can find some promising-looking rocks to put in our bags. If he's curious, we could show him a couple and say we're taking samples to Ajo to get them tested. Would that work?"

"It might. Let's keep thinkin' on it. I'll go into town on Saturday and find my cousin, see if he'll do it. I'll buy a couple of cheap used prospector picks for us, too."

Jimmy's turn at weekend camp chores kept him from going to town the following Saturday. He worried about the plan, but he had to trust Harry's judgment.

When Harry returned Saturday evening, they could only have a brief talk. "It looks good," Harry said. "Let's find time tomorrow to work it out."

They met up the next morning after breakfast when Jimmy had finished his chores in the mess tent. They were sitting under their favorite shady ramada, a short way from the tents. A stately saguaro cactus with upward curving arms stood watch over them under a sky the color of faded blue denim. A red-tailed hawk, looking for a rabbit or ground squirrel, gave a piercing call as it floated overhead on the breeze.

"So here's the deal," Harry began. "I told my cousin we had found some old mine works in the area, and I thought there was some ore worth checkin' out. I asked him if he would be willin' to pick us up some Saturday and take us to Ajo so I could have my dad check out the samples we have."

Jimmy nodded, and Harry continued, "He said he figgered he could borrow his dad's truck for a day, so long as we let him know ahead of time." He paused and went on, "We have to work out how to meet him here without raisin' anybody's interest."

He looked up and saw Reuben and his two Colorado cronies coming toward them. "Uh oh, trouble Jimmy. I'll tell you the rest later."

"What're you girls doing out here all by yerselves? Seems like you two been spendin' a lot of time alone," Reuben said with his

trademark sneer. "I'm thinkin' you're either in love, or you got somethin' to hide. Either way, you go to a lot of trouble keepin' it to yerselves. So fess up. What is it?"

Jimmy said, "Reuben, your imagination is getting away from you. We work here every day, same as you, live in the same tent as you. But, if you have to know, we have been prospecting. Harry knows a lot about that stuff. It beats hanging around here looking at you all weekend!"

He looked Reuben square in the eye and continued, "Besides, Harry and I have been buddies ever since our time at Ft. Huachuca. What's it to you if we like to talk and hang around with each other? How's that any different from you and your buddies here?"

Reuben was surprised by someone talking back to him. He had been taller and heavier than most of the kids he grew up with and used bullying and intimidation to get his way. His mother died when he was young, and his father beat him regularly until he went to prison for a robbery, leaving Reuben angry and confused. After that, he lived with an aunt who gave him little guidance or supervision. He had learned bullying was the best way he could get along in the world.

"Well, I got some idear you two might have an angle on that robbers' loot in the cave. It was you, weren't it Harry, started that rumor about some clue bein' buried by the ranch house—

knowin' full well I'd be lookin' for it instead of watchin' you?"

Jimmy and Harry both laughed, and Harry said, "That was a joke we played on you. We knew you were hot to find that loot, and you'd go after that clue!"

"A joke!" Reuben yelled. "You thought that was funny? I oughta' bust you one in the mouth for laughin' at me!"

"Come ahead and try," Harry said. "But make sure your two buddies stay out of it!"

"Well," Reuben huffed, "we're gonna be watchin' ever' move you two make from now on. We got as much right to that treasure as you. We expect a cut if you find it. If I discover yer holdin' out on us, I'll get hold of that Treasury agent and put him on to you. I'll get a fat reward, and you'll get nothin'—'cept maybe jail time!" With that, he motioned his buddies to follow him and stormed off back into camp. Reuben didn't mention that he'd previously seen the two men sneaking off to the cave and spending several hours inside.

"Damn, that's a wrinkle," Jimmy said. "We better move as soon as we can. The more time that passes, one of those goons might stumble on to something they shouldn't see. And we have to find a foolproof way to do it." He thought a minute and said," We better make a show of poking around some rocks to make it look good."

Harry agreed. "There is a perfect place we could stash the bags at Dad's old mine. My cousin don't have a phone, but I could go to town on Friday night and see if he can pick us up on Saturday. Then I can find a payphone and call my dad. I'll tell him we'd like to come and stay a night and borrow his truck. If that don't work, it might have to be the followin' week or somethin'."

Jimmy said, "We have to come up with a plan for how to get it out of here. I think I have an idea." They discussed it at length, and Harry made plans to go to town on Friday night.

Harry got back late Friday night and whispered to Jimmy, "It's set for Saturday next week! My cousin will pick us up, then leave us in Ajo; we can do what we need to, then catch a bus back to Tucson on Sunday in time for the last camp shuttle. My dad will let us borrow his truck so long as we put gas in it."

The next day they made a show of spending some time up in

the foothills and came back at dinner time with some shiny rocks in their bags. They showed them to a couple of men, who were impressed with their sparkle. Harry said, "We hope there might be some silver worth minin' here. We're gonna take it to Ajo and try to find out."

***

Brian Miller was a quiet man who mainly kept to himself. He was one of Jimmy's tent mates. Of all the men in camp, Jimmy was his only friend. They weren't close, but at least Brian felt

comfortable striking up a conversation with him occasionally. He was impressed by the rocks the men had shown and asked Jimmy if he might be able to go out with them sometime to learn more about prospecting. Jimmy said he'd see if it would be alright with Harry. The partners discussed it later and decided it would be useful to have another person confirm what they were doing. It might even help get Reuben off their backs.

Sunday morning had an early fall chill in the air as Brian left camp with the partners. He was excited about learning something new. They hiked further than he ever had up the Rincon Mountains' rugged foothills, looking for sparkly rocks like the ones Harry had shown him and the other men. Brian stopped and pointed across the canyon they were following. "I thought I saw something shining across the canyon. Is it okay if I take a closer look?" Jimmy and Harry waved him on and sat down to have a smoke. Brian's enthusiasm was amusing. They'd pretend to be interested in whatever he might bring back.

***

The great cat stalked a short way behind Brian. It had seen the other humans before in this area, but was reluctant to attack two of them at once. This one was a different human, with a different scent. The cat continued tracking behind him, slinking stealthily and silently through the brush. It circled around him when he was down in the canyon, far away from the others

Brian felt a prickle of the hairs on the back of his neck. Something was off, but he couldn't put his finger on it. Everything seemed to grow strangely quiet; the birds had stopped singing in the bush, and there was an eerie stillness. He had taken a few more steps when a huge mountain lion slipped out of the brush directly in front of him. For a moment, Brian was mesmerized by the wild beauty of the cat; its sleek tawny body, long tail twitching over the rocks, and feline eyes that looked almost alien. It took a couple of steps toward him. Brian turned and ran in a blind panic.

The enormous cat was on him before he took three steps. It weighed more than the man and easily took him down, its weight holding him on the ground. Brian struggled against the cougar's body and tried to hit it in the head with his fists. But the cat had him pinned too tightly for his blows to have any effect. He screamed just before the animal's jaws closed down on his throat with unbearable pressure. The last thing he saw was one of the cat's merciless yellow eyes looking into his.

The partners heard his scream and ran toward where they had last seen him drop into the canyon. They came upon a scene neither would ever forget; blood was gushing from Brian's throat, the cat had gnawed his face, and now was tearing at one of his legs. They started yelling and throwing rocks. The lion hissed at them before moving a short way off. The men kept at it until the cat skulked off into the brush.

Brian was dead. The cat's attack had torn out the carotid artery on the right side of his neck.; he had quickly bled out from the wound. They could do nothing for him, and they were afraid for either of them to stay alone to keep the cat away. They were not armed and would be no match for it when it returned for its prey. They high-tailed it back to camp for help as fast as they could.

The following morning, during muster, the captain spoke to the men. "You men know that the desert can be a dangerous and deadly place. It's why we have warned you against going off alone. Now a horrible death has occurred. We will arrange a memorial service as soon as possible. I have hired an experienced hunter to track down and kill the lion, which attacked Mr. Miller. I advise you to stay in camp until then and be cautious in the future about going into the hills alone or unarmed."

Jimmy and Harry both felt guilty and responsible because they had inspired Brian with their talk of silver in the hills.

"We shouldn't have let him wander off alone. I feel like it's my fault for letting him go out with us," Jimmy said. Brian's empty bunk and belongings were tragic reminders of what had happened.

"We both made that decision, Jimmy. How were we to know what would happen? It's a terrible lesson for us and everyone here."

"I hope it's not a sign of bad luck to come because of what we're doing. Brian would be alive today if we hadn't encouraged him with false hopes." Jimmy tried to ignore the gut feeling that the treasure might be a source of bad luck.

They decided they would not be making any more "prospecting" forays into the mountains. Or, if they did, they would borrow a rifle to take along.

***

Jimmy was surprised to receive a letter from Kathleen so soon, and there was another one from his mother. He quickly opened the one from Kathleen when he was back in his tent.

October 27, 1934

Dear Jimmy,

I have shed many tears since your last letter, and I am writing with a heavy heart. We seemed to have been growing apart for some time now. I know you are looking for new opportunities in Arizona. We have both changed over the last few months, and I, too, have looked in new directions.

I cannot abide by the idea of living in Arizona. My family is here, and it's where I want to stay. I have decided it's time for us to go our separate ways and do what will make us both happy in our lives.

I guess that's a long way around to say you are free to find someone else that could make you happier. I will always have fond memories of our times together, and I wish you all the best.

Your friend always,

Kathleen

It took him a while to process this news. He had suspected, in the back of his mind, it might turn out this way. Maybe it was his fault for leaving her. He thought about it for a long while, staring into the flickering light from the tent's lantern. The closeness of the tent seemed to make the letter more depressing. Then he opened the letter from his mother:

October 27, 1934

Dear Son,

 I am writing to you with some sad news. Kathleen came for a visit yesterday and told me she intended to end her relationship with you. She was tearful and apologized that it had worked out that way and that she was sending a letter to you to explain it.

She said she could not agree with your idea of staying out there. She didn't want to be that far away from her mother.

But, Son, I want you to know that I heard from friends that she has been seeing that Henry Biggs boy. You know, the son of the Biggs that owns the lumber mill where your father worked. I think it started up pretty soon after you left.

I know this is painful for you. But maybe it's for the best. I don't think she was as sincere in her commitment to you as she let on, or she would have waited longer before seeing someone else. I am broken-hearted for you and sorry that Kathleen was not the girl I thought she was.

We are doing fine. Your brother has found a part-time job sweeping up at Miller's grocery and helping with stocking shelves and such. That extra helps with what you send. I'll close now. I hope all is well with your work there. Write to me when you can.

I love you very much,

Mother

Well, Jimmy thought, that explains why the letters from Kathleen had grown cold. He was surprised he wasn't shocked or sad about it. His earlier guilt turned to anger. He knew Henry Biggs had been eyeing Kathleen and didn't find it surprising now that they had gotten together. But that didn't make it any less painful. Despite his anger, he felt an odd sense of freedom and release from their relationship's worry. Now, at least, he could get on with his life with a clear conscience.

He wrote a letter back to his mother, thanking her for letting him know about Kathleen. He told her that he had not been surprised because they had seemed drifting apart the past weeks; ending their relationship was for the best.

He told Harry about the letters at breakfast. "I'm awful sorry, Jimmy. What a dirty, low-down thing for her to do. Here you are, tryin' to do the best you can for your family, and all the while she's been two-timin' you."

A couple of the other men at their table had heard the discussion and joined in with condolences. One of them said, "Man, if that was my gal, I'd be havin' blood in my eye for that guy she's cheatin' with. That ain't right!"

Jimmy thanked them for their support. "I appreciate what you guys are saying. But I kind of knew it was coming, and I'm not surprised. Yeah, I'd like to get my hands on the guy she two-timed me with. But I think she's more to blame than he is. I'm mostly glad I don't have to worry about it anymore." The conversation continued until breakfast was over, with a lot of grumbling and cursing of untrue women.

***

Jimmy and Harry were up before dawn the following Saturday, walked quickly out of camp and up the hill to the rocks where they had hidden the stash of bags. Jimmy had acquired four large, heavy-duty duffel bags, and they transferred the burlap bags' contents into them. Harry said, "These bags gotta weigh fifty pounds each. I'm glad we're carrying 'em downhill!" They lugged them down near the end of the cave's access road. Rosy dawn started to envelop the Rincon mountains, bathing the foothills in the soft light. They hurriedly stashed the duffels out of sight, then moved off into hiding behind some rocks, waiting for their ride to show up.

The camp was stirring and getting ready for breakfast, and no one paid any attention to the Green Ford Model AA pickup kicking up dust on its way past the camp up toward the cave. Its green paint looked similar to the camp's army vehicles' color in the early light. It reached the turnaround at the end of the road as Jimmy and Harry each grabbed two of the heavy Army duffel bags and chucked them into the back. They jumped into the cab, and Harry said, "Hey, Bill! It's great to see you. This is my buddy, Jimmy. Hit it, and let's get outta" here!"

Two pairs of eyes watched the truck intently as it roared past the camp and away down the road to Tucson—Reuben and J.W. Smart's friend, Rodriquez the LEM. Reuben nodded to himself and said under his breath, "The game is on." He rounded up his two cronies and told them what he wanted them to do. Then he left on the next camp shuttle to Tucson. A friend picked up the LEM, and they headed into town where he would meet Smart and pass on his news.

"Think anyone saw us?" Jimmy asked. They were well down the road away from the camp.

Harry looked back at their cloud of dust. "Maybe. But they prob'ly thought it was one of the camp trucks out on early errands. If they did, they couldn't see us inside, and there ain't no way to identify this truck."

"Reuben and his bunch will surely miss us," Jimmy said. "They'll likely figure our absence is related to this truck when he hears about it. And he'll no doubt hear about it."

"Well, let him speculate. What we do ain't no business of his, anyhow. If it comes up, we'll say we decided to spend the weekend with my family in Ajo and get some of our samples tested. He can worry over that much as he wants."

Bill asked them why they were trying to be so secretive about getting away from the camp. "We're trying to keep them pryin' eyes and gossips from knowin' much about what we're doin'," Harry said. "Any one of 'em would try to horn in on our find if they could. So, the less they know, the better." Bill allowed that made a lot of sense, and there was no more discussion about it.

Jimmy said, "I'm hungry enough to eat a mess of those rubbery eggs Ol' Charlie slings at breakfast. Is there someplace we can get something decent?" They neared Tucson, with a few motels and gas stations scattered along the city's outskirts. "There's a great little place when we get into town," Bill said. "You'll like it!"

The place was a tiny roadside taqueria serving colossal breakfast burros stuffed with scrambled eggs, potatoes, chorizo, jalapeño peppers, onions, and tomato. Harry and his cousin slathered them with a fiery hot red salsa, but that was too much for Jimmy's taste. He thought they were delicious without it. The partners paid for Bill's meal with theirs. Then, they hit the road with full bellies.

They passed through the south part of Tucson and got on what Bill called the Ajo Highway. As they left town, the desert closed in around them. Jimmy said, "The desert here is even more barren on this side of Tucson. There's a lot more creosote."

Harry said, "Yep, and it gets hotter and drier the further west we go. But there's a lot of saguaros and other kinds of cactus further on."

They passed a sign that said they were entering the Papago Indian Reservation. Harry said, "This is a big chunk of Indian land that sits right on the Mexican border for miles. The tribe calls themselves the Tohono O'Odham. One of my Indian friends told me it means 'the people.' The Papago name came from what other tribes called this one, and the Spaniards pronounced it as Papago. They say the word meant 'bean eaters.' These people don't much like the name."

Harry continued, "Ain't nothin' out here but Indian houses and one town you'd miss if ya blink! That funny lookin' mountain off there to the south is called Baboquivari; it's a sacred place for the Indians. My Indian friend told me that they want to build their houses in sight of that mountain because it's the center of their creation." It was a strange-looking mountain, with a pronounced, slightly curved and rugged peak jutting above the surrounding hills.

They passed through the community of Sells, the capital of the reservation. There wasn't much there: A trading post and store, a gas station, the tribal headquarters building, the Bureau of Indian Affairs offices, and a scattering of modest houses.

They covered a hundred miles of empty desert. Jimmy was fascinated by the many rugged and jagged mountains along the way. It was a much different-looking landscape than the mountains around Tucson. They seemed smaller and rougher.

They came to a highway junction at a place called "Why." A gas station and a few scattered buildings made up the entire place. Jimmy grinned and said, "Okay, I'll bite. Why is it called Why?" Harry and Bill both laughed. Bill said he heard it's because nobody could figure out why it's there! Harry explained: "It used to be called simply 'Y,' like the letter, because of the highway junction's shape. Highway 86 joins Highway 85, which runs north to Ajo or south to Mexico, forming a 'Y.' I heard the folks livin' there couldn't get mail 'cause the letter 'Y' couldn't be an official name, so they changed it to the word 'Why.'"

They rolled into Ajo around noon, and Jimmy was impressed with the looming smelter and a large mound of the mine's tailings that dominated everything about the town. Company houses to serve the mine's workers were laid out on neat streets radiating outward from a business plaza. They mostly looked alike, plainly built with no frills. Low, reddish-brown colored hills dotted the landscape. Jimmy thought the place had a lonely, forlorn look about it. It was surrounded by miles and miles of desert.

They parked in front of Harry's house. He said there were three bedrooms and one bathroom, with a covered concrete patio in the back. It looked like its neighboring houses; a nondescript structure, fading brown paint, and a dirt yard with one scrawny Mexican palm tree. A few of the places had brownish patches of bermudagrass, thirsting for water.

The men quickly transferred their duffels into the house. Harry reached inside one and grabbed the bag of rock samples they had brought. He introduced Jimmy to his parents and his sister, Joann. After hugs among the family, Harry's mother sat them down at their dining table for a lunch of baloney and cheese sandwiches. She apologized, saying that it was all they could afford. The men said they were delicious and thanked her for sharing with them. She favored them with a gentle smile. She was a beautiful woman with delicate features and ivory skin, barely starting to show a touch of gray in her red hair. Her voice carried the faintest trace of a Spanish accent.

Jimmy had trouble focusing on the conversation; Harry's sister hijacked his attention. Joann was striking, with red hair like her mother's and cornflower blue eyes that boldly held Jimmy's gaze. She was nineteen years old, a year younger than Harry. Her lithe build gave her the look of an athlete. A light dusting of freckles highlighted her otherwise flawless complexion. Jimmy was smitten at first sight and had difficulty keeping his eyes off her. She seemed keenly aware of his attention and did nothing to discourage it.

After their brief lunch, Bill apologized and said he had to get his dad's truck back to Tucson that afternoon. He left Jimmy and Harry standing in the driveway, watching him go.

CHAPTER 11

ECHOES OF SPAIN

"So, what're you boys up to? You want to see our old silver mine, Jimmy? Ain't much but a deep black hole. Not sure what you'll learn from that." Harry's dad looked from one to the other; the deep sun-squint lines around his eyes made him look intense and intimidating. His years working in the open-pit mine left him darkly tanned. He and Harry were built just alike— thick, muscular arms with a stocky build. They were both about the same height, too, a little under six feet.

Harry said, "We're interested in maybe doin' some prospectin' after we finish our CCC jobs. Jimmy wants to learn more about what the rocks look like; the kind of country that might be promisin'." He brought out the bag of rock samples he had brought and showed them to his dad. "We found these around some old diggins' in the mountains near our camp. What do you think about them?"

"Hell, boy! You know well as me this whole country's been picked clean for years. I heard some stories about some old mines in the Rincon mountains. Everyone says they played out years ago." He turned over the samples in his hands. "This stuff don't look any different than what you find in most tailin' piles around these mines. If the minin' companies don't have any use for it, why should you? I thought I taught you better than this."

He shook his head and said, "If you want to waste your time wanderin' around out there, that's your business. But you better not wander too long 'fore you get to findin' work of some kind.

Harry said, "I wanna show Jimmy around some. Drive out to your mine— give him a better idea about what to look for to find good ore."

His father shook his head again but said, "Go ahead and take my truck. But fill it up with gas when you get back. That stuff ain't cheap!"

"You boys want some more sandwiches to take with you?" Harry's mom asked.

"Sure, Mom. That would be great. We'll prob'ly camp overnight and be back in the morning."

***

They filled a 5-gallon jerry can with water to take with them. Jimmy wasn't much impressed with the apparent condition of the truck. It was a 1928 Chevrolet pickup, a testament to a hard, harsh life in the desert. Its original green paint faded to a splotchy grayish tint after years in the hot Arizona sun. Numerous dents, scratches, and a vertical crack in the middle of the windshield showed a life on rough roads.

Jimmy said, "You sure this will get us there and back?"

"Yep," Harry laughed. "This old crate runs like a top. Besides, it pretty much knows its way out there and back by itself!"

They thanked Harry's mother for the sandwiches and told his dad they'd be back in the morning. Jimmy made a point of telling Joann how nice it was meeting her. He added that he hoped to see her again soon. She blushed and smiled and said, "Nice to meet you, too."

When they were on the road, Jimmy said, "Man, Harry! You never told me how beautiful your sister is. She looks a lot like your mother. She has the same red hair and blue eyes. Is she dating anyone? Your sister, I mean," he said with a chuckle.

"What do you care? You sure you're over that girl back in Denver?"

"I'm over her all right," Jimmy said. "There's no chance of us ever getting back together, not after she two-timed me with that other guy. I'd never trust her again."

They were quiet for a few minutes. "I'm sorry, Jimmy. That had to be painful." Harry teared up and looked away from Jimmy. This was a side of Harry he had never seen. Harry continued, "Our lives are tough enough without somethin' like that happenin'. When I was sixteen, I got dumped by a girl I thought loved me. I didn't see it comin'; thinkin' about it still hurts."

Jimmy nodded and said, "My breakup with Kathleen was painful too, but it seemed like the right thing to do. I feel a lot better about it now, not worrying about what was going on with her. It would never have worked out if she had joined me here. That would have been a lot worse in the end."

"Yeah, I feel the same way about that girl dumpin' me. I know now it was for the best. I haven't had a girlfriend I could trust since then."

They were silent and lost in thought for several miles until Harry turned off on a narrow dirt road. "How'd you know where to turn?" Jimmy asked. "Everything looks the same." There were many cactuses of a type Jimmy had never seen. Harry called them organ pipe cactus because they had multiple tube-like arms reaching up from their base. They were everywhere.

"I watch how many miles we come past Why; then watch for two big piles of rocks right before the turnoff. But I've been here so many times I could prob'ly find it in the dark. Matter of fact, I have found it in the dark!"

They bumped along several miles and crossed some sandy washes. "I'm glad it's not the rainy season," Jimmy said. "These washes look like they can run lots of water."

"I've been stuck out here a time or two." Harry chuckled to himself and said, "You have to wait for the water to go down, or you could wind up bein' here a lot longer than you planned."

They drove several miles on the dirt road, before they turned off onto a dirt track that was no more than two wheel ruts. The truck bounced, squeaked, and groaned over rocks and small drainages that crossed the tracks. "Well, here we are," Harry laughed a couple of rough miles later. "Ain't much to see, but I think it'll suit our needs."

It was late afternoon when they parked next to an old ramshackle tumble-down rock house. It looked like it had been there forever. Jimmy could see it had no doors or glass in the windows, and he suspected the roof was in no better condition. He thought their camp tents might have been better protection from the elements.

It was sitting about fifty yards downhill from what appeared to be some timber works. Everything seemed ancient as if it had been there since creation.

Harry set the truck's brake and put a rock behind one wheel as insurance. He said the brake had failed on one occasion, and he'd had to run down the hill to retrieve it. It ran into a mesquite tree, and that was how the truck came by a lot of its dings and scratches. Jimmy had a good laugh at the idea of that. A large pile of empty beer bottles was off to one side in a haphazard pile. Numerous old whiskey bottles here and there spoke of a long history at the place. Jimmy said, "Holy cow! It looks like some wild party happened here!"

Harry laughed. "Nah. Most of that stuff's been there for years. My Dad and Uncle Fred save the bottles for their deposits, but they never get around to returnin' em. There ain't nothin' to do at night but drink."

Lengthening shadows from the cactus and palo verde trees were a reminder the sun was dropping lower on the horizon. Harry said, "It will be dark soon. Let me show you where I want to stash the bags."

He led the way further up the hill. Jimmy's first reaction to the mine works was one of disbelief. "You mean you actually go down that hole using this contraption? It looks to me like the whole works are likely to tumble in after you!"

"It's a lot stouter than it looks. My dad and uncle have shored it up a lot since they've had the claim for the mine. Besides, it's been here for a hundred years or so, and it's still standin'!"

"Well, all the same, I'd want a good strong rope around me if I went down in it. It's not where I'd like to spend the rest of my days." Harry laughed and told him not to worry.

The mine was a nearly vertical shaft plunging into a black abyss. A large head frame made of heavy timbers was positioned over it. Its two massive beams were held together with thick steel straps. The beams were attached to two substantial tripod-shaped supports on either side of the shaft. In addition, it had another massive beam for support attached and anchored in the ground behind the structure. The whole thing's shape vaguely reminded Jimmy of a giant children's playground swing.

Harry said, "This steel cable connects to the ore car underneath the frame, then goes over the big iron wheel at the top and connects to a winch. That old gasoline engine behind the frame runs a generator for the electric winch to lower and raise the ore car. We always have a safety cable attached when we go down, and there's a long rope ladder we drop into the shaft, just in case." But, he assured Jimmy, they had never had a problem.

He explained, "The mine was first worked by Spanish prospectors a couple of hundred years ago. When the U.S. took over the Arizona territories, some American miners worked it. But by then, the Spaniards had pretty much taken out most of the silver. The Americans rebuilt most of the works used to service the shaft. Then they took out some lower-grade ore for a few years. Eventually, they abandoned it because it wasn't profitable. When my dad and uncle got the claim, they shored up the more recent work to make it safer. Then they replaced the old gasoline engine and generator with this one."

Harry led them beyond the mine's works and around the side of the hill to an old prospecting hole covered with timbers. Harry said, "Nobody ever comes out here, except my dad and uncle, and no one else would have any reason to be around.

This old diggin' hasn't been disturbed in years. Watch your step. These loose rocks are kind of slippery." He bent down and tossed a few of the old timbers aside.

It was a shallow hole that was evidently not promising to the earlier prospector. Harry said, "My dad and uncle have a claim on this whole hill; nobody's ever gonna be pokin' around this old dig. It's the safest place I can think of to store our bags. We can cover them with a tarp to keep 'em dry 'cause it can rain cats and dogs when the monsoon comes."

Jimmy agreed to the plan. "Before we do that, let's count what we have in the bags. We've never had a good look at it."

There was a rickety old wooden table with wooden benches inside the house. It looked nearly as old as the mine works. "Watch out for scorpions," Harry said. "They like to hide in the cracks between the rocks in the walls and under stuff like this table and bench. Don't put your hands where you can't see!"

Jimmy had seen a man in camp who was stung on the foot by a scorpion. It had been in his boot when he dressed in the morning. Jimmy didn't want to have a similar experience. The man was very sick for two or three days, and it took nearly a week for the swelling in his foot to go down enough to get a boot on. One of the LEM old timers said he was lucky it wasn't one of the more poisonous bark scorpions.

They brought in the duffels and started unloading the smaller bags onto the table. They dumped the first one out and sat for a minute, staring at the gold coins. "My God, Harry! Did you ever see such a sight?"

Harry studied one of the coins a moment and said, "This is a ten-dollar gold eagle! My dad had one once." There were twenty of them in the bag, clean and shiny as if they had never been used. They seemed to glow with an inner light when the rays of the setting sun touched them. He went out to the truck and returned with a piece of paper and a dull pencil. "Let's start a tally so we can figger out what they're worth."

They continued opening and counting the contents of the bags. Most of them were gold eagles in various denominations. There were half eagles ($5) and quarter eagles ($2.50) in addition to the 10-dollar denomination. One bag was full of 20-dollar double eagles. Three of the bags held Mexican silver pesos and numerous other silver coins. But the most astonishing part of the loot was five bars of pure gold!

"It's gonna take some work to figure out how much this is worth," Jimmy said. "I'll take this list to the library in Tucson and see if I can find information to help us. But, Harry, I think we are rich beyond anything we had dreamed! I never imagined I would see this much gold and silver in my entire life!"

The last light of day was waning. Harry brought out a kerosene lantern stored in the house, primed and lit it. The lantern cast a harsh white light over the treasure they had spread out on the table. They finished their inventory and put the loot back in the duffels. "We can tuck this away in the mornin' and try to hide any of our tracks around that old pit—just to be extra cautious."

Harry said.

The baloney sandwiches from Harry's mother were a quick and filling dinner, and they sat in the lantern's light. The peace of the desert settled in around them. The breeze was a strangely soothing, subtle hum through the cactus thorns and delicate lacy leaves of the mesquite trees. The quiet was almost jarring after the constant noise of life in the camp.

Jimmy broke the silence. "So, how about it?" Jimmy asked.

"How 'bout what?"

"Is your sister dating anyone?"

"I don't think so. She was goin' with some guy for a while, but it didn't work out."

Harry stood and walked around a little before he continued, "You need to know my mother's family is from Mexico. Maria and me were both born in Mexico— not that we advertise it. It makes us half Mexican, which ain't always a popular thing around here." He added, "I've never told anyone outside of family, but I kept my Mexican citizenship—I have dual citizenship with the US and Mexico.

"Mexico? How can that be? Your mother has that beautiful light skin with red hair and blue eyes. I've never seen a Mexican with looks like that!"

Harry laughed. "Well, I'll allow you ain't seen that many Mexicans, bein' from Colorado. But my mother's family is different. Her mother's family descends directly from the Spaniards who settled in Mexico years ago, and she has a lot of pure Spanish blood. My Grandfather's side of the family has a lot of Spanish blood, too." The darker-skinned Mexicans you are used to seeing don't have as much Spanish blood.

"Wow!" Jimmy said. "I had no idea. All I can say is she and your sister are both beautiful women!" Jimmy paused and asked, "Would it be okay with you if I maybe asked your sister for a date sometime?"

Harry laughed. "Of course, it's alright with me! You are my best friend, and you are a gentleman. But I gotta warn you, that girl's got a redhead's temper. You better tread careful!"

The lantern was burning down, and Harry said, "We best sleep in the truck so's we don't have to worry about critters crawlin' in bed with us tonight. Rattlesnakes like to cozy up with you in a warm blanket when November nights cool off the way they are now. There ain't no doors on this old house, and one might invite itself inside."

Jimmy shuddered at the thought. They had borrowed a few blankets from Harry's parents and arranged them side by side in the bed of the old pickup truck. They took off their boots but slept in their clothes as the desert air's nighttime chill settled in over them.

Sometime deep in the night, Jimmy awoke to the sounds of something moving around the truck. It sniffled and snuffed as it circled the pickup. He sat up and looked around. A half-moon cast a pale, eerie light over the desert. As Jimmy's eyes slowly adjusted to the weak light, he saw shadowy forms moving around them.

He poked Harry. "Harry! Wake up! We've got company!"

Harry groaned and sat up, rubbing his eyes. "Coyotes! It's only coyotes," he said. "They always come around when we're here, looking for scraps and stuff. They ain't gonna bother us." He banged on the side of the truck, and the coyotes yipped and took off at a run.

Harry immediately went back to sleep, but Jimmy lay awake listening to the coyotes yipping and howling in the distance until the sun ate the last of the night's last shadows.

They were up at dawn and brushed the light dusting of frost from their blankets. Jimmy carefully shook out his boots before putting them on— a precaution against unwelcome overnight visitors. Harry laughed and said, "A scorpion ain't likely to find its way into this pickup's bed!"

"Just the same, I'm not taking any chances," Jimmy sniffed.

Harry put away the lantern while Jimmy rolled up and stowed the blankets they had used. Then they carried the heavy duffels up the hill to their new hiding place. They carefully placed them

in the hole, covered them with a tarp, and replaced the boards. Loose rocks and dirt scattered over the planks concealed their recent disturbance. After returning any rocks they had kicked over, they used creosote branches to erase the few footprints in the rocky soil around the spot. They were satisfied that they had done everything they could to protect their treasure and headed back to Ajo.

They had more breakfast burritos and lots of strong coffee at a hole-in-the-wall *taqueria* in the downtown plaza. The Greyhound bus stopped nearby at the Phelps Dodge mercantile store, and they saw it would arrive in about an hour. It was barely enough time to gas up, return the truck, and say goodbye to Harry's family.

Jimmy was most anxious to see Joann again, much to Harry's amusement. He managed to take her aside for a moment and told her he hoped to see her again soon. She said that would be very nice and she would look forward to it. After thanks and hugs around the family, they set off walking the short way back to the plaza to wait for the bus. No one noticed they no longer had the duffels they had with them when they had arrived.

They were back in Tucson in time to grab a cheeseburger before catching one of the weekend shuttles back to the camp. The shuttles ran two or three times each day on the weekend days to give the men a chance for a break from camp life.

They were excited but tired when they arrived back at the camp and headed for their tent to rest up before dinner. Brian's empty bed and belongings were lingering reminders of the tragedy of his death.

More trouble came after dinner.

CHAPTER 12
BRAWL IN A TENT

Jimmy and Harry sat upright on their cots as several men entered the tent. Reuben was in the lead, followed by his two cronies. Reuben's buddies were menacingly holding baseball bats, smacking them in their palms. Reuben had a sneer on his face that spelled trouble. The other men in the tent saw the warning signs and made quick exits.

"Okay, boys," Reuben snarled, "we're done with your cat and mouse games. I watched you leave outta here lickety-split in that strange pickup about daylight yesterday mornin'." He paused for effect. "Now you're gonna tell the truth about what you're up to!"

On their feet, Jimmy and Harry faced the trio. "What we do is no concern of yours, Reuben," Jimmy said. "We told you before you're spitting into the wind with your cockeyed treasure stuff."

Harry said, "Not that it's your business, but we spent the weekend visitin' my family in Ajo. We were findin' out about the ore samples we been collectin'. One of my cousins was kind enough to give us a ride to Ajo, and we rode the bus back to Tucson. Now get off our backs!"

Reuben's face went red, and he shouted, "I don't believe you! I guess we'll have to beat the truth out of you! Show 'em, boys!"

The first man swung at Harry's head, but Harry sidestepped and grabbed the bat. His face turned scarlet red as he twisted the bat away from his attacker. Then, he went after the man with a vengeance. His opponent tried to step out of reach, but he was too slow. Harry swung the bat and struck a hard blow across his opponent's kneecap. The man screamed and crumpled to the floor in agony. Two more hard blows across his chest cracked several ribs, and the fight was gone from the man. He begged Harry to stop as he lay whimpering on the floor.

Jimmy dived into the other man, knocking the bat out of his hands. They tumbled over one of the sleeping cots, with Jimmy ending up on top. The attacker landed an effective blow to the side of Jimmy's head before Jimmy pinned his arms with his knees. Then he pounded the guy's face until he quit struggling. Blood streamed from his nose and soaked his shirt.

Harry, his face a red mask of anger, brandished the bat at Reuben. "If you ever try anything like this again, I'll break both your legs and put you in the hospital. I ought to do it now, you miserable son of a bitch! Now gather up your sorry friends and get the hell out of here."

Reuben and his friend helped the man with a shattered kneecap out of the tent. As soon as he was outside, he yelled,

"This ain't over!" Reuben crept back into the tent late that night. He moved carefully among the sleeping men and slipped into his bed without a sound.

***

Reuben planned to "have his cake and eat it too." He reported to detective Hoag the day before the fight, and the detective gave him another ten dollars for his information about his suspects. He again promised Reuben a hefty reward if his information helped him successfully recover the treasure. Reuben figured he would milk that arrangement for all he could. But in the meantime, he would do everything possible to try to get the prize for himself. He, too, had signed on for another six months with the CCC. He was sure he would find the treasure with a little more time.

***

Jimmy and Harry looked at each other. "Now we're in for it," Jimmy said. "He'll run to the law and put them on us. We better be sure our story's straight."

"Yeah, and that ain't the half of it. I expect we're gonna get a grillin' from the camp commander, too. I likely busted that guy's kneecap and cracked some ribs, so he's gonna be laid up a while. The commander comes down pretty hard on troublemakers. We'll catch hell even though we didn't start it."

Sure enough, the following day before breakfast, the camp commander summoned them to his tent. Neither of them had ever had much interaction with him and didn't know what to expect. The tent was spartanly furnished, with a drab grey metal desk, a couple of matching grey file cabinets, and four matching chairs. A picture of President Roosevelt hung on a wall beside an American flag.

Captain Yoder was impeccably dressed, as always, in his crisp uniform. He sat behind his desk and didn't rise when the two men entered. He didn't mince any words: "I've got two men injured and on sick call. One of them is in the infirmary, and we had to send the other one to the hospital in Tucson." He studied each of them in turn, with a stern look in his eyes. "You men are responsible for those injuries. What do you have to say for yourselves?"

Jimmy and Harry looked at each other. Jimmy spoke first. "Captain, we were in our tent after dinner minding our own business when those three guys came in, causing trouble. Two of them were carrying baseball bats. Reuben Haynes is their leader, and he told the guys with bats to get us. All we did was defend ourselves."

"That seems to fit with what your tentmates told me. Why did Reuben decide to pick a fight with you two? What's going on between you?"

Harry said, "Well, Captain, Reuben has got it in his head that we know where that so-called robber's loot in the cave is hid; or that we found it. He tried to blackmail us into cuttin' him in, or he would call the law down on us."

"Why did he think that?" the captain asked.

Jimmy said, "I think he figured since I was out front most of the time with the Wire Skinners, I would be most likely to find it. I've told him I don't know how many times he's wrong."

"And somethin' else, Captain," Harry said. "As you've no doubt heard, I know a bit about prospectin' and minin'. Me and Jimmy been doin' some of that in the hills on our off days. Reuben told us he figgered we were up to somethin' because we were gone a lot."

Captain Yoder studied them. "Reuben told me he's convinced you have found the stolen gold and wants to report it to the Sheriff and the Treasury agent, hoping for a reward. He said it was suspicious that you left the camp last Saturday in a strange truck. Why did you do that?"

"My cousin picked us up early in the morning and drove us to Ajo to see my family. We also wanted to get some opinions about rock samples we found in the hills. My father is a miner and has an interest in a mine of his own."

Yoder nodded. "Alright. That makes sense to me. I don't believe that old story about the hidden treasure, anyway. I think Reuben is dead wrong, but he is likely to tell his story to the authorities to make more trouble for you. Be warned; I can't be of much help if they get involved." He paused a beat. "And if you get in any more fights, you'd best not send anybody else to the hospital. I think you could have avoided doing so much damage to those two men. If it happens again, I will dismiss you from the CCC."

***

Rodriquez, J.W. Smart's LEM contact, reported the partners' activity. He shared with Smart that he had learned one of them, Harry Taylor, was from Ajo. He said he didn't know for sure but suspected they had carried something away from the camp they wanted to keep secret. It could have been the treasure, but there was no way to know for sure. J.W. said he had friends in Ajo, and he would look into it.

The camp was buzzing, and the men at breakfast were having animated discussions about the fight. Reuben was nowhere to be seen. The men treated Jimmy and Harry like heroes and asked them repeatedly to describe what happened. They thought the idea of Harry taking the bat away from one of the attackers and turning it on him was immensely entertaining.

Jimmy said, in a loud voice, "Look, guys. We're no heroes. We were only trying to protect ourselves. You all know us— we don't cause trouble. We want to keep it that way and get on with our jobs".

"Aww, come on, Jimmy!" one of the men shouted. "We think that bunch got what they deserve. Too bad you didn't take a bat to that troublemaker Reuben, too. It's dang well time somebody stood up to him and his two bit gang!"

There were shouts of agreement as Jimmy and Harry ducked out the door. They knew this was likely the beginning of a lot more mischief and trouble from Reuben. They hoped they would be ready.

Reuben and his one crony who was mobile made themselves scarce over the following days. They ate alone and avoided any conversations among the other men. They ate breakfast, reported to muster, and did their jobs without talking much to anyone. Jimmy thought it was an ominous sign.

***

More problems arrived the following Monday, after roll call. Lieutenant Godwin pulled both men aside and told them they had visitors at the commander's tent. He led them inside, where the US Treasury agent sat next to the captain's desk. Another man stood silently nearby.

"You men remember Mr. Turner here, from the Treasury Department," the captain began, "and this is Mr. Hoag. He is a detective representing the Wells Fargo Company. They would like to interview you about some rumors they have heard. With their permission, I will stay and listen to the discussion. You may proceed, Mr. Turner."

"Please take a seat, gentlemen. I suspect you know why I'm here, so I'll get right to the point." He paused to light a pipe and exhaled a cloud of blue smoke. Jimmy couldn't help thinking he looked too young to be smoking a pipe. "It has come to my attention that there are strong rumors that someone may have found the stolen Wells Fargo Company's property, believed to be hidden in the cave here. The rumors implicate you two men in some scheme to remove it for yourselves."

He looked at each man in turn and took another pull on his pipe. He let the silence settle in, giving the men a chance to think about what he said before continuing, "The Captain has informed me you men are aware of this. He is satisfied there is no truth to the rumors. But, in my sworn responsibility to the US Government, I am obligated to investigate any leads in this case, regardless of their weight. Let me begin by asking you, Mr. Baker, to enlighten me on your part in this."

"Well, sir, we know full well who started the rumors you have heard." Jimmy hoped he looked more confident than he felt, and he continued, "One of our co-workers, Reuben Haynes, has had it in for me almost since we first left Colorado on our way here. He has gone out of his way to make my life uncomfortable since then. Somehow, he got it in his head that I found that old robbery loot. It's simply not so." He paused for a breath. "I think he believes that I was in a good position to find it because of my job with the Wire Skinners. That's about the best I can tell you, sir."

Turner puffed quietly on his pipe as he studied Jimmy. Then he turned to Harry. "Mr. Taylor, I understand you are an Arizona man. How did you get mixed up in this?"

Harry began: "Sir, me and Jimmy been friends since our basic trainin' down at Fort Huachuca. I can say for a fact that Reuben Haynes had a bee in his bonnet for Jimmy back then too. I think he's maybe jealous that me and Jimmy are such good friends." He looked Turner directly in the eye and continued, "I come from a minin' town, as I figger you already know. I grew up with miners. Now and then, I helped my dad work his own claim. Minin' and prospectin' are kind of in my blood. I've heard rumors of valuable ores in these mountains. So Jimmy and I became partners in doin' some weekend prospectin' to see what we could find."

He looked at the captain and back to Turner. "I think Reuben figgered since we were doin' somethin' he didn't know about, maybe we had somethin to hide. I can't see any other reason for him startin' this stuff."

The room was quiet again, the only sound the ticking of the desk clock on the captain's desk. The agent relit his pipe, and the sucking noise as he pulled on his pipestem sounded oddly loud in the tent. He said, "It's my understanding you both made some kind of secret trip out of the camp Saturday last. Mr. Haynes and his associates obviously think you did that to spirit something of value away from the camp." He looked from one man to the other. "What do you say to that?" Harry repeated the same story they had told the captain. The agent asked, "What did you learn about the samples you showed your father?"

Harry didn't hesitate. "My father looked 'em over and said they didn't look like they had enough useful ore to be worth minin'. He said we ought to be spendin' our time on somethin' else. I took Jimmy to some minin' areas around Ajo to show him what kind of stuff we needed to be lookin' for."

"Well, now, that seems fairly plausible." Turner puffed thoughtfully on his pipe. "You wouldn't mind if I spoke to your father about it, would you?"

Harry looked him in the eye and said, "Mr. Turner, you are welcome to make the trip clear out to Ajo to ask my father what I already told you. Seems to me your valuable time might be more useful talkin' to Reuben Haynes and puttin' an end to this stuff. We ain't got nothin' to hide, and it's high time he figgered that out."

Turner said he had no more questions for now, and the captain turned to the detective and said, "Mr. Hoag, what is your interest in this?"

"Gentlemen, my detective agency represents the assets recovery branch of the Wells Fargo Company. The company has a significant interest in the stolen assets supposedly hidden in this cave. I am looking into the possibility of locating and returning them to the company."

He took out his pipe, purposely taking his time filling and lighting it to let what he had said sink in. The captain's tent was becoming hazy with the aromatic smoke. Jimmy chuckled to himself, wondering if smoking a pipe was a requirement to become a lawman.

Hoag continued, "There are laws and doctrine of so-called 'found' money or assets. They mean that any valuables found which have an identifiable rightful owner belong to that owner.

Any cash, precious metals, or other financial instruments that might be found here and identified as Wells Fargo property rightfully belong to the company."

Jimmy and Harry said nothing. Jimmy thought the man looked like a peacock who needed to strut his plumage. His clothes no doubt stood out in the city. But in the desert, they looked almost laughably out of place.

Hoag looked at them and went on, "I listened with interest to your explanations for Mr. Turner concerning the rumors about finding lost treasure. I, too, have heard similar stories concerning you men, and I am glad to know you are so forthcoming about the nature of the rumors. I don't have any more questions, but I must advise you to contact me immediately should you find any of Wells Fargo's stolen property." He gave each of them a business card and told them he could be reached at the Hotel San Carlos in Tucson.

The captain ended the meeting, saying, "These men have shown themselves to be good reliable workers. They have never caused any trouble in this camp. I believe their stories, and I, too, would like to see these rumors put to rest. They are disruptive to the operation of our work here." The captain looked at Jimmy and Harry. "I suggest you men get to your tasks for the day if there are no more questions." Turner and Hoag gave dismissive waves, and the partners walked out of the tent.

Jimmy told Harry as they left that he didn't think it was over with either Reuben or these men. Harry said, "Watch your back with Reuben. He's responsible for this. I wouldn't put anything past him now."

Jimmy noticed Reuben's bunk and living area were empty when he arrived back at his tent before dinner. Harry came in shortly after, and they both wondered what was up. It didn't take long to find out.

An excited murmur was going on when they got to the mess tent for dinner. Word had come out that the captain had assigned Reuben to another tent and pulled him off his work crew. That had never happened in the history of the camp.

Reuben had been sulking and spoiling for a fight. His row in the tent with Jimmy and Harry had left him angry and embarrassed. He was like a stick of dynamite, waiting for someone to light the fuse.

The camp was relatively quiet the next day and seemed to be back to normal. But that night, after dinner, there was a commotion around one of the tents. A large bunch of men had gathered to see what was going on. Reuben and one of his new tent mates had gotten into a fight that had spilled out into the open, and several men grabbed the combatants to break it up. They hauled Reuben off, shouting, "I'll get even! You ain't heard the last from me!"

The men from Reuben's new tent said the same thing; Reuben had started a fight over nothing. Reuben calmed down and crept back into the tent without a word to anyone. He crawled into his covers and watched the other men suspiciously.

The following morning at muster, the men knew something else was up. Captain Yoder was there and addressed them. "Men, I have an announcement that I hoped I would never have to make. You have heard about some recent troubles in camp. I have thoroughly investigated the incidents, including one that happened last night." He paused and looked around at the assembled men before continuing. "I am directing that Mr. Reuben Haynes be dismissed from the Civilian Conservation Corps for his part in these troubles. He will be sent back to his home state of Colorado, effective tomorrow."

There was a lot of shuffling of feet as the men looked around at each other. "In addition, misters Roberts and Henderson are now placed on probation for the remainder of their time here. Any further trouble involving them will result in immediate dismissal from the Corps and their return to Colorado."

With that, he turned it over to Lieutenant Godwin, who said, "I commend you men for doing exemplary work. Hopefully, these unfortunate incidents will not cause you concern." He looked them over and continued, "You are dismissed for your assignments. See me if you have any questions."

Harry and Jimmy had no time for discussion before heading off to their respective work areas. But they both had a sinking feeling in their stomach.

The captain had confined Reuben to his tent except for meals and bathroom breaks. He didn't want to take any chances on more fights and disturbances.

Reuben seethed and cursed to himself, mumbling, "I'll get even," over and over. In his mind, Jimmy had ruined his life. He needed revenge; he needed it before he was shipped off to Colorado.

Reuben's actions were the only topic of discussion among the work crews for the rest of that day. At dinner that evening. The gossip continued with a lot of pointing and gesturing in Jimmy and Harry's direction at their table. Everyone seemed to be relieved to have the problem resolved. Many of the men said it was time Reuben was sent home. Harry asked Jimmy after dinner, "Do you think it's over? Can we relax?"

"I'll relax when that troublemaker is on the bus headed for Colorado. I expect he'll take a parting shot if he gets the chance." Neither man slept, keeping an eye out for someone creeping into their tent in the middle of the night.

Nothing happened overnight. The men were quieter in the mess tent; Harry and Jimmy were able to have breakfast without answering a lot of questions. Jimmy relaxed a little and started to think it was finally over with Reuben,

There were no more announcements during their morning muster, and the men headed out to their work areas. Jimmy and

Harry talked quietly as they rounded the corner behind the mess tent. Reuben leaped in front of them, brandishing a knife. He rushed at Jimmy and made a vicious lunge at his belly. Jimmy jumped aside, and the blade sliced open his shirt, opening a gash in his side. Reuben was off-balance from his thrust, and Jimmy hit him in the face as hard as he could. The blow broke his nose, splattering blood over the front of his shirt. Jimmy was oblivious to his wound and followed up with a hard uppercut to Reuben's jaw, dropping him to his knees. Harry grabbed Reuben's arm and twisted the knife out of his hand. Two more men showed up, and they wrestled Reuben to the ground and held him there.

"Someone get the Captain or Lieutenant, quick like!" Harry shouted. One of the men took off at a run in the headquarters tent's direction.

The Captain and Lieutenant both showed up in minutes. Reuben lay on the ground covered in blood, panting and cursing, vowing vengeance on the entire camp. The Lieutenant sent Jimmy off to the infirmary to get his knife wound tended.

"Well, Reuben," the Captain said, "you're in it now, I'm afraid. You've committed a serious offense attacking someone with a knife. We will detain you until the Sheriff can arrive. Then you will be his problem." He motioned to the men holding

Reuben on the ground and said, "Bring him to my tent. I have a pair of handcuffs I never thought I would need to use. We'll cuff him to a chair until the Sheriff gets here. Someone get a damp towel and wipe the blood off him." Reuben struggled against the men holding his arms, shouting about getting even and killing Jimmy and Harry. They had to drag him to the captain's tent.

CHAPTER 14
PLANS AND SCHEMES

Thanksgiving week marked the impending passage of Jimmy and Harry's first six months with the CCC. They would begin their second six-month period in early December. Many of the men were planning to spend the holiday at home with their families. The partners planned to spend the day off working on details of what they needed to do before leaving the CCC at the end of their enrollment.

The camp quieted down after Reuben had been carted away by the Pima County Sheriff. Word came back that he was charged with armed assault with intent to commit murder and several lesser charges. He would remain in the county jail until a trial date. The Sheriff's office advised Jimmy, Harry, and other witnesses to the attack they would be called to testify at trial. The end of November would have also marked the completion of Reuben's obligation with the CCC if he hadn't gotten himself kicked out.

"Man, I hate this," Jimmy said. Thanksgiving Day was the first chance he and Harry had to talk privately since the previous week's events. They were sitting at their favorite spot under the camp ramada. A cool breeze blowing off the mountains was bracing; Harry said he could smell a change in the air.

Payday joined them and sniffed hopefully around the two

tables, looking for some leftover delicacy. Finding none, he took up station at Jimmy's feet to keep watch over his friends. Jimmy reached down and gave him a scratch behind the ears.

Harry said, "Yeah, me too. I wanna be done with Reuben, once and for all. And I don't like having to be more involved with the law." Harry studied his boots. "Hopefully, they can get the trial done and over soon, so we don't have to worry about it."

They changed the subject and talked about what they needed to do next. The desert wind developed a telling bite as the sun began dropping behind the western mountains. They pulled their wool jackets' collars up and sat with their backs to the strengthening breeze.

Jimmy said, "We've got a little over six months until we finish our second stint with the CCC. We need to figure out a solid plan now." A strong wind gust nearly took Jimmy's cap off. He pulled it down around his ears. "You have any ideas?" he asked.

"Well, I been thinkin' maybe we can divide this into two parts. I think I can figger out how to use our prospectin' and minin' to cover what we need to do. I'll start spendin' more time in Ajo to work on that if you can work out how to do the business end with the gold and silver."

Jimmy considered that and said, "I'm planning on going into the Tucson library to see what I can learn about handling the gold and stuff. I'm thinking we're going to need to set up some kind of business to keep the law off our backs. A mine might be a way to do it."

They talked about the details until the dinner bell rang. Storm clouds had quickly built over the mountains. "Feels like snow," Harry said. "Gonna need that stove in the tent tonight for sure!"

Ol' Charlie had prepared an excellent Thanksgiving meal with turkey and dressing and all the fixings. He even made pumpkin pies for dessert. It reminded the men of the holiday at home before the Depression. Jimmy and Harry ate their fill, then went back to their tent to relax.

The wind howled and beat at the tents' sides that night as the first snarling teeth of a winter storm descended off the Rincon Mountains. Harry's prediction had been right; wet snow fell most of the night. The men woke up the next morning to an unusual scene in the Arizona desert: Snow covered the trees, bushes, and cactuses around the camp with a thick white blanket. It was almost comical to see the stately saguaro cactuses with snow on their crowns and in the crooks of their arms. The diffused light through the cloud cover gave the snow a bluish tint with a strange beauty, turning it into an almost alien landscape. The camp seemed unnaturally quiet.

The men's admiration of the snow soon disappeared when the camp's grounds turned to mud. Their camp-issued clothing and wool jackets were no match for the freezing wind chill from the gusts blowing in over the mountains. Cold, wet boots added to the misery.

Payday had followed Jimmy into his tent the previous night and stayed curled up under Jimmy's bed, refusing to go outside. When Jimmy tried to coax him out, the dog gave him a skeptical look and stayed put.

The men in the camp had nothing to do but huddle around the heaters inside their tents or in the camp's recreation tent. There were board games, and a noisy, smoke-clouded poker game filled many of the men's time. Harry spent most of the afternoon in the game and won a fair amount of money.

One of the men was learning to play the harmonica and set off in a corner blowing melancholy notes. Its reedy tone occasionally sounded like poorly played bagpipes, sharp and out of tune. Finally, someone yelled at him to play something else! The man knocked the spit out of the reeds and grudgingly stuck the harp in his pocket.

Jimmy spent his time in the camp's small reading library. He found a couple of books about business organization and hungrily read through them. The tentative inklings of a general plan began forming in his mind. But first, he would have to wait until the following weekend to spend time in the Tucson library researching the value of gold and silver.

The following Saturday, they went into Tucson. Harry caught a bus to Ajo, and Jimmy visited the library. Christmas was two weeks away, and there were a few festive decorations around the library. The librarian had a red Christmas ribbon tied around the bun in her hair. She remembered Jimmy and said with a smile, "Well, if it isn't the lost treasure hunter. Did you track down those outlaws' loot in the cave?"

Jimmy was taken aback, surprised she might remember those kinds of details. He replied, "No, ma'am. But I'll keep looking for it. I'm trying to understand more about it and learn more about the gold they stole. Can you help me find something about gold coins and such?"

She laughed and said, "Well, you're truly persistent. Come with me, and I'll show you what we have."

He soon found plenty of information about gold and other valuable metals, including a book that described gold coins and their value. He discreetly removed his boot under the table and took out the paper with their coin inventory. His boot was the safest place he could think of to hide it; no one in camp was likely to mess with someone else's boot.

The first book explained how much actual gold was contained in each coin and provided enough information to calculate their stash's value. Another had similar details about calculating silver's values. He applied that to the collection of Spanish pesos and other denominations. He was sure he had enough to do the calculations, but he had to find the metals' current values.

According to what he read; the government had placed a set value on gold. The librarian showed him how to look up current values in the newspaper, and he found the present value of silver there. He borrowed a clean sheet of paper from the librarian and spent the rest of the day reading and calculating the various coins' values. The greatest surprise was the value of the gold bars.

He learned their standard weight was a whopping 27 pounds. No wonder those bags were so heavy! That translated into 400 Troy ounces. One of them was worth about $14,000 at the current government price, maybe more in the open market! The number dumbfounded Jimmy; one of those bars was worth more than he could ever imagine. And they had five of them! He figured it would take him at least twenty-five years working for an average salary to earn the value of one bar—if he could find a job.

Jimmy thanked the librarian for her help and wished her a Merry Christmas. She returned the wish and said she hoped to see him again soon. Jimmy colored a little at the gentle flirtation and walked out into the street to find his ride back to camp.

***

Detective Hoag had followed Jimmy when he arrived in Tucson and watched him enter the city's library. He stood in shadow on the street, puffing on his pipe. He waited several hours for Jimmy to come out and disappear down the road before he went into the library to have a chat with the librarian.

***

J.W. Smart noted Jimmy's movements in Tucson that day, too. His contacts in Tucson and Ajo had told him there was a lot of activity with Harry and Jimmy. He suspected they might have already found the treasure and were preparing to cash in on it. He thought about how he would do that if he were them and decided to visit old 'Skunk' Graves. Graves owned a shop that dealt in precious metals and coins and other not-so-obvious valuables.

J.W. had used him numerous times to fence his most valuable stolen goods and found him a profitable partner in crime. The transactions always required him to keep a healthy distance between them because of the man's bodily odors.

***

After dinner that night, Jimmy lay quietly on his cot. The tent had seemed unnaturally quiet since Reuben's departure; the faint murmur of other men in the tents seemed reassuring. The men had heard no further word of Reuben since his arrest, and Jimmy hoped it stayed that way. He had caused Jimmy enough grief and aggravation for one lifetime.

He had many troubled thoughts about what he had learned in the library that day. Chief among them was worry about dealing

140

with the laws passed the previous year regarding owning and using gold. It was going to be a much more difficult problem than either he or Harry had imagined.

If they complied with the law, they would have to sell most of the gold at the government rate, eliminating any possibility of better profits if the price went up in the future. Worse, they would be breaking the law even if they didn't sell it. He could not yet see how they could begin to cash in on their find without being caught, fined, and possibly sent to jail. And, insult to injury, they would have to pay taxes on the entire amount. His research also revealed a new wrinkle to think about—something called inflation would eat away at the value of the dollars they would receive if they cashed in the gold.

He tossed and turned far into the night—the law seemed supremely unfair in Jimmy's mind. He had found something most people thought didn't exist. And now, to learn he would either have to surrender it to the government or face jail seemed unfair and unreasonable. In his mind, the government was responsible for the hard times gripping the country and the precarious situation it put him and his family in. By his reasoning, that made it acceptable to bend the rules. And, he thought, it wasn't going to hurt anyone.

He had a vague idea of what they might do, but it would be extremely risky. A lot would depend on what Harry learned from his trip to Ajo. Hopefully, between them, they could come up with something workable. He was determined to find a way to keep their dreams within reach.

Harry returned the following evening, but they didn't have any privacy to discuss their ideas. However, Harry did share one piece of exciting news. "My sister was unhappy you didn't come with me this time. She wanted to know why and if you didn't want to see her again." They were at their usual table in the mess tent, and the other men were all ears. Jimmy squirmed in his chair. Harry continued, "I told her you were busy researchin' minin' claims at the library and didn't have the time to come. She didn't much like that answer!"

"What should I do?" Jimmy asked. "I didn't think she cared much one way or another." The other men at the table were chuckling to themselves and elbowing each other, enjoying Jimmy's predicament.

"Hey, Jimmy," one of them said, "sounds like you need some lessons on dealing with women. Of course, the first thing is to show up!" That brought howls of laughter from the others. Jimmy's face turned bright red. "C'mon, Harry! Let's get out of here. I don't need romance advice from this bunch!" They finished their plates and left to continuing laughter at the table. "Dang, Harry! Couldn't you have waited till after dinner to tell me that?"

"Aww, be a sport, man. I just wanted to have some fun. Besides, it'll give that bunch somethin' else to gossip about."

He cuffed Jimmy on the back. "What she said was I better not come back without you next time. You made quite an impression on her. So if you're interested in her, you better get busy showin' it."

Jimmy said he would make plans to go with him next time, and they should do it sooner rather than later. In the meantime, he asked if he should write to her. Harry allowed that it would likely be a good thing indeed.

The days were short, and there wasn't much daylight left after dinner. It was nearly impossible for them to spend time discussing possible plans without being overheard. They both were scheduled for weekend chores the following weekend when many of the men were gone. They made plans to find time to share what each had learned.

They finished their chores by early afternoon on Saturday and met at the ramada, where they knew they would have privacy. The sky over the mountains was intense cerulean blue, and a breeze stirred the leaves on the mesquite and creosote. It had a freshening nip but spoke of spring not far away.

Harry said, "That Treasury agent paid a visit to my dad when he left here. Detective Hoag showed up a couple of hours later that day, too. Thank God all Dad could tell 'em was the same story I told them. He said he heard the men poked around town a while, asked a few people if they knew me. Dad wanted to know what I knew about this lost gold business and why there was this sudden interest.

"Holy cow! What did you tell him?"

"I told him I would have to wait until you were with me, and we'd lay it out. So you and me gotta decide if we wanna tell him the truth."

"We've been careful to keep it to ourselves so far, "Jimmy said. "But we may need to tell him about it to do what we're planning. We don't want to lie to him, and we don't want him being suspicious about us, especially with that Treasury agent and detective poking around. What does your gut tell you?"

"Well, you and my family are the only people I can trust. My dad may disagree with what we are plannin' to do, and he might give us advice we don't wanna hear. But I'd trust him with my life, and I'd trust him to keep our secret."

"I would have felt that way about my dad, too. I trust you, and we're in this together. If you think it's a good idea, I'm okay with it."

They talked about their fathers for a while. Then, Jimmy had a vivid flashback of a conversation with his father: It was the beginning of the depression, and Jimmy had asked him what they were going to do. His father said, "Son, so long as I am able to work, I will take care of our family. Family is all that matters. We can get through this time if we work hard and take care of each other.”

He wondered what he would advise him to do now if he were

alive. It reminded Jimmy that he had to be sure his mother, brother, and sister would be cared for when he was no longer working for the CCC. He hoped what he and Harry planned was successful and that he would accomplish something that would make his father proud.

Harry snapped his fingers and said, “Hey! Where’d you go? You sorta” blanked out there for a minute.”

“I was thinking about my dad and our family. I have to make this plan work so I can keep helping my family.”

They continued talking about what they were going to do. “I think there’s two possible ways we can set up a cover,” Harry began. “The first would be to locate and stake a new claim for minin’. We’d have to spend some money to get it set up like a real minin’ operation, assumin’ we found somethin’ we could make a legitimate claim on.” Jimmy waited for him to go on. “The second would be to buy out the mine and claim from my dad and uncle. It would give us an established business.”

“Have you talked to your dad and uncle about it? I don’t know about involving your uncle.”

A roadrunner hopped up on the other table nearby. It had a distinctive bright blue and orange spot behind its eye, which stood out distinctively from its grey feathers, indicating a mature male. He studied the men curiously. Then he scraped his beak across the table a couple of times before dashing off in search of a lizard.

Harry said, "I told my dad we were lookin' to go into business together when we're done here, and we're lookin' for opportunities. I asked him if he thought him and my uncle might be interested in working out some kind of arrangement with us. He asked me why we would wanna get involved in that old mine. It barely paid for their gas and beer when they worked it once in a while. I told him we thought we could make it pay if we put more work into it. He said he would consider it and talk to my uncle. We need to go there soon and talk about it with them.

Besides," he said with a sly smile, "my sister is anxious to see you!"

Jimmy laughed and said he wanted to see her, too. But first, they had to figure out what to do with the gold. He told Harry what he estimated the gold and silver value to be. Harry whistled. "A hundred and fifty thousand or more! You can't be serious!" Jimmy assured him it was an accurate estimate based on the information he found at the library. "A hundred and fifty thousand!" Harry said again, shaking his head in disbelief.

"That's way more than any estimates we heard the robbers took."

Jimmy said, "Well, it's worth more now than it was in those days. And I don't think the old stories about the loot mentioned anything about gold bars. It's way more than I expected!"

They sat in silence for a few minutes, thinking about what that meant. During the Depression, the average salary was around five hundred dollars per year. The men had a hard time understanding how much a hundred and fifty thousand dollars was. They could work the rest of their lives and never come close to saving that much money.

"Wells Fargo never admitted how much the robbers took," Jimmy said. "I think they were probably embarrassed by the loss." He described what he found out about their risk of breaking the law. "I know we agreed we didn't care before, but we didn't know at the time how serious the government was about it. They've put several people in jail for doing what we're talkin' about."

"So what're you sayin'? You gettin' cold feet?"

"No, not that. I'm saying we have to come up with a foolproof plan if we want to stay out of jail. I've studied it a lot, and I think maybe the best way is to take the gold to Mexico and exchange it for dollars there."

"Mexico! You got any idea how dangerous that might be? We could lose everthin' and wind up in jail anyway!"

"I'm aware of that, but I can't find any way to do it here. We can't use an American bank or any places here that buy and sell gold. They'd report us in a heartbeat or try to beat us out of our gold."

Harry said, "Sounds like what we need is to find a Mexican bank or some kind of business in Mexico we can trust to make this work. But findin' a business we could trust with that kind of money in Mexico is gonna be tough. They do things a lot different down there."

They wrestled with the ins and outs of it until the sun began to set over the Tucson mountains, turning a bank of clouds flaming orange. The air grew colder, and Jimmy wondered if another storm was coming.

The captain gave the men the day off for Monday, Christmas Eve, and Christmas day. That gave the men a four-day holiday weekend. Harry's uncle in Tucson let them borrow his truck for the holiday, so long as they were back by evening on Christmas day. The partners stopped at a market to buy a turkey, cranberry sauce, and an apple pie to take to Harry's parents' house for Christmas dinner. Harry said his mom had told him that would be the best Christmas present they could bring.

They burned up the road headed for Ajo. No one paid much attention to speed limits on the reservation, and patrolmen were pretty scarce. They pushed the truck as fast as they felt safe. The rough pavement gave them a jarring ride and rattled their teeth. They were in Ajo by lunchtime.

Mrs. Taylor gave them both a hug, wished them Merry Christmas, and said Harry's dad would be home shortly. She thanked them for the turkey and said it would make it a truly wonderful Christmas for the family.

Joann came into the room with more Christmas wishes and hugged Harry before turning to Jimmy. "It's nice to see you again, Jimmy. And thank you for your kind letter. I've been hoping you would be able to visit and spend some time with us."

Jimmy turned bright red and felt like his tongue was stuck to the roof of his mouth. He was finally able to blurt out, "It's nice to see you again, too." Mrs. Taylor rescued him, telling them to come and wash up for lunch.

Harry's dad returned, and they sat down for another lunch of baloney sandwiches. Harry's mom apologized again for the sparing fare, but it was all they could afford. They were receiving some government assistance, and with the twenty-five dollars a month from Harry's work, it was barely enough to pay the rent for the house and keep meager food on the table. The planned Christmas feast would be the first extravagant meal they shared in over a year.

Harry offered to buy a beer after lunch, and the men left for the local bar. The smell of stale beer, Pine-sol, and dirty ashtrays greeted them at the door. The dingy bar showed no signs of holiday cheer; the room had its usual smoky dim glow. The bartender was busy polishing the counter even though they were the only customers in the place. Harry got three bottles of Coors and took them to the table. The condensing moisture on the cold bottles left spreading water rings on the table.

"So, what are you two up to?" Harry's dad asked, "And what about that Treasury guy and detective snoopin' around askin' questions? I don't like the sounds of that!" He looked from one to the other and asked, "How are you figurin' on startin' a business on the salary the government's been payin' you? What the hell's goin' on?"

Jimmy looked at Harry and nodded. Harry said, "Well, Dad, what we have to tell you has got to remain secret between us. I trust you more than anybody, and Jimmy agrees that it's okay to tell you. But, once we tell you, you could be in danger like we are."

His dad looked from one to the other again and said, "If you're in danger, I want to help. Tell me what I can do. Start at the beginnin', and don't leave nothin' out!"

Jimmy said, "Mr. Taylor, what the agent was asking you about is true. About the treasure, I mean. I found it, Mr. Taylor. Hidden, like the old stories said, in a secret place in that cave where we've been working." Harry's dad looked at Jimmy with disbelief.

"It's true, dad," Harry said. "I've seen it with my own eyes. More gold than you could imagine!" They told him how Jimmy found it and how they got it out without anyone knowing. They finished by telling him they had hidden it out by the old mine.

John looked thoughtful. "I wondered what you boys were up to, makin' that hurry-up trip out to the mine. It smelled pretty fishy at the time. Damn wonder you both ain't in jail already. So, now you got it, what are you gonna do with it?"

Jimmy explained that government rules made a challenging problem for them. They needed help to make their plans work to keep or use the gold.

"Damn government! Tellin' us what we can and can't do with our gold," Harry's dad fumed about the new laws. "So, what do you think you're gonna do?"

They told him about the idea of buying the claim to the old mine and using it as a cover for the money they planned to have. When they told him about the idea of using a business in Mexico to exchange the gold, he chuckled and shook his head.

"You boys ain't got a clue what you're gettin' yourself in for, tryin' to do business in Mexico. I learned about that when I worked down there before I met your mother. People you can trust down there's few and far between, and ever one of them's got their hand out for *la mordida*."

Jimmy had a blank look, and Mr. Taylor explained, "*La mordida* means 'the bite' in Spanish, and it's a way of life in Mexico. *Mordida* is their word for the bribe, or the payoff. Nothin' happens down there without it. You might even have to pay the border guards to enter the country. It depends on their mood, and whether they need the money, I guess."

They were quiet as they sipped their beers, thinking about the risks they were preparing to take. A couple more men drifted into the bar and sat at the counter. One of them got up and put a coin in a music-making machine, and the Carter

Family's scratchy recording of 'Can the Circle Be Unbroken' filled the room.

Harry asked, "What about mom's family down there. Are there any of them that might be able to help us? Is there anyone we could trust?"

John Taylor eyed the two men at the bar and said, "Let's finish our beers and move on. There's too many ears in here for what we need to talk about." He left a quarter for a tip on the table and waved goodbye to the bartender.

They sat outside on Taylor's tiny patio the rest of the afternoon, wrestling with what the men proposed. Harry brought out more beer from the refrigerator.

John took a long pull on his Coors and said, "Harry, your mom's family in Mexico has been pretty standoffish all these years. I'm the one to blame for that. They never forgave me for marrying her and moving out of Mexico after you kids were born."

He took out a pack of Zig-Zag cigarette papers and gently blew one loose. The rich aroma as he opened a red can of Prince Albert tobacco drifted across the table. He made a gentle fold in the paper and tapped a little tobacco into it. Then he licked the edge of the paper and sealed it closed. The ritual completed, he struck a match on his boot sole and lit the cigarette.

He gazed thoughtfully into its smoke and said, "Your mother

keeps in touch with her parents and goes down for a visit about once a year. She took you and your sister down there when you were younger. Do you remember that?"

"I barely remember my grandparents," Harry said. "It's been a long time since I was there. Why did you move out of Mexico? I've never heard the story."

"Well," he began, "her parents didn't think much of me back then. I was workin' at the smelter and doin' farm work on the side. They thought their daughter deserved better than what I could give her. So we dated secretly for a while, and her dad was furious when he found out; told her she had to stop seeing me."

He took another pull on his beer and sat lost in his memories before continuing. "So we did what foolish kids do; we ran off and got married anyway. Her father almost disowned her. But then he thought better of it because she is his only child. Instead, he told me we were on our own; we would have to get by on what I made." He stopped and rolled another cigarette. It was obviously hard for him to talk about it. Harry and Jimmy sat silent, waiting for him to continue.

"About a year later, you were born, and your sister followed the next year. I couldn't earn enough in Mexico to support my new family, so I decided to move here. I heard there were good jobs in the mine. It helped that Ajo was close enough your mother could see her family once in a while. Her parents still resent me for taking away their little girl. But they have grudgingly accepted me."

He stood up and said, "I'll talk with your mother later and see what she says. I'll have to tell her some about what you're doin'. Is that okay with you boys?"

Jimmy said, "Mr. Taylor, I trust you, and I will trust Mrs. Taylor, too. If we can make this work, it will be good for all of us."

Mrs. Taylor stuck her head out the back door and said, "Are you going to sit out here all day gossiping like old women or come in and have dinner?" The men laughed, and John said they were only waiting for an invitation.

There was no more discussion about their plans and schemes at dinner. Jimmy was seated next to Joann, who was wearing a particularly pretty blue dress that matched her eyes. Jimmy was entirely smitten, much to the rest of the family's amusement.

After dinner, Jimmy asked her if she would like to take a walk. She suggested a stroll down to the town plaza. They chose a bench with a beautiful sunset view as the sun dropped behind the big white Catholic church facing the square. Tall palms lined the plaza, and their stiff leaves rustled in a light breeze.

She said, "I was pleased you wrote to me. I was afraid I might not hear from you or see you again."

Jimmy once again had trouble finding his tongue. "I was afraid you might not want to see me again," he said. "I was only here a short time, and we rushed off without any time for us to get to know each other."

She smiled at him, and he was mesmerized by the depth of her eyes. "I felt as if I'd known you my whole life, Jimmy. How can that be?"

Jimmy was again speechless for a few seconds but was finally able to say, "I feel the same way, Joann. It's kind of like we were supposed to meet."

They huddled close together to ward off the evening chill and talked about their lives. Jimmy told her about what had happened with Kathleen in Denver. He breathed into the silence, then said, "I wondered if I would ever find anyone else. She had been my first love."

"I've never been in love," she said. "I can't imagine how painful that must have been for you." Jimmy looked away, and she continued, "I've only had one steady boyfriend, and that didn't last long. He had eyes for too many other girls, and I told him it was over after a couple of months." She laid her hand on his arm, and they sat looking at each other for a moment. The setting sun highlighted the gold flecks in his hazel eyes, and she thought he was the most handsome man she had ever met. They had chemistry she'd never felt before. She decided then he would be the man she would marry.

Jimmy looked into her eyes again. It was like an electric current passing through him—at that moment, he, too, knew they would be together forever.

***

The following day, Sunday, Jimmy attended mass at the Catholic church with the family. It was his first experience with the church, and he felt awkward with the various ceremonies. He did his best to mimic Joann and the others. She gave him a big smile for his efforts.

After church, the men went to talk with Harry's uncle. His uncle Fred was a burly, balding man, darkly tanned from years working in the Arizona sun. He was in a cheerful holiday mood, and the deep smile wrinkles around his eyes belied his otherwise gruff demeanor. He was the kind of man who didn't mince words, and Harry's dad got right to the point.

"Fred, these boys have a proposition for us. They're lookin' to get into business together when they get done workin' on that government project in Tucson, and they want to try their hand at minin'. They've been savin' money and want to buy our claim on the old mine".

Fred looked from Jimmy to Harry and burst out laughing in a deep rumble. "You wanna do what? Hell, we barely get enough out of that old hole to buy a few extra beers and pay for our gas drivin' out there. Harry, you been down there with us; you know what it's like."

Harry was ready for that reaction. "Well, Uncle Fred, the way I got it figgered is you guys only work it a couple of days every few months. If we work it steady, we can make it pay and establish ourselves. Then maybe we could pick up some other claims and go from there."

Fred scraped his hand over the beard stubble on his chin while he thought. It sounded like a rasp dragged across a rough board. "What are you proposin'?" he asked.

Harry said, "We can put a little down and pay you a percentage of whatever we take out. It might take us a while to get to where we can do that, but it should be worth your while. If it don't work out, you can keep what we pay you, and we'll turn the claim back to you."

Fred asked Harry's father if he agreed with the idea. John said, "If these fool boys want to try it, I'm okay with it." They finally decided to take fifty dollars each for their part of the project and receive ten percent each from whatever profits there might be. Jimmy said they would have the cash soon. They shook hands all around, and the deal was done.

On their way out, Fred said, "I expect you boys are gonna be needin' some help to get started out there. Me and John can give you a hand with that. I hope you can make somethin' out of that old hole in the ground."

Jimmy and Harry thanked him for the opportunity. On the way

back to Harry's house, his dad said, "I talked some with your mother last night, Harry. She's pretty nervous about it, 'specially about gettin' in trouble with the law. But she said she's willin' to help if she can and will make a trip to see her parents soon." He put his arm on Harry's shoulder and told him he needed to go with her. Harry said he'd try to arrange a couple of days off from work so he could join her.

Harry's mom had made a batch of pork tamales, a traditional Mexican dish at Christmas time. There were spicy black beans to go with them, and delicious, creamy flan was desert. There was plenty for lunch and dinner.

Jimmy bunked with Harry during their stay in town. They talked far into the night about everything they had to do to get started with their operation. Everything would hinge on whether they could work something out in Mexico to exchange gold for US dollars. But in the meantime, they were going to need cash.

Jimmy said they had 300 or so Mexican silver pesos that they could exchange lawfully in the US. He figured they'd bring slightly over $3,000 after paying the exchange costs. "It's lawful," Jimmy said, "but we have to be careful where and how we do it so's not cause any suspicion. I think that government agent and the detective are watching us all the time. They don't act like they'll give up, in spite of Reuben's proof being laid to rest."

Harry said, "I'll leave it to you to figger out how to do that. Meantime, I'll work on this Mexico stuff and what we'll need at the mine to get started. We're gonna need a truck right off. I'll put the word out with my cousin Bill in Tucson that we're lookin'."

The partners didn't have any plans for that Monday, Christmas Eve. Jimmy wanted to spend some time with Joann, and Harry handed him the keys to the pickup. Joann was quick to accept the offer of a ride, and they drove around while she pointed out the sights of the town. The smelter and mine dominated everything else, and there wasn't much else to see. They stopped at an overlook, and Jimmy was astounded at the size of the open-pit mine. He had never seen anything like it, and the equipment he could see parked at the bottom looked like children's toys. Joann told him it was called the New Cornelia Mine, and it had been yielding copper ore since 1915.

Back in the truck, Joann leaned into him, and they shared their first kiss. Jimmy felt like his life had new meaning.

He told her their plans for the old mine. "I'll find a place to live in Ajo after I finish my work at the cave. It's only a few more months."

She said, "Oh, Jimmy! That's wonderful news. I can hardly wait!" She dabbed tears away and kissed him again.

The family invited Jimmy to attend the traditional midnight Christmas Eve mass at the Catholic church. Jimmy said he was honored to join them. Christmas lights strung on the palm trees in the square opposite the church gave it a festive look. Many candles lighted a nativity scene in front of the building. As on his previous experience with the church, he was entirely in the dark about the proceedings. But he did the best he could. The music provided by a choir was a type of music he had never heard before—he thought it was beautiful.

On Christmas day, Harry's mom and sister were busy preparing their Christmas feast. It was getting close to lunchtime, and the mouth-watering aroma of the cooking turkey filled the house. It turned out to be the best meal any of them could remember in a long while. They lounged around with stuffed bellies for a couple of hours afterward.

Before they left for Tucson, Jimmy thanked Mrs. Taylor and told her it was the best meal he'd had in a very long time. She hugged him and told him she was glad he enjoyed it. She packed up a bag of leftover turkey and fixings to take along for their dinner that night. Jimmy shared another embrace and a long kiss with Joann and told her he would see her as soon as possible.

On the road, the men were quiet for a few miles until Harry said, "Jimmy, this is gettin' complicated. I can see it's gonna take some good business plannin' to make it work. I gotta depend on you for that part; I'm not so good with readin' and math. When I got to high school, I found out that I have something called dyslexia. I see words and numbers backward. It's been a struggle my whole life. I only got through high school because I'm a good wrestler, and the coach wanted to keep me on his championship team."

"I had no idea, Harry. It doesn't slow you down any!"

"I can do the leg work organizin' people and equipment, doin' mechanical stuff we need, but I'm no good with details. I trust you to make the business end work."

"I'll do my best!"

They passed the miles continuing to talk through plans and various problems they would face as they rolled into Tucson with enough time to return the truck and catch the last shuttle back to camp that evening.

CHAPTER 16
TRANSITIONS

Jimmy and Harry sat on their favorite ramada bench with their backs to the wind on a Saturday morning. The winds were strong most afternoons, kicked up dust, and blew hats and caps off men's heads. The men who worked outside the cave complained about it incessantly. It was a dry wind, sucking moisture from the skin and causing the eyes discomfort.

Harry said, "I talked to my cousin Bill last weekend, and he says he thinks he's found a pretty good deal for us on a pickup truck. The guy who owns it will lose it to the bank if he can't sell it to make good on his loan. He says it's a like-new two-year-old Ford. The guy needs two hundred dollars to pay it off."

Jimmy nodded. "That sounds like a pretty good deal, but we'll need to check it out. We'll have to find a way to cash in some silver pesos. I've got to get a day off to go into town on a weekday to do that." A gust of wind grabbed his cap and sailed it away into a nearby creosote bush.

Harry said, "Yeah, and we'll have to make a trip to the old mine to get what we need from our stash. I'll work on that; you figger out the rest."

Jimmy retrieved his cap and said, "What have you learned about our prospects in Mexico?

"I got approval this mornin' from Lieutenant Godwin to get two days off week after next. A letter from my mother said she'd be ready to make the trip whenever I could get the time. We'll know soon enough if that's gonna work out down there."

"There's something else I'm thinking about," Jimmy said. "I have to find a place to live when we leave here. Do you think we could fix up the old house at the mine and make it fit to live in?"

Harry laughed. "I don't think you want to be stuck way off out there. You'd go nuts with nobody to talk to but rattlesnakes and coyotes! I'll talk to my uncle Fred when I'm there. His kids are gone, and they have a spare room. I'm pretty sure he'd be willin' to put you up until we can do somethin' else. You might need to help out with food and such. I'm gonna have to stay with my folks, so it would work out pretty good."

The men went into town the next day. Jimmy visited the library while Harry went to look at the pickup his cousin had found. Harry said, "If the truck looks good, maybe we can make a deal to help the guy with his bank payment until we have the rest of the cash. It sounds like he's pretty desperate to get out from under it."

The same librarian was on duty and called Jimmy by name. She was an attractive and shapely but plainly dressed girl, with her brown hair done up in a bun in the back. Her round silver-colored wire-rim eyeglasses gave her a studious look perfectly suited to a librarian. She was about Jimmy's age, and it was apparent from her smile that she would be open to more than simply helping him in the library.

"What can I help you with today, Jimmy? More treasure hunting? Or something more down to earth?" He blushed and smiled at her teasing and said he just wanted to read the local papers because he would need a new job soon. She asked if he planned to stay in Tucson, and he told her he didn't know yet. He said he knew where the newspapers were and would let her know if he needed any help.

The librarian looked around for other patrons, then said in a low voice, "There's something I need to tell you. When you were here last, a detective came in after you left and asked me many questions. He wanted to know what kinds of information you were studying. He left me his card." She handed the card to Jimmy.

Jimmy didn't need to look at the card to know who it was. "I'm sorry he bothered you. He heard some false rumors from the camp that I might have found the outlaws' treasure. He claims it belongs to the Wells Fargo Company."

"I only told him you seemed to be interested in information about mining and such. He wanted details, but I told him I didn't remember any specifics. I hope you are not in any kind of trouble."

"I'm not in trouble and don't expect to be. Thanks for letting me know about that guy. He's chasing false rumors, hoping to make a quick buck. Let me know if he bothers you again. And thanks for telling me!"

Jimmy pondered this development. The detective was getting way too close to piecing together what the partners were doing. He wondered who had tipped him off about the library. Apparently, there were spies everywhere. He and Harry would have to be doubly careful now.

He found what he was looking for pretty quickly: a shop dealing in rare coins and two businesses advertising their services to exchange, buy and sell precious metals. He noted their phone numbers and addresses, found the Tucson phone directory, and looked up banks. He added that information to his notebook and put back the materials he had used.

He stopped at the desk and chatted with the librarian for a few minutes. He knew she wanted him to ask her out. Before he met Joann, he certainly would have. But he dodged the unspoken invitation and thanked her for her assistance. "I'm always happy to assist you in any way I can, Jimmy." She patted the bun in her hair, gave him her best smile, and said she hoped he found a job in Tucson.

He found a payphone and called Harry's cousin. They had returned from looking at the truck, and Harry said to meet him at their favorite greasy spoon restaurant for burgers and cokes.

"That truck's perfect for us, Jimmy. It's only two years old and ain't got many miles, no dents or anything. It started right up and ran like new. I don't think we could do any better for two hundred dollars."

"Is the guy willing to work with us on the payment?"

"He jumped at the offer. He don't have the next payment. I told him we'd get the money to him and have the rest before another payment was due."

"It's gonna take my savings plus to cover my half," Jimmy said. "Can you cover yours?" Harry nodded, and they made plans to get the money to the truck's owner.

Jimmy said he thought he had found some good possibilities for exchanging their silver. But it was Sunday, and he would have to wait for a weekday to contact them. The camp had recently installed a payphone; he thought he could use it to find out what he needed to know.

Harry would retrieve some silver pesos when he went to Ajo the following week. Their plans were starting to come together, and they ate their burgers and fries in quiet thought.

***

The Lieutenant pulled Harry and Jimmy aside the next morning after muster and told them the captain wanted to see them in his tent. They looked at each other, worrying about what he might want.

167

"Please sit, men," the captain said. "I have some disturbing news from the Sheriff — Reuben was killed in jail last night. He apparently started a fight with another prisoner and was stabbed multiple times with some kind of shiv. He was dead when guards found him."

Shock registered on the men's faces. "Oh, my God, Captain!" Jimmy exclaimed. "I didn't wish him harm, much as I disliked the man. That's horrible."

"Yes, it is. But he brought it on himself," The Captain said. "You men are not to blame. He seemed to be destined for constant trouble in his life." There was nothing more to be said, and he dismissed them to their daily duties.

A somber mood enveloped the camp the rest of that day as word of Reuben's death spread.

***

Jimmy used the camp's payphone to check out his library research prospects. The banks weren't interested and referred him to the metal dealers in town. They told him to bring in what he had, and they would make him an offer based on the silver content of the coins. He also contacted a shop that dealt in rare and collectible coins and thought that might be worth checking out. Spreading his business around between those sources seemed a good idea; they might get suspicious if he brought too many coins in at once.

Harry would join his mother the following Saturday for their trip to Mexico. Jimmy told him to bring back 50 silver pesos. He figured that should give them enough cash to pay off the truck and the mining claim. They could use the rest to buy supplies and live on until they could sell some gold or make some money from their mine.

CHAPTER 17

CABORCA

Harry rode the bus to Ajo. He and his mother set off in his dad's pickup truck, heading south for the forty-five-mile drive to Mexico. After crossing the border at Lukeville, Arizona, they entered the Mexican state of Sonora. Mexico's Route 2 took them through the town of Sonoyta. The farm town of Caborca was another 90 miles south.

The desert country between Caborca and the border was foreboding, arid, and barren for miles. Harry imagined the mountains in the distance might be what mountains on the moon might look like, otherworldly and alien. They rose abruptly from the desert floor in tortured shapes, some sharp and jagged, some rounded, mostly black rock.

The irrigated fields made Caborca look like an oasis compared to the barren desert around it. The climate was excellent for growing cotton, which was the business Harry's grandparents had been in for many years. Workers were planting the fields in orderly furrowed rows in preparation for the next season.

His grandparents always welcomed his mother back when she visited and doted on her children when they were young.

Harry secretly hoped their goodwill toward him and his mother would overcome any ill feelings they held for his father. They met him and his mother with many hugs and much laughter. A big *fiesta* was planned that night to welcome them.

Harry's grandmother, Yolanda, was a beautiful woman. Only a touch of gray in her dark red hair belied her age. She was tall, well-proportioned, and carried herself with poise and grace. Her fair skin and blue eyes were strikingly similar to her daughter. Harry was amazed at the resemblance between them.

His grandfather was a tall man with a natural air of authority, but smile wrinkles around his brown eyes softened his stern appearance. A full, well-trimmed mustache echoed his hair's salt and pepper color. The contrast was striking against his darkly tanned features; it was apparent he had spent most of his life in the sun. He dressed in dark slacks with a short-sleeved dress shirt, open at the collar with a bolo tie made of fine silver and turquoise. Finely tooled black western boots completed his casually elegant appearance.

They lived in a rambling *hacienda*-style home on one of their farms about two miles out of town. The large, beautiful adobe structure was finished in white stucco, glistening in the sun. The quarters included a half dozen bedrooms and expansive living areas. A shady central courtyard was a lush, relaxing place to linger. Its beautiful pond with a fountain and many tropical plants made it the perfect place for the guests to gather that evening.

Harry struggled to keep everyone's names and the relationships straight. Several of the men were his grandfather's age and appeared to be successful people. They were all well-dressed, similar to his grandparents. Harry judged from the diamonds, emerald, and gold jewelry some of the women wore that they were probably wealthy. They all seemed to know his mother and all about her marriage to his father.

They greeted him warmly in Spanish. He spoke the language, but it was rusty from lack of use and not nearly good enough for an extended conversation. He was embarrassed by it, but most of the guests spoke much better English than he spoke Spanish, so it worked out okay.

It was a festive gathering with a *mariachi* band and plenty of local *cerveza* and tequila. Harry was careful not to let the tequila get the better of him. He had to be clear-headed the next day to take care of business.

That night Harry reviewed his plans, waiting for sleep. He was encouraged by the reception they had received. Hopefully, it meant everything would go well. He finally drifted off to the gentle lullaby of the fountain splashing in the courtyard.

The next day was Sunday, and the family expected Harry to attend services with them at the Catholic church. There would be no discussion of business before church. It seemed like the whole town was there for the services, including most of the people he met the previous night. His mother had forewarned him, and he had brought what he hoped were appropriate clothes from his old wardrobe for the occasion. He felt like everyone was looking at him. The ill-fitting dress clothes he brought made him feel very self-conscious. He had gained weight from a steady diet of Old Charlie's cooking. The clothes didn't fit well and caused him to squirm on the hard church pew, hoping his pants wouldn't rip when kneeling during the service. He sighed with relief when it was over.

During lunch, Harry's grandparents wanted to know about his work at the cave. They were intrigued by the idea of a cave that stayed at a cool seventy degrees year-round. His grandmother laughed and said it was probably too cold for them. Then his grandfather asked him what he intended to do when he finished his work there. It was the opening he wanted.

He told them of his plans with Jimmy and said he hoped to make some business connections in Mexico. They didn't seem particularly pleased by this news. They turned the conversation to how the Ajo mine's shutdown affected Harry's family's welfare and prospects for the future. Harry said he wanted to help the family if he could and thought his plans would be a way to do that.

His grandfather said it was time for a *siesta*, and they would talk more about it later. Harry was uneasy, unsure how this was going to turn out. His mother told him to join her in the courtyard while the household was in its afternoon rest period.

When they were alone, she said, "Harry, your grandfather is quite familiar with mining. He even owns interests in some mines down here. One of his brothers has a successful mining and smelting operation in Chihuahua. He is rightfully concerned about what you have told him."

Harry watched goldfish in the pond. "I don't know how much to tell him. You know the risks we're facing. I need his help, but I am afraid he will flatly turn me down if I tell him the truth." The fountain's splashing filled the lull in conversation while his mother considered what she would say.

"My parents were never happy about me marrying your father and leaving Mexico, but they have always loved me— and they love you children. They have shown us much kindness. He is family, and he loves you." She reached over and touched his arm. "And, son, never forget that you, your sister, and I are his only heirs. He wants us to have what he has worked for all his life when he is gone. I would trust him with my and my family's life. But you must decide if you are willing to take him into your confidence."

***

After dinner, Harry asked his grandfather if he could speak with him privately. Esteban led him into his den and closed the door. He had sharp features with high cheekbones, a hawk nose, and he wore his sixty years well. His brown, almost black eyes calmly took in everything around him, and he had a disconcerting habit of looking directly into a person's eyes as he was speaking.

The room smelled of years of cigar smoke embedded in the walls and carpet. Two oversized armchairs covered in well-worn leather over hand-carved mesquite wood frames sat in the center of the room, facing a massive wood desk. A painting of a beautiful young woman hung on the wall behind the intricately hand-carved desk.

His grandfather handed him a snifter of brandy and motioned Harry to sit in one of the chairs as he sat in the other. "Who is the lady in the painting?" Harry asked. The woman in the painting looked out at Harry with beautiful and penetrating blue eyes set in a face with a milky fair complexion, and he was sure he knew the answer to his question.

"Your grandmother. She was an exquisite, lovely, and charming woman when she was young. She still is, after all these years. That painting was done the year we were married." He took a sip of brandy. "I am happy to see you. It has been a long time since you visited."

"*Lo siento, Abuelo.* I'm sorry it's been so long."

"What is on your mind that brings you way down here? I sense there is something much more than the mining enterprise you've been talking about."

"*Abuelo*, I need your help with somethin'. It is dangerous and

risky for me and maybe for my family. For that reason, I am cautious about sharin' it, but I know I can trust you with my secret." He told the story from beginning to end, leaving nothing out.

When he finished, his grandfather got up, went to a humidor behind his desk, and took out two large and expensive Havana cigars. He clipped the ends and gave one to Harry, and struck a match to both. They sat in silence while Esteban stared into the smoke, deep in thought.

After a few minutes, he said, "My grandson, *mi Nieto*, you are family. *Sangre de mi sangre.* So I will tell you some of my family secrets, known only to a few. Perhaps it will help with your problem."

He blew a large cloud of blue smoke, took a deep pull on his brandy, and began, "When I was a young man, my family was extremely poor. We were *campesinos*, peasants barely making a living working the fields for a prominent *hacienda* owner. Your grandmother and I were just married, and I ached to give her more than a peasant's life."

He sipped more brandy and continued, "There began to be talk of revolution, and it lit a fire in my heart. The Mexican government was terribly corrupt, controlled by wealthy landowners and business people. It was a lot like it is for you, now, with the Great Depression in the United States. There were not many opportunities for men like me."

He paused, and the room was quiet except for the ticking of an ancient ornate clock in a bookcase. It sounded like loud blows from somewhere far away. "'The rumors of revolution grew strong, and I heard armies were forming to change the country. So I traveled to Juarez and joined with Pancho Villa's fighters."

A smile crossed his face, thinking of his adventures as a young man. He said, "In the beginning, we were only small bands of fighters, striking at the government and withdrawing. I think now it's called guerilla warfare. One day my band stopped a government train, traveling south. We had quite a shootout with armed guards, and in the end, they ran away. We were surprised to find they were protecting a large shipment of silver and gold from the north's mines. It would have been used to pay for more government soldiers to try and stop our rebellion."

Jimmy was astounded. He'd never heard about his grandfather's role in the uprising; he knew next to nothing about the revolution. He thought he might have some inkling of where his grandfather's story was heading, but he stayed quiet and let him finish.

"Those of us in my band of fighters had never seen so much wealth. We were faced with a choice: We could turn it over to Villa to continue the fight. Or we could keep it for ourselves.

We decided to give half to the revolution and use the other half for our families. After all, we had risked our lives in its capture. That seemed only fair to us."

He drained his remaining brandy and sat quietly for a moment. He waved his arm expansively and said, "All this, all you see here in our *hacienda* and our lands, and more, was paid for with my share of that train's cargo. Many of the others around here are successful farmers, business owners, lawmen, and high government officials who owe their positions to that action so long ago. We guard our secret to this day."

"*Abuelo*, I had no idea you were a fighter in the revolution. My mother has never told me any of this."

"Your mother has never heard this whole story. She only knows that I came into some land at the end of the revolution. I want to keep it that way."

He puffed up the embers on his cigar. "I have told you this so that you can know that I understand what you are trying to do. And I will help you in any way that I can."

"I'm grateful, *Abuelo*. My partner Jimmy will be grateful, too. We've worked hard to get to this point."

"What do you need?"

"I'm sure you know the U.S. government has made it illegal to keep more than one hundred dollars worth of gold. We need to find a bank we can trust to exchange what we have. No US bank can do what we need. And we need to find someplace in Mexico we can bring our ore to be refined — one that won't ask too many questions."

"Let me think about this. We'll talk more tomorrow. Go and have a good night's rest, *nieto*."

***

The next day, after breakfast, his grandfather pulled Harry aside. "I think I have some friends who can help with what you need. Come, let's take a ride."

Harry drove his father's truck, and his grandfather gave him directions. They arrived at some mine works about twenty miles out of town with a smelter operation at the entrance. Esteban said, "The man who owns this company is one of my *compañeros* from our time with Villa. He came by this business in the same way I came by mine. We can trust him."

Harry stopped in front of an adobe headquarters building that looked like it had been there forever. His grandfather led the way in, and a man about his age came out and grabbed him in a big embrace. "*Hola*, my old friend. It is wonderful to see you. And who is this you brought with you?"

"*Señor* Arredondo, this is my grandson, Harold Taylor. Everyone calls him Harry!"

He shook Harry's hand. "He's a fine-looking lad, Esteban. He favors you."Arredondo brought them coffee, and they settled in to discuss why they were there.

Harry said, "*Señor* Arredondo, I am takin' over a silver claim from my father near Ajo. It's a small operation with some profitable ore. I am going into business with a partner, and we plan to start workin' the mine. I'm lookin' for a smelter to process a limited amount of ore for us 'til we get more established."

"This seems a long way to haul your ore, young Taylor. Is there nothing nearer your mine you could use?"

"No, *señor*. Only the big copper smelter for the mine at Ajo. It is closed down now, and I don't think they would do jobs like ours. Besides, we are hopin' that we might develop other business relationships in Mexico."

Harry's grandfather interrupted. "Humberto, my grandson's situation is like the situation you and I found ourselves in many years ago. The US government won't look favorably at what he is proposing. I told him you are a man of great integrity that I trust and that you might be able to help him."

Arredondo nodded. "Young Taylor, I believe I remember your father. He used to work for me. And after he moved to Arizona, he brought silver ore for me to process from a mine he acquired. This is the same mine you are now working, yes?" Harry said it was. "Your father is a good man," Arredondo continued. "I understand what you need, and I think I can arrange it without too many questions. I will have to charge you a nominal fee for the smelter to keep my books accurate."

"I would expect no less, señor. I will be very grateful for your help."

Arredondo gave Harry a business card and told him to call when he was ready to schedule the work. After thanks for the coffee, the old friends had a parting embrace. Harry and his grandfather left for another meeting.

They headed back to Caborca and stopped at a white, flat-roofed building with a sign out front that said *Banco Regional de Caborca*. They stepped inside, and a man in a business suit, obviously the manager or owner, came out of his office and shook Harry's grandfather's hand. "Esteban! How nice to see you! Please, come into my office and have a seat." He was another man about Harry's grandfather's age, and Harry saw the logic of his grandfather's plan. He hoped this banker would be as helpful as the last man. This part of the plan was the trickiest and carried the most significant risk.

"Pablo, I would like you to meet my grandson, Harold Taylor. Harry, this is *Señor* Estevez." Estevez shook Harry's hand and motioned them to sit in front of his desk. Harry could already feel droplets of sweat beading on his forehead despite the cool February day. A floor fan stirred the air; Harry was thankful for the light breeze to dry his sweat.

Harry's grandfather began the conversation in a seemingly indirect way. "Pablo, do you remember the time in Juarez you and I drank so much tequila we became lost until the next day?"

Pablo burst out laughing. "How could I forget, Esteban? We were young and foolish!"

Esteban continued: "Indeed we were. But we had a serious purpose, you and I, which led us on many later adventures. One of those adventures played a large role in helping you become the successful banker you are today. I expect you remember that day, as well, Pablo."

"I do, Esteban. What has that to do with your visit today?"

"You and I, and the others, made decisions back then we thought would be in the best interests of the future of our families. My grandson faces a similar decision, and I would be grateful if you could help him."

"By all means, *Señor* Taylor. I would be happy to help you if I can. What is it you need?

Harry was now sweating and embarrassed to appear so nervous. He began, "*Señor*, the US government has restricted owning and selling gold in my country. Me and my partner have come into a substantial amount of gold. We need to exchange it for either Mexican pesos or American dollars to make use of it."

Estevez sat back in his chair and studied him. "You are aware that this is illegal in your country, and your government could put you in jail for it?"

"I am, *señor*. But conditions in my country are desperate right now. There're no jobs and no prospects for any I can see. My partner and I need to take care of our families and ourselves. We are in a position to do that if we can make use of our gold. We're also working a mine and would be exchanging some silver with you, too."

Estevez looked from him to his grandfather and back at Harry. "What you ask is indeed risky, for you, and for my company and me. It would have to be financially worthwhile for us to take this risk."

"I understand," Harry said. "We would make it worthwhile for you and your business."

"As your grandfather has so eloquently pointed out, my business, as well as his, was established with significant risk. I will agree to assist you with this as a favor to your grandfather and your family. You and your partner will need to meet with me to work out the details of the transactions."

He, too, gave Harry his card and told him to contact him to make an appointment. Harry exhaled a big sigh of relief when they were outside. His grandfather chuckled and said, "You did well, *nieto*. But I suspect you will have many more stressful encounters in the coming months!"

They arrived back at the *hacienda* in time for lunch and a *siesta*. Harry was ecstatic as he described the morning's success to his mother. She smiled at him and took his hands. "Thank you for believing in my father. It means a great deal to me. I know it does to him, too."

***

Harry and his mother left early the next day to return to Ajo. Harry told her he needed to stop at the old mine on the way but wouldn't be there long.

"I've never been to that mine," she said. "Your father always said it was no place for a lady. But I knew he and your uncle didn't want me along to interfere with their drinking." She laughed, but Harry could tell it had a serious note.

Harry laughed. "Wait 'til you see the pile of beer bottles! But don't tell Dad I took you there. I'd never hear the end of it!" She said it would be their secret. Harry showed her the two rock piles that marked the turnoff to the mine's road and chuckled, "I'd never find it without those, coming from this direction. We're about ten miles south of Why."

Everything appeared as the partners had left it; there was no reason for anyone to be out there. It was blazing hot in the sun. Harry found his mother a shady place inside the old house for her to wait for him.

184

He quickly went to the old dig where they had hidden the treasure. There was no sign of any disturbance around it. He moved aside two of the boards and pulled out one of the duffels. He found one of the smaller bags and counted out 50 silver Mexican pesos as Jimmy had instructed. He put them into the canvas prospector bag he carried and put the covering boards back as they were.

They arrived back at his parents' house. Harry told his father that his grandfather had been incredibly helpful by introducing him to the people they needed for their business there. He told him Mr. Arredondo at the smelter sent his greetings.

His father laughed and said, "That old dog! I wish I had every dollar he squeezed out of me over the years. Be careful with him, Harry, and don't let him cheat you." He reminded him again to be wary of their dealings in Mexico and trust no one but themselves.

As he was preparing to leave, Joann took him aside. "Don't you come back here without Jimmy!" Harry said he would do his best. "We have a little over four months to finish our time with the CCC. Then, I expect you'll be seein' more of both of us than you might like."

She laughed. "That is highly doubtful. I can't wait to see Jimmy again!"

He caught the afternoon bus back to Tucson, anxious to share his good news with his partner. Back in camp, they had a few minutes of private time before dinner. Harry said, "Everything went great in Mexico. I think it's gonna be everythin' we need." He filled Jimmy in on the details and said, "Uncle Frank said he'd be happy to have you stay with them, and you're welcome as long as you like. But you'll have to help out some with expenses."

"I'm more than happy to do that. Great news! Thanks!"

"And be ready—Joann is really gunnin' for you! She told me I better not show up again without you. Better be prepared!" Jimmy turned nearly as red as the sunset and smiled.

CHAPTER 18
LOOSE ENDS

Jimmy asked for and received permission for a day off to go to Tucson. He told the Lieutenant he needed to make preparations for leaving the CCC during regular hours in the workweek. There was to be a lull in his crew's work on Wednesday, and he made arrangements to use that day to go into town.

He had the 50 silver pesos in his daypack. His first stop was the shop that advertised dealing in rare coins. A kindly-looking older man sat behind a desk with some cardboard coin holders in front of him. He was balding and wore eyeglasses with lenses that looked like magnifying glasses. He motioned Jimmy to the seat across from his desk and asked how he could help him. Jimmy took out four of his coins and laid them on the desk. "Would you be interested in these?" he asked.

The shop owner scrutinized each coin and said, "These are nice coins with minimal wear. But they are quite common here and don't have any value as collectibles. I would have to discount them substantially to make them worth my while. To be truthful, you could probably do better at one of the shops that deal in bulk metals." Jimmy thanked him for his honesty and left.

He went to the first of the two shops that advertised dealing in coins and precious metals. It was a small, dingy place on a side street. Jimmy looked inside through a dirty fly-specked window. There was a single counter facing a couple of old chairs with stuffing coming out of the seat covers. He expected a more prosperous-looking business. A tiny brass bell over the door jingled when Jimmy opened the door. The owner emerged from the back and asked what he could do for him.

Jimmy laid one of the pesos on the counter. "I inherited some of these, and I would like to exchange them for dollars. Can you do that?" The owner looked the coin over carefully. He was a short, heavy, balding man with a mustache badly in need of a trim. His lips were pulled back slightly from his teeth, displaying discolored and rotting teeth. He exuded a rather pungent body odor that was powerful even from across the counter.

"How many of these do you wish to exchange?"

"I have twenty-five of them,"

"I'll give you seven dollars apiece for them, less my normal 15% cost of an exchange. How would you like your bills?"

Harry's research had prepared him for this. "According to the newspaper's current quote, they are worth eleven dollars each. I will take ten dollars each, and that includes your exchange fee."

The man studied Jimmy for a moment with close-set, intent, and greedy eyes. He hadn't expected this rube to have done any homework and said, "Let me check on something," and slipped into his backroom. He picked up his phone and made a call. J.W. Smart answered, and "Skunk" Graves told him he thought the man he was looking for was in his shop to exchange silver coins. They had already discussed terms of splitting anything J.W. recovered. J.W. told him to stall the man a few minutes until he could get there. Graves returned to the front a few minutes later and said, "I can offer you eight dollars, but I will need my customary fifteen percent fee."

"Fine. I'll take my business somewhere else, maybe to Phoenix." He put the coin back in his pocket, picked up his pack, and started for the door.

"Wait, wait," the owner called after him. Jimmy stopped. "I can offer nine fifty, including my fee. It's the best I can do."

Jimmy returned to the counter and said, "I believe you would make a nice profit at ten dollars. Take it or leave it."

The man exhaled a cloud of fetid breath, which caused Jimmy to step back. The man's rotting teeth, combined with his body odor, were almost overpowering. "All right, all right. You look like you could use a favor, and I will help you out this once. But don't expect me to do it again!"

He counted out twelve twenty-dollar bills and slapped them on the counter. Jimmy watched carefully as "Skunk" laid out the bills. He waited a few seconds and said, "I believe the count is ten dollars short." Graves feigned embarrassment and said, "Oh, my! I'm so sorry. I only keep twenty-dollar bills out front. Let me get a ten from the back." Jimmy smiled to himself at the man's blatant attempt to cheat him. He would do no more business with this man. "Skunk" returned with the ten-dollar bill and placed it with the stack of twenties.

Jimmy kept his distance from the man's obnoxious odors. He took twenty-four more coins from his pack and laid them beside the dollars. The owner made a show of carefully examining each one and finally nodded, scooping them off into a tray.

Jimmy collected his money and left. Neither party exchanged thanks. Back on the street, Jimmy instinctively knew he now had to move quickly. He suspected that the shop owner likely had some unsavory associates who would soon come looking for him. He would be easy prey in that neighborhood.

He quickly walked several blocks across town to the second shop. He noticed two men in an old, black decrepit looking Hudson Super-six sedan who pulled up across the street as he entered the shop. Mud and debris caked its spoked wheels; it likely hadn't been washed in many years. They were watching him—his suspicions about the last shop owner were correct.

This shop appeared more successful; it was larger and cleaner than the first one. Jimmy found the owner and his son working the front. He told them what he wanted and showed them one of the coins. They went into their backroom to confer, came out, and made Jimmy an offer similar to the one made by the last shop owner.

Jimmy went through an almost identical haggling conversation as he had in the first shop. Finally, he threatened to take his business elsewhere, perhaps to Phoenix. He eventually haggled out a deal for another two-hundred-fifty dollars.

He put his money in his backpack. Glancing out the front window, he noticed the two men in the car still waiting on the street. They were intently watching the door. He asked the owners if there was a back door he could use. They looked at him quizzically but didn't ask any questions. The owner showed him into their back office. The door opened onto an alley lined with trash cans and discarded wine bottles.

It took Jimmy a moment to get his bearings before he started running as fast as he could in the direction of the safest place he could think of: the county courthouse. He came out of the alley on the main downtown street. He could see the famous blue dome on the courthouse building a few blocks away.

His followers turned into the alley as he ran out the opposite end; they gunned the old Hudson's six-cylinder engine to try and catch him. Jimmy ducked into another alley and continued running toward the courthouse. His pursuers missed his turn and were momentarily confused at losing their prey. It bought Jimmy the time he needed. He reached the courthouse and ran through one of its arched entryways, across a courtyard, and into the front doors.

The pursuers' car screeched to a halt on the street, and the two would-be robbers jumped out—but they were too late. They saw

Jimmy dash through the door of the courthouse; their target was out of their reach for now. J.W. Smart cursed and kicked a tire before getting back in the car.

Inside the courthouse, Jimmy looked around for a courtroom with a trial in session. He slipped inside and took a seat. His appointed time to meet his return ride in the nearby plaza was a half-hour away, but he thought he was reasonably safe sitting in the courtroom.

Smart and his associate parked in front of the courthouse, hoping for another try at robbing Jimmy. J.W. had spent far more time in the ornate old building than he cared to remember. He cursed and said, "Damn! We almost had him. Maybe we can catch him when he comes out." A Tucson police officer took an interest in them and told them they couldn't park there. They left and hung around the plaza, pretending to look in some shop windows, hoping to catch their prey when he emerged.

Jimmy waited until the last minute and dashed out a side entrance. He met his campmates loading up in one of the camp's army trucks. Jimmy was thankful he had spotted his would-be robbers when he did, or the episode would have had a far different ending.

J.W. watched as the truck pulled away. Their prey was gone along with a big payday, but, he told himself, there would be another time.

***

The partners went to Tucson the following Saturday to meet with Harry's cousin. He took them to see the man who was selling them the truck, and Jimmy looked it over carefully before nodding to Harry. The truck was a light maroon color—a nice change from the typical black of most pickups in town. It looked practically new; its black interior was as clean as the day it rolled off Ford's assembly line. The tires showed almost no wear. Jimmy thought it was a great-looking rig.

They paid the money and received a signed title. The partners now had their first key piece of equipment for their plans. They took their new truck to Harry's cousin's house and parked it. It would be safe there until they could use it.

It was late February, rodeo week in Tucson. The annual *Fiesta de Los Vagueros* was a big celebration that brought many people into town for the parade and rodeo. Any diversion from the continuing bleakness of the Depression was welcome. The parade featured many horse-mounted riders, the local polo club with white helmets and bright shirts, two local military bands, two mariachi bands, a group of Native American dancers, and assorted colorful floats.

Jimmy had never been to a rodeo. He was especially fascinated by the roping events. They fit right into his dreams of someday having his own ranch. Riding a fine horse, twirling a lasso, and bringing down a calf for branding were precisely the kinds of things he wanted to do.

***

The rodeo brought a lot of money into the town. J.W. Smart, still angry over his failed attempt at robbing Jimmy, thought there would be an opportunity to make up for his loss. He staked out one of the busiest bars in downtown Tucson. Then, when most of the customers were gone at closing time, he made his move. He walked into the bar and threw a canvas bag on the counter. He leveled his pistol at the bartender's chest as he told him to empty his cash drawer.

The bartender was also the owner, and he had been robbed before. He had sworn never to let it happen again. He grabbed a sawed-off twelve-gauge shotgun from under the bar and managed to fire both barrels into J.W.'s chest. The robber fired his revolver as the shotgun's discharge hit him, but his shot was forced high by the force of the blast. The bartender suffered a shoulder wound; J.W. died almost instantly.

The partners never knew anything about J.W., his connection to their treasure, and the man responsible for it.

Trouble showed up again on Monday morning when the captain summoned Jimmy and Harry to his tent. Treasury Agent

Turner, detective Hoag, and the Pima County Sheriff were seated

around the captain's desk. The captain motioned the partners to chairs alongside his other visitors and said, "These men have some additional questions for you."

Jimmy looked from one to the other, speculating what this was about now. The Treasury agent spoke first: "Gentlemen, The Sheriff and detective Hoag are here at my request because I believe this discussion is of interest to both of them. Mr. Brown, it has come to my attention that you were in Tucson the last week where you visited three coin and metals shops. My sources say that you exchanged somewhere around 50 silver Mexican pesos. Is this correct?" Jimmy nodded. The agent continued, "My interest here is that silver coins are supposedly part of the lost treasure hidden in the cave. Would you care to explain how you came to be in possession of that number of silver coins?"

Jimmy looked from one to the other of the men while he thought. "First off, I don't see how any of this is your business. But if you must know, those coins were a loan to Harry and me from Harry's grandfather to help us get started in our business when we are done here."

"And do you happen to know how his grandfather accumulated these coins?" the agent persisted.

Harry said, "He told me he had them many years from his businesses in Mexico. My grandfather is a very successful farmer in Mexico. I never asked anything else about them. "

"And, Mr. Baker, why is it you were the one doing this transaction instead of Harry?"

"Harry and I have an agreement that I will handle the business end of the mine while he handles the other details. We are partners."

"How about you, Mr. Taylor? Anything you care to add to this?"

"No, sir," Harry said. "We are partners and share in the work we are doing to prepare for our mining business when we leave here. Like Jimmy said."

"And do you have any other information about the silver coins your grandfather had?"

"No, sir. I didn't know anything about 'em until recently. I tried to talk him out of lettin' us use 'em, but he wanted to help us get started right. He knows we'll repay him when we can."

It was apparent the agent didn't believe what he was hearing. Turning to Detective Hoag, he asked, "Sir, do you find this story believable?"

"I think it's quite believable that a grandfather would want to help his grandson get ahead," Hoag said. "I've looked into this since you called me, Agent Turner, and Wells Fargo has no way of identifying the coins in question. However, they are quite common, as you know. So, with nothing concrete to go on, I can see no reason for me to question these men's story."

The Sheriff said, "I have no reason to question what these men have said, either. Those kinds of silver coins have been common around here for as long as I can remember. But, since you have no way of identifying them and therefore no way of proving they are of interest, I'd say we're done here." He smiled at Jimmy and Harry and continued, "Besides, I have good reason in my experience with these men to think they are honest and reliable. I hope you men are successful in your mining ventures."

The Treasury agent was not happy or satisfied with this conversation's outcome. He clearly thought he had the partners dead to rights in their scheme to cash in the robbery loot.

The captain asked if there was anything else and dismissed Jimmy and Harry to their daily tasks. Before the other men left, he said, "Agent Turner, I realize you are only doing the job you are hired to do. But, I believe it has been amply shown by recent circumstances that these men have not done what you believe. This idea resulted from ill-founded rumors started by one man with a grudge. You have been taken in by them."

The agent replied that the captain was entitled to his opinions, but he would continue to do his job. He wished all the men a good day and left the tent in a huff. The Sheriff followed along behind him, still smiling.

Harry made for the camp's payphone and called his mother as soon as the agent, detective, and Sheriff were gone. He told her to

look out for the agent snooping around again. She asked what the agent wanted this time, and Harry filled her in on what they had told the agent about the coins. He said he figured the agent would be less likely to contact his grandfather, so they should be prepared for questions. She laughed and said she would pass the information on to her father, just in case.

CHAPTER 19
INTO THE BLACK MAW

The partners were anxious to finish their CCC obligation and move on with their plans. But time seemed to grind along at the speed of mold growing on a wall. Spring was passing into summer, and the temperatures in late May hovered around one hundred degrees in the afternoons.

The camp had a tradition when a group of men had completed their enrollment terms; during morning muster, the captain would call each man forward, hand him a certificate of completion, and say a few kind words of encouragement for their future. He called Jimmy, Harry, and the other enrollees they had started with a year ago to come forward. It was the last Friday of Jimmy and Harry's time in camp.

Jimmy and Harry accepted their certificates. The captain offered them both extra words of encouragement, saying he hoped their new business would be successful. It seemed unreal to Jimmy that a year had passed since he left his home in Denver.

Surprisingly, he found it bittersweet. He had enjoyed most of his time and the work, and he had many friends among his coworkers. But, on the other hand, he was excited and anxious to start on the plans he and Harry had so carefully made. Now it

was time to do everything in his power to make his dreams
happen.

***

Jimmy and Harry said their goodbyes to friends in the camp.
Jimmy made a special effort to speak to the two men from
Colorado as they traveled to Tucson on the camp shuttle. "I
want you guys to know I have no hard feelings for you, and I
hope you do good back in Colorado. It would be a kindness if
you could find time to visit Reuben's family and let them know
what happened." The pair didn't reply, and Jimmy didn't press
it, thinking he had done what he could— maybe more than he
should.

Harry's cousin met them at the downtown plaza and took
them back to his place to get their truck. They thanked him and
his family for their help. Harry gave Bill a few dollars to cover
the gas cost for shuttling them around.

The truck started on the engine's first turn, and they were
gone. Harry and Jimmy stopped at the Douglas and Sons
grocery store for supplies: tuna fish, corned beef, Spam, two
tins of real ham, peanut butter, spaghetti, various kinds of
beans, three boxes of saltine crackers, applesauce, peaches,
other fruits, assorted vegetables, and canned soups. Two red
one-pound tins of Hills Bros. coffee and a bag of sugar rounded

out the list. Harry said they could pick up some homemade tortillas and tamales in Ajo before going to the mine.

Next, they stopped at a hardware store and bought assorted gear: cookware and eating utensils, two decent cots, four wool blankets, and some cleaning supplies for the mine's old house. The Western Auto store downtown had a good stock of firearms, and the partners bought a Revelation bolt action .22 rifle and three boxes of long rifle ammunition. Harry picked out a used Smith and Wesson Model 27 .357 magnum revolver with a six-inch barrel. It was heavy but well balanced and came with a holster. Then they bought a couple of boxes of .357 magnum ammunition for the pistol, plus a box of .38 caliber snake loads. The gun could utilize both calibers. It was in used but like-new condition. At twenty-five dollars, it was by far the most expensive item they purchased. Harry said it would likely be valuable in the coming months; he said it was powerful enough to stop a mountain lion or anything else they might encounter.

Jimmy said he didn't have any experience with guns and shooting. Harry told him it was high time he learned. It was important to know how to shoot if he was going to live in the middle of the desert. Target practice would be high on their to-do list!

They filled the truck with gas, bought a couple of ice-cold RC Colas, along with two bags of salted peanuts, and headed for Ajo.

They pulled into Harry's parents' driveway about four in the afternoon. Joann ran out to meet them. She threw her arms around Jimmy, kissed him, and said, "Why'd you wait so long?"

"Dang, Sis! Give the man a break," Harry said. "He's been workin' his tail off!"

"That's no excuse! You could have brought him with you last time!"

Jimmy felt like a soccer ball being kicked back and forth. Harry's mother saved him again, telling them to settle and clean up for dinner.

Harry's mother had prepared a special meal to celebrate the completion of their CCC time and return to Ajo. She had made some fresh green corn *tamales* and splurged on some beef for filling *enchiladas*. Dessert was Harry's favorite—delicious homemade *flan*.

Harry chided her for spending so much on them, but she said they deserved it, and she and his father were happy to do it.

The men drove to Uncle Frank's house. He was waiting for them and introduced Jimmy to his wife, who Jimmy could call Aunt Rita. She was a stout woman with a cheerful face, a quick laugh, and mischievous green eyes. Rita welcomed Jimmy like family. She showed him his room: a tight but comfortable space, a good bed, a dresser with a mirror, and a tiny closet. A beautiful picture of the famous Yosemite Falls hung on the wall; the picture's water and greenery seemed out of place in the desert. The room was luxurious after the spartan quarters Jimmy had lived in for the last year. He unpacked his few belongings, washed up, and combed his hair. Then he went back to Harry's house to find Joann.

They went for a long walk around the plaza, catching up. The businesses around the plaza were closed, and they had the area to themselves. A light breeze made the warm June night almost comfortable. Venus was glittering in the west, and the darkening night sky became powdered with a dusting of stars. They felt as if they were the only ones on the planet.

Jimmy said, "I couldn't wait to see you again, despite what Harry said. We had too much to do for me to get away."

She laughed. "I know, but I had to tease you. These last few months passed so slowly it seemed like they'd never end. I truly did miss you and was anxious for you to be here. It feels like we've known each other forever— not just these past few weeks."

Jimmy held her close in the dim light of a distant streetlamp. They shared a long kiss. Then another. He felt the same warmness he experienced the first time they had kissed; it gave him a feeling of great peace and comfort. "I feel that way, too. Harry and I will be very busy for a while getting organized. I'll be spending a lot of time at the mine. But I hope to be with you as much as I can. That is if you'll let me."

She kissed him again in answer. They sat for a while, drinking in the beauty of the star-filled night. Jimmy wished the moment didn't have to end. But it was growing late, and he walked her back to her house. They shared more kisses on her front porch. Jimmy did not want to leave. He hated to break the spell of holding her. They had one more long goodnight kiss, and Jimmy headed to his new home.

The next day was Sunday. Both Jimmy and Harry attended the services with the family at the local Catholic church. Jimmy was self-conscious; he had no dressy clothes. Joann told him not to worry about it.

Harry's mother was very devout in the religion. She'd been raised in Mexico, where the church was a large part of life. Jimmy knew next to nothing about the Catholic faith, or any other religion for that matter. His only experience had been attending the Christmas time services with the family. He did the best he could to be respectful and follow along with the prayers and rituals. Occasionally Joann would smile at him and reach over to take his hand. Jimmy was relieved when the service was over.

Back at his new home, Jimmy asked Frank and Rita if it would be okay to phone his mother in Denver. He said he'd pay the charge, and they told him it was fine. It was a relief to hear his mother's voice. He hadn't had a chance to speak to her in a long time.

He could hear the surprise and relief in her voice when she answered: "Oh, Jimmy! It's wonderful to hear your voice. I've been so worried about you out there in that desert. It's hard to imagine how far away you are. I hope you are alright!"

"Everything's fine, Mom. In fact, it's great! I finished my time with the CCC, and I've gone into business with my best friend, Harry Taylor. He's from a town called Ajo, and I'm living there now too. We are starting a mining business."

"Son, do be careful! I've heard so many awful rumors about men working in the mines around here. I couldn't bear to have something happen to you."

"It's okay, Mom. We will have a small operation, nothing like the mines around Denver. We are going to take out silver-bearing ore. I'll tell you more about it later. But I don't want you to worry about that or about money. The money I earned for you in the CCC's will stop soon, but I will continue to send you some money to make up for it as soon as our business is going well."

He told her about Joann, how much he liked her, and that she would hear more about her. He gave her the house's phone number to reach him and said he would call her again when he had more news.

His mother's tone turned somber, and she said, "I have some distressing news. Your sister has been extremely ill, and the doctor says he thinks it may be polio. She is so ill, Jimmy! I don't know what we will do. Her care is going to be expensive, and I will have to be with her nearly all the time."

Jimmy was stunned. Polio! He didn't know much about it but had heard it was a horrible and frequently fatal disease. "Mom, I

am so sorry. I wish I could be there with you. Please tell Sarah I love her and see she gets the care she needs. I will find a way to pay for it. My business will be making good money soon, and I will help any way you need me to."

He could hear her sobbing and waited for her to regain her composure. Finally, she said, "Jimmy, I don't know what we would do without you. Take good care of yourself. I will phone you when I have more news about your sister."

Jimmy sat quietly by himself, trying to process this new information. It made it more critical that he and Harry be successful with their plans.

***

The men got together on Harry's parent's patio after lunch to discuss what to do first. Harry's dad said, "You were right about that Treasury agent. He showed up here later that day after you called. I told him it was none of his damn business where you got those coins and to stop pesterin' us about his goofy lost treasure. He was pretty huffy about it, told me HE was a representative of the US GOVERNMENT, charged with enforcing its laws, and stormed out of the house. It's good you warned us."

"That guy's a real bulldog," Jimmy said. "For some reason, he believes there's something to the rumors he heard. I expect we haven't seen the last of him."

"And something else," John continued, "There was a detective here later that day too, said he represented Wells Fargo. Asking the same kind of questions. I gave him the same answers."

The partners knew the treasure was well hidden with virtually no chance of discovery by their pursuers. But it was apparent the extra scrutiny on them would continue. They realized they would have to be doubly cautious not to do anything to arouse more suspicions.

The men decided to spend the next two or three days at the mine. First, they would make arrangements for overnight stays, and then Harry would check out the mine's equipment. After that, they would have a look in the mine itself. Jimmy was excited to get inside it despite his early trepidation.

Jimmy sat with Joann that evening and told her he expected to be back by the end of the week and hoped to spend more time with her. "You barely got here," she said, "and now you're running off again! Come back to me as soon as you can, and in one piece, if you please!"

They loaded up their supplies plus several jerry cans of water and bought some eggs and bacon for breakfast. Harry's mom sent some tamales along with enchiladas and tortillas leftover from the previous dinner. After one more stop at a gas station, where they filled two more five-gallon cans with gasoline to power the mine's lift engine, they headed south out of town to the mine. They found everything as they had left it.

The silence of the desert descended around them. There was nothing for miles around, and the isolation was complete. The truck's engine made a quiet ticking as it cooled. Eventually, Jimmy's ears started to pick up the distant calls of a covey of quail and the rasping call of a cactus wren perched nearby. The wren's call reminded him of the sound the truck's starter made when it was cranking. There was no breeze, and, already, the late morning heat was stifling.

An old metal picture with a thermometer mounted on it hung in the shade of one wall on the house. Harry said his Dad bought it for twenty-five cents from a gas station going out of business. It looked completely out of place in the hot desert. The picture showed a pretty girl with large breasts in a white swimsuit lounging beside a cool-looking swimming pool. She smiled provocatively while holding a dewy bottle of Coca-Cola. Despite the refreshing scene, the thermometer read 103 degrees.

They spent the rest of that day storing their supplies and cleaning up the old house. The house had a partial roof over part of the main room, which afforded some shade from the intense sun. The long ribs from several dead saguaro cactuses made up the original roof. They were laid across thick mesquite limbs for beams and covered with a layer of adobe mud. Most of the mud had deteriorated and crumbled over its long life. The floor was dirt, cobwebs dangled from some of the saguaro ribs and in the corners of the room.

Sweat drenched the men's clothes. Jimmy frequently wrung the moisture out of his saturated cap.

Harry said, "Wait 'til we go down in the mine. You might be cravin' a bit more of this heat to take the chill off!"

"I don't think I'll ever complain about being too cool again," Jimmy laughed.

They knew what was left of the roof wouldn't keep out any rain, but they set their cots up under it anyway. "We'll have to do somethin' about the roof soon. The summer monsoon will be startin' up any day now, and those rickety beams will be useless. Dad is bringin' some tarps for cover." Jimmy wasn't sure the old place was any better than the tent they had slept in the past year. At least that tent had a flap that could be secured from the weather and local desert denizens when necessary. Unfortunately, the old house had long since lost its doors and windows. Fortunately, there were no rattlesnakes in residence.

Several scorpions scurried out of the debris as the men cleaned. The eight-legged pests met quick ends under the men's boot soles. They cleared out assorted garbage and junk that had provided them many hiding places. It was a reminder to shake out their clothes and boots in the morning. Harry said, "Hang your clothes on the hooks in the wall, but it ain't no guarantee a scorpion won't bed down in 'em. And check the covers on your bed, too. Always give your boots a good shake before you put 'em on. For some reason, those tricky little devils like hidin' in 'em!"

"Maybe they're attracted to the smell," Jimmy joked, and they had a good laugh.

Harry said, "Let's do some target practice before dinner. Grab some of those empty bean cans, walk about 20 paces up the hill, and line 'em up. We'll see how good your eye is." They had brought both the .22 rifle and the pistol. "Let's start with the rifle. That will get you used to pullin' a trigger and makin' noise." He showed Jimmy how to check that the weapon was not loaded, how to put in the clip, and how to work the bolt to put a cartridge in the chamber. Lastly, he showed him how to position his feet and sight on a target.

Jimmy went through the motions a couple of times. Then Harry said, "Take your time, line your sight up on the first can on the left. Take a deep breath, let it out slow, then squeeze the trigger with an even pull."

To both men's amazement, the can spun up into the air. Harry laughed. "I don't believe it! Some beginner's luck! Okay, put in another shell and do another one. Let's see if you can do two in a row." Again the target spun up into the air. Jimmy repeated it on the other three cans in the row, only missing once.

"You're a natural," Harry said. "I think you've been puttin' me on about never usin' a gun! Let's try out our new pistol; see how you do with that."

The revolver was much different to handle. It took several tries for Jimmy to get used to it. Harry showed him how to stand and brace his arms and hands for a steady aim. It was much louder than the rifle and had a vicious recoil; it almost kicked back into his face the first time he fired it. But he kept at it until he could pick off a can consistently at about 15 feet.

Harry said, "Let me shoot a few." It turned out he was a crack shot, adept with both weapons.

"Wow! You're like a professional or something, Harry!"

"I been doing this since I was a kid. My dad started teachin' me when I was about ten. When we came out here, there was always target practice involved. You're pretty good for your first time, and you'll get a lot better with practice, too. That's prob'ly enough for your first lesson. We need to practice some every evenin' to get you comfortable with the guns. Let's put 'em away now and break out somethin' for dinner."

Jimmy's ears rang despite the cotton he had stuffed in them before shooting. The recoil from the revolver made his wrists sore.

Harry said, "The rifle's mostly fine for picking off any small stuff around here, and we want to keep it handy. The pistol will be better for protecting us whenever we might need it. If a rattlesnake comes around, you put in a couple of the snake loads to take care of it. They're filled with little pellets that are really effective. Maybe most important, there's some rough *hombres* in Mexico. We need to be prepared in case any of them get ideas. The size of that pistol is likely to scare off a problem. We'll keep practicin' in the evenin's until you get used to handlin' it."

A red drop of sun on the horizon faded as they primed and hung up two kerosene lanterns for the night. Harry made a mesquite wood fire in the outside pit to heat some dinner on its grill: tamales, left-over enchiladas, some fresh tortillas, a couple of beers each. Their bellies were stuffed when they finished. They ate in silence, enjoying the newfound privacy and the night sounds of the desert. It seemed odd not to be surrounded by the coughing, snoring, and murmuring of many men around them.

Jimmy said, "I guess I never paid much attention to how noisy the camp was. We got used to it, and it was part of life. I think it's gonna take some time to get used to the quiet of this place."

"Wait 'til my Dad and Uncle Fred show up and start drinkin' beer! It won't seem so quiet and peaceful then!" They both laughed about that and made preparations to call it a day.

Sometime deep in the night, Jimmy awoke to something snuffling and moving outside the house. He got up and could see several coyotes milling around the area of their now dead campfire, sniffing at the grill. There was a sliver of moon hanging over the hills to the west. It cast a weak, surreal, pale glow over the scene. One of the coyotes apparently saw or smelled him, gave a yip, and the whole pack moved away into the shadows. He guessed it was the same pack that had come to visit on his first stay here. He lay on his cot, listening to them howl and bark. They gradually moved away from him, and he drifted off to sleep. Harry had been oblivious to the night's activities.

They were up at first light. Harry fired up the old kerosene camp stove on a flat rock by the fire pit. They had a huge breakfast of bacon and scrambled eggs wrapped in homemade tortillas, washed down with a steaming pot of cowboy coffee. The sharp smell of the coffee reminded Jimmy of home. It had an aroma like percolating coffee on the stove in his mother's kitchen.

Harry said, "My dad taught me that the secret to makin' good coffee this way is to take your time. You boil the water to a roll first, let it cool slightly, put in a pinch of salt, dump in the grounds, and stir. Let it sit for a few minutes before you put a splash of cold water in to help settle the grounds." They drank the whole pot from tin cups, burning their fingers on the hot metal and continually blowing on the steaming liquid to cool it enough to sip. Jimmy thought it might have been the best breakfast and coffee he ever had.

Their first task was to check out the gasoline engine and generator that powered the winch for the mine's ore car. The metal was already hot to the touch when they removed the canvas tarp covering the equipment. It would sear the skin after a few more hours in the direct sun.

The fuel tank had been drained after its last use. Harry took it off and rinsed it out with fresh gas to remove anything that might clog the fuel line. Next, he took apart and cleaned the carburetor to get rid of dust and any particles that might cause a problem. Finally, he cleaned the ignition points, the spark plugs, and the air and fuel filters.

"You can't be too careful about keepin' this ol' engine clean," he told Jimmy. "The heat and dust in the desert can cause lots of problems when an engine sits for a time. We don't want problems with it when we're down in the hole, 'cause it's a long climb out!" Jimmy didn't know whether this reassured him.

When he finished cleaning, Harry gave the engine a couple of good cranks. It roared right to life and ran smoothly, much to Jimmy's amazement. Harry explained the winch's controls to Jimmy and then tested the ore car lift. It worked smoothly in both directions. The winch had a simple forward, back, and stop control on a long, heavy electrical line. The line and control were placed in the ore car, then the slack was played out as the car descended. It allowed for lowering and raising the ore car from inside the mine. Jimmy thought it was an ingenious system.

Satisfied with his work, Harry shut off the engine and went to check out the other parts of the mine's equipment. He pronounced it safe and said it was ready for them to go down and have a look after a break for lunch.

Jimmy peered into the black maw of the mine. It was darker than the cave entrance had been, and the walls were much closer. The shaft went almost straight down, plunging out of sight in only a few feet. He wasn't afraid of the dark, but that drop into the unknown was a little unnerving.

Harry diverted his attention and said, "Look at this," pointing to an outcrop of rock beside the shaft. Barely visible, after long years weathering in the wind and sun, Jimmy could make out an inscription etched deep into the stone: Felipe Diego Lopez, MDCCLXXVIII.

"Wow! What does the date mean?"

"My dad had someone translate it, and it means 1778. The name might've been the main guy or one of the workers here. No way to know. They prob'ly took out everythin' that seemed like easy pickin's and moved on."

Harry had hung a canvas sack nearby with the name "Desert Water Bag" printed on its side in large red letters. He took a couple of swallows from it and gave a satisfied sigh. "These bags will keep water cool for hours. You just wet the canvas and then hang 'em in a shady spot."

He took another swallow and said, "There were others after the Spaniards left. Mexicans likely worked it for a while. Americans came much later. No tellin' when the last time was somebody worked it before my dad got hold of it. But I can tell you what's left is a lot of work to take out."

The mine's supplies included miners' helmets with lamps similar to those they used in the CCC cave project and a pair of flashlights. They loaded a few tools and some water in the ore car before climbing in themselves. Harry lit one of their lanterns and pulled the winch control cable. The ore car descended slowly into the abyss. Jimmy took some comfort in hearing the engine running loudly and smoothly.

They didn't go far before they disturbed a colony of bats that fluttered around them. Jimmy was startled at first, but he had become accustomed to them in the cave.

The biggest surprise was the temperature. It was much cooler than the cave had been; Jimmy guessed somewhere in the high sixties. It was inching toward one hundred ten degrees in the shade on the surface. He shivered with the abrupt change from the midday heat outside the mine.

Harry stopped their descent about forty feet down. He shone his light into a dark passageway branching off to the side, and carefully climbed out of the car, motioning Jimmy to do the same. He led Jimmy further into the side shaft. It reminded Jimmy of working his way along the floor of the cave, with only his helmet lamp to light the way. The floor was uneven in places, making it easy to trip or stumble. There was utter and complete blackness outside the circle of the lantern's white light.

"There's two side shafts like this," Harry explained. "They was started by the Spaniards who first dug this hole. The shafts followed the ore vein." Timbers supported the shaft along the way. They came to the first of several rooms, shored up by more timbers. Harry continued, "These rooms were made where they found the largest deposits of good ore. They'd clean it out and move on, leaving an open space. My dad and uncle have been doin' the same thing. Most of the work is on the next shaft below this one." They followed that tunnel to its end, then went back to the main shaft and got in the ore car.

Harry took them down another thirty feet to the next side tunnel, which they explored in the same way. "We'll likely start workin' here," he said when they reached the furthest room. There were some tools there and evidence of more recent activities. Two old wooden wheelbarrows that looked like they had been worn out decades earlier leaned against the rock wall.

They played their lights over the rock surface at the front of the space. Even to his untrained eye, Jimmy could see the rock's color appeared much richer than the surrounding walls. It was a vein about two feet wide and a foot high. Harry ran his hand over it. "This is what we're after. We'll keep workin' this vein so long as it holds out. And here's where the hard work starts. We gotta break out this ore-bearin' rock, shovel it into the wheelbarrows, and carry it back out to the ore car. After a day doin' this, you won't care if there's coyotes or a herd of buffalo wanderin around our camp at night. You'll be dead to the world soon's your body hits that cot!"

Jimmy laughed. "There's no buffalo around here!"

Harry cracked up and said, "If there was, you'd never know it if they come around at night!" Jimmy tested the rock with a pick. It hardly made a mark. Harry said, "We got a way to break it up some. You'll see when the others get here. Let's go back up to the surface."

The ore car's controls worked smoothly, and they slowly went up to the shaft's opening. Jimmy thought it was like traveling toward the sun as he looked up in the ascending car. The heat hit them like an iron fist when they reached the surface. It was more of a shock than going into the chill of the mine's darkness had been.

After dinner that night, they could hear the coyotes over the hill from their camp. They would no doubt pay another visit that night. Harry said he had never known them to venture into the house; the smell of man might be too much for them. Jimmy hoped that was right as they settled in for the night.

John and Fred showed up about nine the next morning. They brought more mining gear, food, tarps for the roof, and lots of beer. "Beer's the most important thing," Fred said. "Can't get much done without a cold one at lunch and several more after dinner!"

Jimmy asked how they were going to keep it cold. Fred laughed, "Why, we'll take it down in the mine, of course! Bring some up with us when we come back. Keeps it plenty cool enough to drink!" Fred and John's first task was to load up their beer supply in the ore car.

The ore car could only accommodate two at a time. The two older men went down first and unloaded the beer. Then they signaled Harry and Jimmy to come down. They loaded up the rest of the equipment, along with a jerry can of water, and joined them at the end of the deepest tunnel.

Harry's dad demonstrated the method for breaking out the ore-bearing rock. First, they used a large star punch, which one man held while the other struck it with a nine-pound sledgehammer. After each blow, they twisted the punch and hit it again. They continued until they had chipped out a hole around eight or ten inches deep, with a slight downward incline. Then, they repeated the process on the opposite side of the vein.

They opened a bag of expanding grout which was a mix of dry cement with fine aggregate. It formed a viscous slurry mixed with water in a bucket. The men funneled some of it into each hole. Then one of them hammered a piece of rock into place to seal each cavity. Fred said, "Well, that's that. All's we gotta do now is wait. It's time to break out some beers!"

Jimmy showed his confusion, and Harry's dad explained, "The grout will harden and expand inside the holes and put pressure on the rock around 'em. That causes stress fractures in the rock, which we can break out with our hand tools. It's a slow and tedious process. But it beats the way the Spaniards did it with nothin' but pickaxes."

They made their way to the surface, along with plenty of beer. Harry's dad had brought an ample supply of canvas and poles. They used some to rig a shade beside the house away from the worst of the late afternoon sun. The rest was lashed down across the saguaro cactus ribs on the roof. The men hoped it would keep out the rains when they came. Then, they spent the rest of the afternoon talking. The pile of beer bottles beside the house grew steadily.

Harry's mom had sent along a mess of burros filled with beans and cheese and more enchiladas for their dinner. Jimmy was feeling pretty relaxed from the beer, and more so with a full belly of delicious Mexican food. He thought this mining enterprise might be okay, after all.

The next morning, they took out their first load of silver-bearing ore and began a stockpile at the side of the ore car's works. Harry and Jimmy took turns punching out two holes for the cement slurry. The other men broke out the ore from the previous day's cement fractures, loaded the loose ore in the wheelbarrow, and transferred it to the ore car. They were all exhausted after a grueling day. It was back-breaking work, and they were ready for some rest and chilled beers.

They spent another day with the same routine. Their ore pile was growing gradually. By the end of the day, they judged they had about as much ore as their truck could handle. They decided to wait until they could make appointments with their Mexico connections before loading it.

They were tired and ready to head back to the conveniences of town. Besides, they were nearly out of beer. Jimmy was most anxious to get home and spend time with Joann.

CHAPTER 20
A FAMILY MATTER

On their drive back to Ajo, Jimmy confided to Harry that he had fallen in love with his sister. "I haven't known her that long, but I think it's long enough. I've never felt like this about a girl before, not even my old girlfriend in Denver. I'm going to ask Joann to marry me!"

Harry sat for a moment in stunned silence. "Man, you don't know what you're gettin' yourself into! You sure you wanna tie yourself down like that?"

"I'm sure, Harry. I think there was a reason it didn't work out with my girl in Denver, and that reason is I'm meant to be with Joann. I believe she feels the same way."

"I'm sure she does. She pretty much told me as much. I think she'll marry you in a heartbeat. And I'll be proud to have you for my brother-in-law. But there's somethin' important I expect you ain't thought about, though."

"I know. I don't have a ring, but I'll get one soon as I can."

"That ain't it. My mother raised my sister and me in the Catholic church. She and her family will want a wedding in the Catholic way. I don't think you have a clue what that means."

He was right, Jimmy thought. He hadn't thought about that. "Tell me what that means," he said.

"Well," Harry began, "it's complicated. First, you gotta get our parents' blessin'. Then you will have to go with Joann to an interview with the priest and ask for his blessin'. That's where it may get sticky for you."

"How so? I'm not afraid to talk to the priest!"

"Well, he's gonna tell you that you will need to join the church to receive the church's blessing for marriage. That means you have to go through a lot of stuff for that to happen." He described the various steps Jimmy would have to go through to become a full member.

"What happens if I don't want to do all that? Can't we get married anyway?"

"You could, but I'm fairly sure it would be a problem for Joann and the family. Our mother is serious about her religion. Her family in Mexico is the same way, too. She'd take it pretty hard."

Jimmy was pensive for the remainder of their trip back to town. Harry was right. This was something new to him—a potential problem he hadn't considered. His understanding of Joann's religion was vague. He had only attended church a few times with her family. He didn't see a current solution for the problem.

His parents had not been particularly religious. Attending church was a rarity for him growing up. He thought his mother was a Methodist, but he didn't recall that his father had any affiliation with religion. Religion mainly had been an afterthought for Jimmy. Now he faced a situation for which he had no experience or actual frame of reference. All he knew was he loved Joann and wanted to marry her. He resolved he would do whatever was necessary to make that a reality.

Jimmy had dinner with Harry's family that evening, and afterward, he and Joann went for one of their long walks around the plaza. The area was deserted; most people were holed up in their houses, avoiding the heat. It was over one hundred degrees with no hint of a breeze. The crimson light from the setting sun gave the buildings and trees a reddish glow. Jimmy was sweating profusely, and not just because of the heat. He hoped Joann didn't notice. They sat on a wooden bench in the plaza, and Jimmy took her hand.

"I'm not much for words, so I'll come right out with it. I love you, Joann. More than I've ever loved anyone before."

She smiled at him, her eyes reflecting the last twilight glow from the sun. She had never been more beautiful, Jimmy thought.

"I feel the same way, Jimmy. There's never been anyone else in my life like you."

"Will you marry me, Joann?"

Her eyes welled with tears, and she nodded her head. "Yes,

Jimmy. Oh, yes!" She put her arms around his neck and kissed him, and they held each other that way for a long while.

"I don't have a ring for you yet, but I'll get one soon as I can."

"It's okay, Jimmy. It's not the most important thing.

They drifted back toward her house arm in arm, taking their time, savoring the last of the time they would have together that night. She stopped and said, "You know I'm Catholic. How do you feel about getting married in the Catholic church?"

"I don't rightly know, Joann. All I know is I love you, and I want to marry you. Can I ask permission from your mom and dad?"

"Absolutely, but they are going to want to talk about the church. They will want you to become a member, too."

"How do you feel about that?"

She held his hands and took a deep breath before she answered. "I've never told this to anyone else, and you must keep it between us. I don't believe in the church anymore. And I don't want you to join it to marry me—that wouldn't be right for you. I think there's another way."

Jimmy stood with his mouth agape, his surprise preventing a response. Joann continued, "It wasn't always that way, but as I got older, I was frustrated by the rules and restrictions it placed on me. It simply didn't seem right for me. I don't want to tell my parents; my mother would be devastated. So I've kept up the pretense of being a good Catholic girl. It was the only way I knew to get by." She squeezed Jimmy's hands more tightly and said, "You can never speak of this."

She told him more of what it was like growing up in the church. "There were some good things, too," she said. "I had many Catholic friends, and I loved the social activities. But in my heart, Jimmy, I knew it wasn't the way I wanted to spend the rest of my life. I felt like it was stifling me."

"What do you want me to do?" Jimmy asked.

"If you agree to raise our children in the church, I think the priest would be satisfied. We can have a church wedding and get on with our lives."

Jimmy walked her home, kissed her goodnight on the front step, and returned to Uncle Fred's house. The heat was oppressive in his bedroom. The old electric fan only had one speed and did little to cool it. Black flies buzzed around and clung to the window screen; the cooler interior air drew them to the room.

He had a restless night. He tried to sort out everything he had heard that day and what his true feelings were. He lay there sweating through the sheets. A sense there might be some trying times ahead niggled at the back of his mind. He was still awake when the first light of dawn shone in his window.

Jimmy had a breakfast of oatmeal, toast, and coffee with Harry's aunt and uncle. Then he walked to Joann's parents' house and asked if he could speak with them about something important. Harry had gone out. Jimmy knew Joann listened from down the hall in her bedroom. John and Maria shared a knowing look, and John said, "Sure, Jimmy. What would you like to talk about?"

Jimmy sensed they already knew what he wanted—this was a game he would have to play. He decided the best course was not to mince words and get it out in the open. "I'm in love with Joann. I'd like to ask your permission to marry her." They both smiled at him, and John spoke first, "Jimmy, you are as fine a man as I have known, and I would be proud to have you as a son. Yes, you have my permission."

Maria said, "I would be thrilled to have you as part of our family. I couldn't hope for a better man for my daughter." They stood, and she hugged him tightly. John shook his hand vigorously. Jimmy felt as if he'd passed some kind of test.

Joann joined them, and the women cried and alternated between hugging Jimmy and each other. Joann said it was the happiest day of her life and couldn't wait until they were married. They sat around the kitchen table as Maria made coffee.

"I'll go and see the priest today," Maria said, "and make arrangements for you to talk to him. I'm sure he will welcome you into our church, and we can start making plans for the wedding.”

John asked, “What is your religion, Jimmy? Are you familiar with the Catholic church?”

“Well, Mr. Taylor, I have to confess I’ve never been a member of any church. My parents were not church-going folks, so I don’t know a lot about religion. All I know about your church is what I’ve learned from going along to services with you folks a few times and what Harry has told me. That’s pretty much it.”

“Did Harry tell you that you would need to become a member of the church for your marriage to be sanctioned by it?”

“Yes, sir. We talked about that, but I don’t know enough about it yet. Is it possible for us to marry if I’m not a member?”

An uncomfortable silence followed as John and Maria exchanged glances. “Perhaps it would be best to let our priest explain that to you,” Maria said. “It would be our wish that you become a member. But you need to learn about what that means. The priest is the best one to help with that.” She said she would arrange a meeting as soon as possible.

It happened quickly. Maria made arrangements for them to meet with the priest after Sunday’s services the next day.

Jimmy needed a little stress relief after his talk with John and Maria. He and Harry went to the local bar for some beer and privacy. There were seldom more than one or two customers in the place in the early afternoon. They sat at a corner table with a couple of bottles of Coors. They wanted to be out of earshot of the bartender and one other customer. The room was steamy hot, making the bar's always offensive smells almost overpowering.

Jimmy said, "Man, I don't know how that bartender can stand the smell in here all day and half the night. This place smells worse than our camp tent after everyone had beans for dinner!"

Harry laughed. "I reckon he's used to it! How'd it go with my folks this mornin'? You don't look too beat up."

"It was fine. They were happy with the news. But Joann and I have to meet with the priest tomorrow. Not sure how that's going to go."

"I'm sure it'll work out fine, whatever you two decide to do. But right now, we need to talk about what to do next week. We'll need to make appointments with the smelter and bank people before we go down there. You ready for that?

"As ready as I can get. We can't do much until we get that set up. How about we make calls on Monday, see if we can arrange some meetings, maybe Wednesday or Thursday. That should give us time to get everything together and load up the truck before we go."

"We should see my grandfather first; let him know what we're doing. Besides, "Harry chuckled," he needs to meet his new grandson-in-law."

"Do you think we could stay with your grandparents while we're there?"

"They will be offended if we don't!"

***

Joann and Jimmy met with the priest after the services the following Sunday. His dark, cramped office had scarcely enough room for a desk. There were two chairs between bookcases overflowing with books and papers. Jimmy felt like a caged animal.

The priest asked Jimmy if he wished to join the church. Jimmy looked at Joann. She held his hand as he said, "I can't join something I don't believe in. Why can't we marry without me joining the church?"

The room's walls seemed to grow closer in the ensuing silence. The priest's eyes felt like hot coals burning into Jimmy's face. Finally, he broke the silence, launching into a long discussion about the religion's benefits. Jimmy listened respectfully but said he still didn't feel it was right for him. In the end, after the couple said they would raise their children as Catholics, the priest agreed that he would help them. He said Joann would have to seek permission from the church bishop in

Tucson to have their wedding in the church. That would require a trip to Tucson. He said he would arrange for her to do so.

Joann and Jimmy were greatly relieved by the outcome of the discussion. On the drive back to Joann's house, she said, "We'll explain all this to my folks. I'm sure they will be okay with it. I'll meet with the bishop as soon as the priest can arrange it. If he approves, we can set a date. My mom will be anxious to make lots of plans and arrangements.

They shared the news with her parents. After lunch, they talked about wedding plans. If all worked out, they wanted to set a date in early October. Maria wanted to allow plenty of time for her family from Mexico to plan to attend.

Later, Jimmy said, "I hate having to wait so long. But I understand the reasons. I appreciate your mother being so helpful, too."

Joann laughed. "She's practically been waiting for this since the day I was born. She's had plans in the back of her mind forever, and she's excited to be able to do something with them. All we need to do is stay out of her way when we get approval from the church!"

The partners stockpiled enough ore to take their first test shipment to the Caborca smelter. The process would determine the silver content and help them decide how to proceed with the mining operation.

Jimmy said the most critical step was to make arrangements with the bank. He was nervous about sharing too much information with the banker. He wanted to establish a relationship and gain some experience with him before giving him many details.

"We have to be sure this man is completely reliable and honest with us. Our success, and likely our staying out of jail, will depend on him. You think we can trust him?"

Harry said, "My grandfather trusts him, and that's the best recommendation I think we'll ever get. He's known him most of their lives, and they have a secret history together. My feelin' is he wouldn't betray that trust with my grandfather."

"All the same, I want to go slow with him and get a good idea of how he'll handle our business. We can't afford to make any mistakes."

"We can talk more with my grandfather when we get there. I think he can give us good advice on how to proceed."

Their first stop was the mine. They put some wood planks in the bottom and sides of the bed of their truck to protect it from the rock. Then, they backed up the hill to their ore pile and shoveled in about what they thought it could handle. Harry kept a careful eye on the springs to not overload them. They figured they were pretty close to the truck's half-ton capacity.

They spent that night at the mine and headed for Mexico early the next day. The truck's handling was sloppy due to the load's weight, and they were cautious crossing the washes between the mine and the highway.

Harry said they would likely get a shakedown at the border crossing because they were hauling cargo and had a reasonably new truck. He explained the concept of mordida again: "Wages in Mexico are even worse than in the US. The cops don't make much, and they depend on bribes to make a livin'. They call it *la mordida*, 'the bite,' because they're takin' a bite out of your money. It's normal and expected and part of doin' business down there."

"So, don't get upset or anything if we have to pay for somethin' you don't think we should," he cautioned. "The border cops look for people like us to squeeze. Don't worry, it won't be much, and I'm prepared for it. Let me do the talkin'."

Jimmy took the precaution of hiding the sample gold coins he brought in his boots before reaching the border. He hoped that would be the last place the border police might look.

Harry's dad had insisted they bring along his Smith and Wesson .38 revolver, though Harry said he wasn't expecting any trouble. "Trouble is where it finds you in Mexico," John said, "and you need to be prepared for anything. Take the pistol and keep it out of sight".

"I guess we're well-armed," Harry joked to Jimmy later. They stuffed the .357 down into the bench seat's fold and scattered some snack wrappers over it. The .38 was hidden in Harry's waistband and covered by his shirt. It would be Jimmy's first time crossing the border, making him uneasy to think about leaving the United States. Harry's description of *la mordida* hadn't helped.

They rolled up to the border crossing in mid-morning. The sun was already sending heatwaves dancing across the desert. Two guards stepped up to the truck—one on each side. "*Buenos días*," the guard on the driver's side said to Harry. "What is your purpose in Mexico, *señor?*"

"*Buenos días, señor*," Harry replied. "We have a small amount of ore we are taking to a smelter near Caborca."

"You have no smelters in your country?" the guard asked.

"The smelters there won't take small amounts like this. My friend and I are just startin', and we can't mine the large loads other smelters require. My friend has a smelter here who can help us get started."

"And who is that friend, *señor*?"

"*Señor* Humberto Arredondo owns a mine and smelter south of Caborca. He is an old family friend."

The guard nodded knowingly, as if the mine owner were his best friend, too. He looked across the truck to the other guard and back at Harry. "This looks like a nice truck for just starting your business. Are you hauling anything besides these rocks I can see, *señor*? Maybe we need to give it a close inspection. Only take two or three hours."

This load of ore is all we have, *señor*," Harry said, "but you are welcome to take it all out and check if you want to. But we have an appointment with *Señor* Arredondo we need to keep." He held out a US five-dollar bill. "Perhaps this can help?" He knew that was several days' wages for both guards. The head guard took the bill and quickly slipped it into his pocket. He smiled and said, "We don't need to keep you any longer today. Give our regards to *Señor* Arredondo." Both guards stepped back and waved them through.

They drove on, and Harry said, "That's your first lesson in *la mordida*, Jimmy. A lot of respect and a few dollars go a long way. It was a lot to give them, but it will help us out in the future. I don't think they will give us trouble the next time we come through. But we will likely have to pay them each time."

"I'm sure glad you were with me," Jimmy laughed. "I would

have been stuck there all day and with no idea what to do! And, hey—some of that conversation was in Spanish. I didn't know you spoke it."

"My mother made sure Joann and me learned it as we were growin' up. She always said we needed to be proud of our roots, and we should know how to speak the language, 'specially since we live so close to Mexico. I'm kinda rusty 'cause I ain't been using it a lot, but I can get by."

They passed a few irrigated fields and went through the sleepy town of Sonoyta before moving on into the desolate desert. The landscape was largely barren with scattered vegetation, scraggly desert shrubs, a few struggling mesquite trees, and cactuses. It was far drier and hotter than the desert around Tucson, and the highway crossed many dry washes. The mountains in the distance, some sharp as wolve's fangs, shimmered and shivered in the heat.

"I can't imagine being stuck out in this country," Jimmy said after a few miles.

"Well, there's two ways to die in a desert like this," Harry replied. "Thirst or drownin'. Most of the time, thirst would be the killer. But you see these dry washes we cross? When the monsoon rains come, they can become rivers, and you don't wanna get stuck in one."

"I remember that truck getting washed away and a guy drowning near our camp a year or so back," Jimmy said.

"Looking at these washes now, it's hard to imagine enough water in them to do something like that."

Harry studied the landscape and said, "Remember two simple rules of gettin' along in the desert: take plenty of water, and never, never drive across a flooded wash."

They drove on in silence most of the way to Caborca. Harry turned off on a dirt road before they got into town. "My grandfather's *hacienda* is about five miles down this road. His farm fields are scattered along the *Concepción* River, where they have irrigation wells. The river don't have much water; most of it's underground here. It goes all the way across this part of Mexico and dumps into the Gulf of California."

Jimmy thought the *hacienda* was a green jewel after passing through the miles of bleak desert they had crossed. There were citrus and olive trees, tall date palms, and brilliant red bougainvillea vines everywhere. Rows of plants Harry said were oleanders, were covered in pink, yellow, and white blossoms. As they got closer, their cloyingly perfumed fragrance was almost overpowering at times. Those plants are pretty to look at, but don't use 'em for nothin'," Harry said. "Ever' part of 'em is poison, so don't go roastin' no hot dogs with 'em. My grandfather had 'em planted to break the wind that blows through this valley."

They pulled into the wide circular driveway and stopped in front of a beautiful white house. It seemed to go on forever. Red

Spanish tiles covered the roof, and there were numerous arches at various entrances. Jimmy was stunned by its beauty.

Harry's grandparents stepped out of the main entrance to greet them. His grandmother hugged and kissed him, and his grandfather shook his hand and put his arm around his shoulder. "It's good to see you again, *nieto*! And this must be your partner you've told me so much about!" Harry introduced Jimmy, and they greeted him warmly. His grandmother said, "Come in the house where it's cool, and we'll have some lunch."

They caught up on various family members over lunch, and when they finished, Harry said, "Jimmy has some wonderful news to share with you!"

Jimmy hoped he didn't look as nervous as he felt. "Well, first, I want to say how nice it is to meet you. Harry talks about you all the time, and I feel like you are my family, too." They smiled and waited expectantly for the news he had for them. "I have proposed marriage with your granddaughter, Joann, and she has accepted. We plan to marry in October, hopefully with your blessings."

Jimmy was ready to bolt for the door in the silence, but Esteban got a broad smile on his face and stood. Jimmy stood, too, and Esteban shook his hand. "We will be proud to have you join our family. *Un otro nieto*!" Another grandson!

His wife stood and hugged him warmly. "We've heard so much about you! This is wonderful news." She laughed and said, "I must confess my daughter has already called to share this news. But it was far better to hear it from you. I am so happy for you and Joann."

"This calls for a toast!" Esteban went to his liquor cabinet and returned with glasses and a bottle of his finest tequila. "I've been saving this tequila for a most special occasion," he said as he poured each of them three fingers. "To my new grandson and your marriage to my granddaughter! May you share many years of health and happiness!" They touched glasses and downed the liquor. It went down smoothly, but Jimmy felt like his belly was on fire.

They visited a while, and Harry said they had an appointment at the smelter. They took their leave, promising to return later to help his grandfather finish off the bottle of tequila.

They arrived at the smelter, and Mr. Arredondo came out and looked at the ore in their truck. Harry showed him an assay report from the previous year, which indicated the ore should yield around 70 ounces of silver per ton. Arredondo picked up a couple of pieces and looked them over carefully. "Yes, I can see this will yield some silver. We will soon find out how much."

He waved over one of his men and said, "This is Luis, my smelter foreman. I told him you were coming, and we are ready for you. Luis will help you." They shook hands with Luis, and he showed them where to back in the truck to unload.

Harry asked him for shovels, but Luis waved him aside. "No, *Señor* Harry, we do this for you." He waved over two of his helpers and directed them to unload the ore. "*Muchas gracias*, Luis," Harry said and handed him 3 US dollar bills. Luis smiled broadly and set about helping his men. "You come back in the morning, yes? We have this done for you."

They had it unloaded in less than 15 minutes. The partners stopped at the office, thanked *Seño*r Arredondo, and told him they would be back in the morning. They headed back to the *hacienda* to clean up and have a siesta before dinner.

The men retired to Esteban's study after dinner for cigars and tequila. Jimmy and Harry were fascinated by Esteban's stories of riding with Pancho Villa. He said, "I was with Villa when he "invaded" the United States. We occupied a bar on the main street in Douglas, Arizona. Everyone drank a lot of beer and whiskey, made lots of noise, and had a good time."

Esteban laughed deeply and puffed thoughtfully on his cigar. "Those were times when men could truly be men. Not like today, when the government tells us what to do and when to do it!"

The partners talked about their plans. Jimmy asked Esteban if he had any advice about dealing with the banker. Esteban thought while he smoked. "Pablo Estevez is a good man, but you must always remember he is first a banker—money is his business, and he is very good at making it. I believe his promise to Harry and me is good. But you can count on him to try and squeeze every ounce of profit from it that he can. You must be prepared to drive a good bargain, one in which both of you benefit."

They finished most of the tequila, and it was growing late. Jimmy's head was swimming from the alcohol. Beer was his usual drink; the tequila hit him pretty hard. He didn't look forward to the hangover he would no doubt have in the morning.

***

A splitting headache greeted Jimmy when he awoke, and his head felt like a leaden weight. He drank two cups of strong black coffee before breakfast; eggs, beans, and tortillas helped clear his head. He passed on the spicy chorizo the others were having. Harry was in about the same shape, red-eyed and grouchy. His grandfather showed no outward signs of their overindulgence and was as cheerful as ever.

Their first stop that morning was back at the smelter. As promised, Mr. Arredondo had completed refining their ore and had their silver on a tray in his office. "Your ore weighed in at 920 pounds, enough for a good test. We extracted 33 ounces, which is good. I believe that is close to what your assay predicted."

"That's great news, *señor*," Harry said. "It will make it practical to continue working our mine. *Muchas gracias* for doing it so quickly. How much do we owe you?"

"We have poured the silver into these sixteen two-ounce ingots plus the remaining ounce in a split ingot. I can accept three ounces as payment for our services if that is agreeable."

They indicated it was, thanked him again for his service, and promised to bring him more business in the future. He gave them a cloth bag to carry the remaining ingots.

They headed back to town but had gone only a few miles when Harry said, "Trouble, Jimmy! Be ready!" A car and pickup were parked at angles blocking the road. Harry took the .38 revolver out of his waistband, and Jimmy brought out the .357 from its hiding place.

Two men stepped forward, waving them down. They rolled to a stop a couple of truck lengths back from the roadblock. One of the men carried a shotgun; the other had a pistol in his belt. The man with a pistol stepped to the driver's side while the other man covered the truck's passenger side.

The man on the driver's side spoke to Harry in broken English, "This nice truck, *señor*. We take off your hands, *si*?

Harry said, "Not for sale. Sorry. Please let us through."

"I no tink so, *señor*. I tink we keep you truck, and you silver too, eh?" The other man smiled and shifted the shotgun up into the crook of his arm.

"Jimmy, show the other gentleman your persuader while I explain things to this one." Jimmy brought up the .357 and leveled it at the shotgun carrier's chest. His eyes bulged; he was so startled he dropped the shotgun.

Harry's face turned the same shade of crimson Jimmy had seen in their fight with Reuben's men. He reached out and grabbed the other man by his shirt front, pulled him close, and stuck his .38 in his face. The muscles stood out in his neck, and he said through bared teeth, "Here's what's gonna happen— toss your pistol away where I can see it." The man did as he was told.

Harry's voice was full of menace as he said, "Now, step up on the runnin' board and put your hands on top of the cab. My pistol will be in your belly, and I WILL shoot you if you don't do exactly what I say. Tell your men to move out of the way and let us pass. My friend will take the wheel as we drive."

The robber was taken entirely by surprise and did as he was told. Harry kept a wrestler's iron grip on the man's shirt to keep him from jumping away. The robber's source at the smelter had told him these two *gringos* would be easy pickings— now here he was with a pistol stuck in his gut.

Harry said, "I'm going to drive slow, and my partner will steer. If you try anything, I WILL shoot you." The robber shouted instructions, and the other bandits backed their vehicles out of the road. Harry proceeded slowly. Jimmy steered them with one hand to pass between the robbers' car and truck.

Harry shoved the bandit off the running board. Then he grabbed the steering wheel and floored the accelerator as soon as they were clear. They roared off, leaving the would-be robbers in a cloud of dust. The robber's leader grabbed a pistol from one of the other men and fired several rounds at the truck as it moved away. All but one missed—it left a hole in the pickup's tailgate as a memento of the close call.

The partners were both shaken, and neither could speak for a couple of minutes. Then Jimmy started laughing, and Harry joined in. They laughed almost hysterically for a minute, shaking off the adrenaline overdose they were experiencing.

"Damn, Harry! I didn't know you had it in you! I thought we were done for!"

"I was angry that someone was tryin' to rob us. I reacted by instinct, but I was scared to death, too. We couldn't let 'em take the truck and our silver!"

They headed toward Caborca and decided to stop at Harry's grandfather's place to relax before meeting with the banker. Esteban was incensed to learn what had happened. "I have an idea who those men are," he said. "They have been hanging around this area, causing trouble for a while. I will talk to our police chief and insist they do something about them before someone gets hurt. You boys were incredibly lucky!"

Esteban said he was happy at the news of their first run of silver ore. "It sounds like that old mine has some value after all. But I think you will have to work awfully hard for it."

Harry said, "That's true, *abuelo*. But we are willin' to do it. I hope we don't have to fight off robbers at gunpoint each time we bring down ore. I'd like to know how they knew we had silver.

"I had the same thought, *nieto*. I'm guessing someone who works at the smelter set you up. I will speak to *Señor* Arredondo about it."

***

The bank had a couple of customers when they arrived. The partners waited while Mr. Estevez took care of someone in his office. There were two other employees: a young man at the counter and a middle-aged woman working at a desk. The young man motioned them to take a seat.

Estevez's customer left, and he came out to greet the two men. "It's good to see you again, *Señor* Taylor! And this must be your partner you told me about." Harry introduced Jimmy, and they went into the banker's office. Estevez asked, "How can I help you today, *señors?"*

Jimmy said, "As Harry has told you, we have a large amount of gold and silver we would like to exchange for US dollars. We want to open an account with you to do that. These are samples to show you what we would be exchanging." He spread the gold coins he brought on the desk and laid out the silver ingots they had received at the smelter. The banker showed no emotion as he studied each gold piece and a couple of silver ingots.

"How many of these do you have?"

"We don't want the exact amount known," Jimmy said, "but it will likely be more than fifty thousand dollars. We expect to exchange it in smaller quantities. How many would be practical for you to handle?"

The banker's eyes grew wide at the prospect of substantial profits. "Fifty thousand dollars is a significant amount! This exchange involves, shall we say, a rather delicate procedure for my bank. We have to be careful not to get into trouble with the United States government. They could cause many difficulties for us. I recommend exchanging no more than twenty-five of these coins at one time to start."

Jimmy said he understood and waited for him to go on. "We can accommodate you as a special favor to your grandfather, Harry. Otherwise, I would not do this. This is not a typical banking transaction, and we will have to charge you a premium over a regular exchange rate to facilitate handling your coins."

Jimmy expected something like this. "Can you be more specific?" he asked. "And how about the silver coins and ingots from our mine? Won't those be easier and cheaper to handle?"

"Our normal exchange rate would be five percent. But, I will need to charge fifteen percent to handle the gold transactions. Your silver coins and locally mined silver, however, I can handle for our standard five percent."

Jimmy studied him intently. "I think fifteen percent is too high for what we are asking. We are talking about a significant amount of money we will be passing through your bank. Naturally, we expect to pay a premium, but I believe ten percent would be the most we should pay."

"*Señor*, as I explained, we will have many additional costs to handle the quantity of gold you have outside normal banking channels. I believe fifteen percent is what it would require to meet the interests of my bank."

Jimmy looked at Harry and said," I think we should talk to our contact in Tucson again. It would be more trouble to use his service, but he already said he could do it for substantially less than Mr. Estevez is telling us." He looked at the banker and said, "We appreciate your time and willingness to work with us. But we simply can't afford your price. Let's go, Harry."

They stood up to leave, but the banker stood and said, "Please, *amigos*. Have a seat, and let's discuss this a little more."

In the end, they settled on ten percent for the gold coins and five percent for silver coins and ingots. They opened an account in the name of "J and H Mining" and used the gold coins they brought as an opening deposit. The silver ingots netted thirty dollars after expenses. They split it between them, then shook hands with the banker and left.

"Wow, Jimmy! That was some bluff. We ain't got nowhere else to exchange that stuff!"

"I could see the greed in his eyes. It was like playing poker with the guys back in camp. You could always tell the greedy ones. They hated losing and were pretty easy to bluff. I gambled on this one, and it paid off. I think this was a fancy version of *la mordida!*

"You're a quick learner, partner!"

***

The young teller had busied himself with something near Estevez's office door and heard most of the discussion. The mention of a large amount of gold riveted his attention. He watched the two gringos leave with speculative interest.

"You shoulda' seen Harry!" Jimmy laughed. "He was like the toughest guy in Mexico. He jerked that guy up by his shirt front and stuck the pistol in his face. I bet he wet his pants!" They were back in Ajo at Harry's parents' house excited and happy everything had worked out well.

Harry said, "Yeah, but it was prob'ly stupid of me. I reacted without thinkin'. We're lucky the other guy didn't let fly with that 12 gauge he was packin'. He was so surprised when Jimmy hauled out that big revolver, he dropped it and backed away."

"I told you trouble finds you in Mexico," Harry's dad said. I'm damn proud of both of you, but next time, you may not be so lucky. It took a lot of guts to do what you did. That bullet hole in the tailgate of your truck is a clear warning: Be prepared—there will be a next time."

Everyone was quiet, letting that soak in. Harry said, "You're right, Dad. I've thought a lot about it. We gotta find a better way to protect ourselves when we're down there."

His mother brought up the idea of hiring some guards. "Your grandfather could help you do that. Find some honest men who would help you. I don't want you going back until you can be safe."

Both Harry and Jimmy thought that was a good idea. It wouldn't cost that much. The security and peace of mind would be well worth whatever the cost. Harry said he would call his grandfather and discuss it with him.

When Jimmy and Joann were alone, she hugged him tightly for several minutes. "I'm so afraid for you, Jimmy. For both of you. No amount of money is worth losing you."

"We'll be okay. Next time we'll be a lot more prepared. And we'll hire some guards, too."

Jimmy went to the Western Union office in the plaza and wired ten dollars from his silver proceeds to his mother. Later, he and Harry met with Harry's father and uncle. They gave them each three dollars, their ten percent share of the profit.

They were surprised the silver content was so high. "Dang, John," Harry's uncle laughed, "if I'd a" known it was that good, I might not have been so quick to sell!"

They had a good laugh, and John said, "Yeah, but we know from our experience that it's unpredictable. One pocket might be rich, and the next one will be almost nothin'. I think we got the better end of the deal!"

"Hey! We can afford more beer with all this money we earned from that first shipment!" Fred said with a mischievous smirk. John and Fred said they would join the partners for a few days to help them in the mine.

The men planned to spend the next week working the mine, taking out as much ore as possible. At least a couple of tons were needed to make it worthwhile to hire a truck and haul it to the smelter. If the silver-bearing vein held up, they could make a good return. It was what they needed to make their fledgling business look good.

The next day the partners stocked up on supplies they would need for a week. They filled several jerry cans with water and bought more gasoline for the mine's engine and kerosene for the lanterns and stove. It was sweltering hot as they headed out of town.

Billowing thunderheads were visible to the south. Harry said, "Looks like we might get an early start on the monsoon rains. Them clouds look promisin'; I think they are movin' this way."

***

Detective Hoag watched as the partners headed out of town. He started his rented black Dodge sedan and followed. All his instincts told him he was close to the truth with these men; his major payday was not far off. He hadn't believed the men's story about the silver coins they exchanged. They were no doubt beginning to cash in the stolen Wells Fargo robbery loot. It was time to put on more pressure.

***

As Harry turned off the highway onto the road that led to the mine, he noticed in the rearview mirror that a car had turned off behind them. It followed along at a distance, trying to stay out of the dust. "There's a strange car behind us," he said. "Better be on the lookout. Could be trouble."

Jimmy craned his neck to try and get a look at the car. "It looks pretty new," he said. "Too new to be out wandering around here. I think it's someone following us. Maybe that Treasury agent."

Harry said, "Well, if it turns up the track to the mine, we'll know it's trouble!"

The suspicious car turned and followed them up the track leading to the mine; the driver parked a short distance from the old house. The partners got out of their truck. Harry tucked the .38 in his waistband; Jimmy did the same with the .357. The other car's driver sat and briefly watched them. But there was too much sun glare on the car's windshield for the partners to make out his face.

When the driver got out of the car, there was no mistaking his identity. "It's Hoag," Harry growled. "He's just here to harass us!"

Hoag had abandoned most of his fancy suit in the baking heat. He was now wearing only his trousers, shoes, and undershirt. Jimmy thought the man looked like a plucked rooster without his fancy clothes— but this rooster had a revolver in a shoulder holster.

"Well, well," Hoag said as he came up to them. "So, this is your big mining venture, eh?"

Harry said, "What do you want now, Hoag? You got no business here."

"Why, I simply came to pay a friendly call to see how you boys are getting along. I've never seen a genuine Spanish mine before."

Harry said, "Well, you ain't seein' this one, either. This is private property, and you're trespassin'. Get in your car and get out!"

"That's not a very friendly way to greet a representative of the law. And besides, I didn't see any No Trespassing signs on this property. You men have something to hide?"

"We have nothing to hide and a lot of work to do. Get on out of here and leave us alone," Jimmy said.

"You men wouldn't mind me having a look around first, would you? I just want to see this big operation of yours. I understand you're doing business in Mexico, too, and I'll be looking into that."

Harry rested his hand on the .38 at his waist and said, "We do mind. You need to leave. Now."

Hoag noted that Jimmy was armed, too, and said, "I'll leave. But next time I come, I'll bring the Sheriff and a warrant. We'll search your operation here top to bottom. You men need to come clean with me now before it comes to that." The partners stared him down and said nothing.

Thunder rumbled across the desert and reverberated off hillsides; the clouds were moving up rapidly. The Mexicans called them *chubascos*—high, boiling white cumulonimbus clouds with dark, ominous-looking bottoms. They formed along the Gulf of California and traveled northward into the deserts. The men could see the storms were pushing a towering line of dust in front of them. Harry said the storm would hit them soon.

Hoag got in his car and left as the first of the wind-driven dust and sand hit. His car disappeared into the brown wall of dust that enveloped them. "Jimmy, grab the bedrolls and put 'em in the truck cab," Harry shouted over the wind. "This storm will soak them! I'll put the supplies undercover!"

The wind and dust backed off after a few minutes. Clouds the color of bruised plums closed in around them. The light changed to a kind of twilight as lightning split the sky. Torrential rain came, followed by hail the size of golf balls.

They barely had time to get their supplies under cover before the storm hit. They ran for the truck and jumped inside. The hail beating on the metal sounded like the banging of a hundred drums by a bunch of drunks. The wind howled again, and more blinding rain followed the hail. A blinding flash of lightning struck something by the mine's works. It was followed instantly by an ear-splitting crash of thunder.

The storm moved on, and the rain began to subside. The hail had cracked the truck's windshield and dented the hood in several places. It would have likely injured them badly if they had been caught in the open.

"Wow!" Jimmy breathed. "I never saw anything like that. Even the winter storms in Denver couldn't hold a candle to it. What do you suppose happened to Turner?"

"He's prob'ly stuck in some wash between here and the highway. That big ol' *Sin Nombre* wash before you get to the highway is likely runnin' pretty good. Serves him right."

"*Sin nombre?*"

Harry chuckled. "It means without a name."

Jimmy laughed. "Sounds about right! But I'd sure like to be shut of that guy. Never knew anybody so annoying."

They found that the lightning had struck an old ore car off to the side of the mine works. It melted the metal in places. The ground around it had a black, scorched look.

Harry said, "Man, it's lucky it didn't hit the frame or engine! It could've put us outta business for a while.

The men spent a restless night. There were more passing clouds with drizzles of rain and rumbles of thunder for a few hours. No coyotes came to visit. Harry said they were probably hunkered down somewhere, waiting for the lightning and thunder to stop.

John and Fred arrived the following morning. Fred immediately unloaded his beer supply to stow in the mine shaft. John said, "Looks like the washes ran a lot last night. We passed a car that had washed a ways down the *Sin Nombre* Wash. It was a black Dodge. You know anything about that?"

Jimmy and Harry exchanged glances. Harry said, "That detective followed us out here yesterday in a car like that. He left as the storm hit. Did you see anything of him?"

"There was nobody around the car," John said, "and we didn't pass anybody on foot."

Harry said, "Jimmy, we better go have a look. That fool may have got caught in a flood!" They left the other two men to unload their supplies and get organized for the day's work. New gullies in the road slowed them down as they drove back toward the big wash.

"See them buzzards circlin'?" Harry asked as they drove. Four or five large black birds with wide wingspans were lazing around in closing circles." That ain't a good sign. We better hurry!"

They found Hoag's car about a hundred yards downstream wedged in some heavy brush and rocks. There was still a trickle of water flowing in the wash, and the bottom was muddy and slippery. The turkey vultures, which Harry called buzzards, were circling over something further down.

The men picked their way along and found Hoag's body. The

force of the water had wedged him about four feet up in a mesquite tree. The vultures had already been at him; bloody sockets stared back where his eyes had been. The men gagged at the damage to his face —scavenging birds had torn strips of flesh from his cheeks. They had also begun tearing at the skin where his arms were exposed by his undershirt.

A pair of the vultures had moved off a few yards. Fresh blood glistened on their beaks; their beady eyes watched the men expectantly. Several more of the scavengers continued circling overhead.

It took a few minutes for the men to regain their composure from the shock of the gruesome sight. Harry said, "Poor bastard. I hope he was dead before the buzzards got to him." He looked up and down the wash. "Musta been a helluva flow through here yesterday. He prob'ly drove right off into six or eight feet of fast-movin' floodwater. He likely couldn't see much past the hood of the car. City slicker wouldn't a knowed any better."

They stood there in silence, pondering the finality of the scene. Harry tested a branch on the tree and said, "Let's see if we can get him down and carry him back to the truck."

Jimmy hesitated. "I think it might be better if we leave him here and go into town to get the sheriff. They need to see for themselves what happened. This guy's been asking a lot of questions about us."

Harry said, "I didn't think about that. You're right. We don't need any suspicion about us being involved. I'll grab the tarp out of the truck and cover him. You try to keep the buzzards off him until I get back."

They covered the body as best they could. Jimmy said he'd stick around to deter the vultures. Harry headed off to Ajo to find the sheriff.

The deputy on duty grilled him about what they were doing out there. Harry explained about their mining operation. The deputy said, "I met that guy a while back. He asked a bunch of questions about you and your family. Said he suspected you of trying to sell illegal gold. What about that?"

Harry explained, "That whole business was started by a guy at the CCC camp. We had heard the old stories of outlaw treasure being hid in the cave, and he figured my partner was likely to find it because of his job on the crew. He was the first one into a new section most of the time, stringing lights for the other workers to follow."

"Yeah, I heard something about that, too. I heard a man attacked some guy with a knife at the camp, too. Was that you got stuck?" Harry said it was his partner. The deputy continued, "That detective probably believed the rumors and figured you guys were good for a crime or would be. He wanted us to keep an eye on you for him, but my boss told him we had better things to do."

The Deputy finished his notes and said they'd send an ambulance for the body and a wrecker to bring in the car. "You stick around 'til they get here so you can lead us to the scene."

"Better bring a long cable for the wrecker, "Harry warned. That wash is wet and muddy, and it would be easy to get stuck in it."

***

Simon Gregory sat at his desk in the Wells Fargo Co. office in San Francisco. He was growing increasingly agitated at not hearing from the detective he hired to chase the company's stolen property in Arizona. Hoag had indicated in their last phone conversation that he was following a solid lead. Gregory was starting to suspect he may have found the treasure and run off to Mexico. It would make a tidy retirement.

There had been no communication from him for two weeks. The clerk at Hoag's hotel in Tucson told him the man had not been seen for some time and still had an unpaid bill. Gregory grew more concerned and contacted the Pima County Sheriff's office. After being transferred several times, he learned that Hoag had died in a flash flood in a desert wash.

Gregory asked if the sheriff's office had information about a lost shipment of Wells Fargo's gold from train robberies supposedly hidden in a cave. The sheriff laughed into the phone. He said, "The rumors about that lost robbers' loot are just that—

rumors. People have searched that cave for as long as I can remember and never found a trace of any treasure. I believe your man was taken in by the rumors. Unfortunately, he met an untimely accidental end in the desert. I suggest you not waste your company's money chasing this old legend." Gregory thanked him and hung up. Perhaps he was right—there was no profit in pursuing this particular "lost asset" any further.

***

Treasury agent Turner sat in the Phoenix office of his boss, Agent-In-Charge Harrison. Harrison tapped a file of papers on his desk and said, "You've spent months chasing what appears to be an old cowboy legend of lost treasure. So far, you've provided no evidence of anyone finding any gold, much less doing anything illegal. As you state in your reports, even local law enforcement sees no value in pursuing unfounded rumors."

Turner said, "Sir, I believe there is good reason to continue this investigation. These men have acted suspiciously. There would be a significant amount of gold involved. I believe it's only a matter of time until they make a mistake."

Harrison reddened and slapped his fist down on the stack of reports. "There will be no further investigation! This is a complete waste of your time and the agency's resources. You should have known better than to put all your time into something this flimsy!"

Turner was stunned as his boss continued, "As of now, I am reassigning you to the Chicago office with a recommendation you receive additional training. Make whatever arrangements you need to. See that you report there in two weeks."

Turner was speechless, but he could see he didn't have any good arguments that would sway his boss. So much for his hoped-for promotion for capturing a pair of criminals involved with illegal gold sales. But, when he thought about it, Chicago wouldn't be so bad. He was tired of this desert, anyway.

CHAPTER 23
A DIFFERENT VEIN

"Dang, Harry! I always get chicken skin when we first come down here." Jimmy shivered as the partners made their descent into the mine shaft's darkness. John and Fred had left for Ajo.

"Chicken skin? I never heard that one before. But, yeah, I get goosebumps, too. It sure beats the blast furnace heat on the surface.

Jimmy couldn't shake the thoughts in the back of his mind: what if the cable broke, what if the whole surface structure came crashing down on them, what if the engine died and their ladder wouldn't hold them? It was always like that when they made their first descent. Thankfully, the worries passed as they worked.

Harry broke out the material they had loosened the previous day. Jimmy scooped it into the wheelbarrow and took it down the tunnel to dump in the ore car. He was making his second trip with the wheelbarrow when there was a terrible roaring commotion from the tunnel. A blast of choking, dust-laden air followed.

He ran back down the tunnel shouting for Harry, choking and coughing in the dust. A section of rock had collapsed and taken out a support beam. "Harry! Harry! Where are you?" He heard a low moan and shone his light through the dust toward the sound. Another groan and Jimmy was able to locate his partner partially buried in the rubble. Jimmy could see blood covering his face but couldn't tell anything about the rest of his body.

"I'll get you out, Harry! Hang on!" Jimmy cried as he began to shovel away loose rock. The beam had fallen across Harry's chest. Jimmy had to move a lot of rock to loosen it. He worked as carefully as he could; he didn't want to dislodge more rock. Finally, he worked the beam clear that had pinned Harry. It took all his strength to lift the beam off his friend.

"Harry! My God, Harry! Can you talk?" Harry's eyes fluttered, but he could only moan. Jimmy could see he was in a bad way. He only knew little of first aid from his training in the cave. "I'm going to get you out of here, Harry. Hang on!" Harry's body was limp as he lifted him from the rubble. Jimmy placed him over his shoulder as gently as he could. Harry made low moaning noises as Jimmy staggered under his body's weight. He moved cautiously—careful of each step on the uneven tunnel floor. Harry's arm's flopped loosely against Jimmy's back.

He finally got him back to the ore car and said, "Hang on, buddy, this is going to be tough." He managed to get him into the car, climbed in with him, and raised the car to the surface.

Jimmy raced down the slope to get the truck. Its tires spun on the slope as he backed it up as close as he dared to the shaft. He lifted his friend out of the ore car and placed him as carefully as possible on the truck's seat. He tried to give Harry some water from a canteen, but he couldn't swallow it. "This is gonna be a hard, bumpy ride, Harry, but I gotta get you to the hospital in Ajo!" He had grabbed a couple of blankets from the house and used them to cushion Harry's head on his lap.

The dirt road back to the highway had never seemed worse. The recent rains had made new gullies and scoured the banks of the washes where they had to cross. Jimmy was cautious not to get stuck or stranded on high center. They bounced over rocks and ruts on the flats at a reckless speed, only slowing to get across the washes.

Jimmy gunned the truck through its gears when they reached the highway. He pushed it faster than it had ever gone. They blew past the few cars they overtook. A couple of drivers honked their horns and shook their fists at the reckless behavior. The truck's tires squealed as they pulled up to the hospital's emergency entrance. Jimmy ran inside, shouting for help.

Two nurses and an orderly rushed outside with a gurney. They gently lifted Harry onto it, then raced back inside. Jimmy followed as close as he could.

When the nurses chased him out of the exam area, he found a phone and called Harry's house. His mother answered immediately. She knew something was wrong from the sound of Jimmy's voice. "Jimmy! What's wrong? What's happened?"

"Harry's in the hospital, Mrs. Taylor. He's hurt pretty bad. You best come quick!"

She dropped the phone and yelled for her husband, and they raced to the hospital. "Where is he, Jimmy? What happened?" Harry's father shouted when they ran into the emergency room. "Was it the mine?"

Jimmy did his best to explain what had happened and tried to calm them down. They were both peppering him with questions, for most of which he had no answers. All they could do was wait.

The minutes ticking by on the waiting room's wall clock seemed to Jimmy to be moving in slow motion. Others came and went in the austere room: a mother with an injured child, an older man gasping for breath with a heart attack, and a man who had cut off a finger with an electric circular saw. Jimmy hardly noticed them. All he could think about was his injured friend. The thought haunted him that he should have done more for him.

A doctor came to talk to them several hours later. "His condition is critical but stable. He has a concussion, several broken ribs, and possibly other internal injuries. We are doing everything we can for him, but we need to keep him in intensive care tonight. It's a miracle he's alive."

Maria collapsed, sobbing into John's arms. Jimmy didn't know what to do or say. They sat in stunned silence for a few minutes before Jimmy said, "Joann! Where's Joann? I need to find her!"

John said she had gone shopping and was probably home by now. "I need to go to her," Jimmy said. "I'll bring her back here."

He found her putting away some groceries and said, "Harry's hurt bad. There was a collapse in the mine," and he started sobbing. The stress of it descended on him like a dark smothering curtain.

"Oh, Jimmy! My God!" She started crying too. They held each other until their sobs subsided,

Jimmy said, "Let's get to the hospital. I need to be there when he wakes up!"

Harry was unconscious for the next three days. Jimmy sat with him for hours, talking to him. "You're not going to die, Harry," he told him repeatedly. "We have too much to do."

Harry woke up on the morning of the fourth day. That afternoon when all his family and Jimmy were there, he said he would have died without Jimmy. "I thought I was dead. Then I heard Jimmy's voice as if it came from a long way off. The next thing I knew, he was loading me into the pickup. I don't know where you found the strength to do it, Jimmy. I owe you my life." He gave Jimmy a weak smile and went back to sleep.

The nurses shooed them out to do some tests, then the doctor came in and examined him. John caught him when he came out. "Is he going to be okay, doctor?"

"I'll be honest; I think so. But Harry's going to need a lot of rest. He's young and strong. Hopefully, he won't suffer any long-term damage. You and your family should keep him in your prayers."

Harry was released and sent home with strict bed rest orders for at least a week. He said, "I've already been in bed too long. We got too much work for me to lay around on my backside!" His family and Jimmy quickly overruled him.

Jimmy said, "The work will wait. You have to get better, get your strength back. You don't want to wind up back in the hospital!"

***

Two days later, Jimmy, John, and Fred went back to the mine to see what had happened. They barely made it to the house before another monsoon gully washer struck. John said, "Whew! Glad that didn't catch us out there on the road. A flooded wash would have stranded us overnight, waiting for the water to go down!"

The following morning, they descended into the mine. They very cautiously approached the area where the collapse had occurred. John examined the rock face.

He shook his head and said, "This is my fault. I should have seen that fracture line headed toward that support beam. Look here. See these spider web cracks? That weakened the whole area around the beam. I should have seen it!"

Fred said, "You can't see everything down here. We always knew somethin' like this could happen. I bet it happened to others before Harry, too. It's a lesson for us all. From now on, we will inspect the areas around these beams before we do any more work. Now let's get this one back in place and clean this up."

Jimmy had been looking around the area of the collapse. He grabbed a pick and broke out a piece from the wall opposite the active work area. It had a different look than he had seen before. "Look at this," he said to the others. "Why does this ore look different?"

John and Fred studied the ore and exchanged knowing looks. "I'll be damned!" John exclaimed. "This is a much richer ore than any we've seen here before. We need to get more samples for assay. This vein could be the mother lode!"

They first replaced the fallen beam and made sure it and the surrounding rock were stable. Then they broke out several pieces of ore from the wall. It was clear the collapse had exposed a more significant, and perhaps much more extensive, vein of ore.

"I think we've done enough, "John said. "Let's wrap up here and take these samples to the assay office in town and see what we've got."

They had a lot of excited discussions on the way back to Ajo. John cautioned them not to get carried away with wild speculation until they knew more about what they had. They

agreed to keep it to themselves until they had more information.

Two days later, the assayer handed the paper with his test results to John and said, "John, you might have finally found what you've been looking for all this time. Those were the richest samples I've seen in years. And not only silver – there's a fair amount of gold mixed in it, too."

John asked the assayer to keep the results confidential. When he showed the report to the others, they were speechless. It showed silver content of ninety-two ounces per ton and two to three grams of gold per ton.

They talked about what the results could mean. John said, "We shouldn't get too excited until we take out a larger amount of ore, see if the results hold. It could be a fluke and peter out in only a few feet. But we need to keep this among ourselves. There'll be a bunch of people trying to horn in on it if word gets out. We don't want to start a rush for new claims out there."

Harry was excited by the news. Maybe the accident had at least brought some benefit. He was recovering well, and his strength was coming back rapidly. He was anxious to get back to work, but his broken ribs made him cautious.

Jimmy and the others continued working with the mine's new vein of ore. It seemed to be holding up well, and they were taking a substantial amount of material out. They spent much of their time improving the old works on the surface to prepare for larger-scale mining operations.

CHAPTER 24

BIG BUSINESS

Jimmy said, "We need to decide what we need to do to take out more ore. Hopefully, that will give us more income until we can sell more gold." Harry had recovered enough to go back to the mine, but Jimmy knew he needed more time to recuperate from his accident. "How about if you concentrate on finding better equipment? We'll need to hire a couple more men to work the mine, too. And, we'll need a bigger truck to handle the shipments to the smelter."

Harry readily agreed to that plan. It was clear they needed more help. They were not going to be able to keep their operation secret. Harry bought NO TRESPASSING signs and posted them on the access road and all around the mine area. It would be his job to chase off anyone who ventured too close. He was glad to have something to do until he could help more with the mining operations. Jimmy would work with Harry's father and uncle to rework and improve the surface equipment to handle the ore more efficiently.

July brought a particularly active monsoon period with frequent heavy rains. The men and workers had to time their operations to avoid the flooding washes carefully. Severe thunderstorms sometimes made it dangerous to work at the surface, and they had to stop work when storms were nearby. It wasn't safe to be near electrical equipment or the metal mine works. The partially melted ore car from a previous storm was a stark reminder.

Jimmy and the others had the mine's works in what they considered reasonably good working condition. They had shored up the old timbers in the mine, reconstructed the ore chute, and rebuilt the ore holding bunkers used in previous mining operations. Material from the ore car could then be dumped into the chute and collected in a bunker at the bottom.

They resumed work in the mine. After a few hours of work in the shaft, John said, "If this pans out to be as rich as it appears, we should buy a gas-powered pneumatic system for drilling and breaking out the ore. It would make it go a lot faster."

Jimmy stretched his back muscles. "I'm for that! This back-breaking labor will make old men of all of us!"

First, they had to prove that the ore would be profitable enough to justify investing in new and expensive machinery. They judged there was enough ore after a solid week of hard work for a good run at the Mexico smelter. They went back to Ajo for a rest, and Harry made arrangements to rent a dump truck for the following week.

Harry also spoke to his grandfather about hiring security when they transport their silver from the smelter. Esteban said he had already made arrangements to hire a couple of off-duty police officers in Caborca. They would only need to be paid for their time.

Jimmy would drive the truck, and Harry would lead in their pickup. As usual, Harry handled the negotiations at the border crossing. *La mordida* was satisfied, and they rolled into the smelter in mid-afternoon.

They had called ahead, and *Señor* Arredondo met them. "It's wonderful to see you again, my young friends! I see you have brought me much more to work with this time. You have been very busy, eh?"

They exchanged pleasantries and dumped the ore from the truck into the smelter's processing facility. Arredondo told them it would be ready in two days. Jimmy parked the dump truck, and the partners went back to Caborca. They had another appointment at the bank.

Estevez greeted them when they came into his bank. He motioned them to his office as an attractive young woman was coming out. "Please allow me to introduce my daughter, *Angélica*."

She was a gorgeous girl with silky blue-black hair falling around her shoulders and huge brown eyes. Her smile could break men's hearts; she turned it on both men as her father introduced them.

She said, "My father has talked a lot about your adventures

in an Arizona cave. And he says you are doing very well with your mine! So when he said you were coming, I wanted to meet you!"

Both partners reddened and were suitably embarrassed. Jimmy looked at his feet, but Harry met her gaze and returned her smile.

Harry said, "It is a pleasure to meet you, *señorita*. It sounds like my grandfather has been telling your father tales about our time working in the cave. It wasn't as exciting as it might sound. But our mine is doing well."

She turned her devastating smile directly on him and said, "I know you have important business now with my father. Perhaps sometime you can tell me more about your adventures!"

"I would enjoy that very much! I hope to see you again soon, Señorita."

"That would be very nice," she said. She favored Harry with a smile filled with dazzlingly white teeth as she was leaving. He stood in a daze, watching her gentle lilting walk as she left the office.

Her father broke the spell and said," Please come into my office, *señors*."

They were all seated, and Jimmy said, "We have twenty gold coins this time. We want to exchange them and have the dollars placed in our account. "

"Certainly, *Señor*. I have already calculated the current gold price, and it will only take a few minutes." Harry handed him the bag of coins and said, "We will have more silver to exchange the day after tomorrow. And it looks like our silver production is going to increase substantially."

"That is excellent news! I will look forward to your continued business."

They finished the exchange and left. When they were back in the truck, Harry said, "Jimmy! Did you see the way that girl looked at me? And her smile? It's good you had to do most of the talkin'! Did you ever see a more beautiful girl?"

"Only your sister! It sounds like you're already hooked!

"Her voice was like honey; I could listen to her for hours. I can't wait to see her again."

"Yep. You're done for."

"I want to stick around for a while and get to know her better. See if I can arrange a date."

Jimmy guffawed loudly. "I told you so! I knew it would be this way as soon as we left the bank." Harry turned red, and Jimmy continued, "By all means. Stay as long as you want. I'll take the dump truck back to Ajo. You come when you're ready."

"You're a good friend, Jimmy. Thanks!"

Jimmy went back to Ajo, leaving Harry in *Angélica's* seductive clutches. He had a pretty good idea of how that would turn out. Jimmy busied himself with the others at the mine, and Harry showed up four days later. He had a glow about him Jimmy had never seen before.

"You were right, Jimmy. I'm head over heels for that girl."

No surprise there!" Jimmy laughed. "So, what now?"

"I've made arrangements to see her again when we take the next shipment down to the smelter."

"In that case, we better get busy!"

***

They purchased a pneumatic drill and other tools, and the work in the mine proceeded much faster. Harry supervised the operation on the surface and hired a couple more men to help haul the ore out of the tunnel.

He had not been back down the mine since his accident. His mother begged him to stay out of it. But he knew he had to face the fear that had taken root deep inside him. How would he face other challenges that would surely confront him in his life If he couldn't face this?

"Jimmy," he said one morning, "I want to go down with the crew today. It's time."

"You sure, Harry? There's no rush. We have it well under control and working smooth."

"I'm sure. I just wanna have a look around, get used to the idea of bein' underground again."

"I'll go down with you."

Harry climbed gingerly over the edge of the ore car with Jimmy after the day's first load was emptied. The descent went smoothly. A new generator on the surface powered many new lights; the shaft was not nearly as daunting.

Harry cautiously climbed out of the car when they reached the level where the current work was going on. His ribs and back muscles were sore and stiff, and let him know anytime he overdid it. They moved down the side tunnel and stopped where the cave-in had occurred. Harry stood for a minute, rubbing his hand over the beam that had collapsed.

"I would have died here, Jimmy, if not for you. I am amazed you were able to get me out of here— I'll always be in your debt."

"You don't owe me anything. You are my best friend and partner, and I would lay my own life on the line for you. You would have done the same for me."

They moved on to where the men were working and watched the new pneumatic drill and jackhammer in operation. Jimmy said, "Great improvement, eh? It sure beats hammering on those hand drills for hours. And look how far they've come!"

Their new crew was working smoothly, and there was nothing they needed to do there. Jimmy gave Harry a hand stepping out of the car back on the surface. Harry pretended not to notice.

They had enough for a shipment in four days; everything was working well. So well, it made Jimmy a little nervous. He had learned to expect the unexpected with their activities

That night after dinner, Jimmy said, "I keep thinking, Harry. We've been through so much. It makes me uneasy when things are going well for us. I keep looking for something else to happen."

"Yeah, sometimes I feel like that too. But right now, I think we've done everything right. The mine work is goin' perfect, and the rich vein is holdin' up. You're fixin' to get married, and I've found a new girlfriend. We got a lot goin' our way."

They sat quietly, gazing into the embers of their dying fire, listening to the coyotes howling and gabbling in the distance. An elf owl had taken up residence in a woodpecker's hole in a nearby saguaro cactus. Its hooting sounded hauntingly lonely in the night.

One of their workers ran up to them before they left the next day. He was so excited he could barely blurt out, "*Señors*! Come quick! You must see!" He ran back toward the mine before they could ask any questions. They went back down to where the men were working. Harry's dad and uncle met them with toothy smiles on their faces.

"Look at this!" John said. He shined his light on an excavated area beside the place they had been working. "It looks like

another, much larger vein! Maybe much richer than the one we've been working!" They could see the silver veins clearly in the rock. They were much more pronounced than what they had been mining.

They stood looking in amazement. Jimmy and Harry both ran their hands over it as if they might somehow probe its secrets.

John said, "This changes everything, boys. This vein will require another side shaft, and we're going to need more timbers to shore it up. It looks like it might be running at a 45-degree angle to this one."

They left the workers to continue pulling out ore while they went to the surface to plan what to do. Their business was about to become much more significant if the new vein held up and was as rich as it looked.

When Jimmy and Harry were alone, Jimmy said, "I've been thinking. We're hiring people to be working out here when we're not around. What if someone gets snoopy and goes nosing around that dig where we hid our stuff? We need to do something else with it."

"Yep. You're right. Maybe we can figger a safe way to get it to Mexico. We can't take a chance on border guards findin' it. It might be the time they decide to shake us down if we move it. We'd be done for if our stuff was out in the open. Let me think about it some."

The day after they returned to Ajo, Harry said he had a solution for moving their "material." "I found a local shop to fabricate a steel box that could hold the four duffels. We can bolt it into the bottom of the dump truck's dump bin, put the bags inside, and cover it with silver ore when they load the truck. We can retrieve the bags when we dump the ore in Mexico, then take them to my grandfather's place to hide them."

Harry chuckled to himself at his cleverness and continued, "I doubt any border guard's gonna dig down and root around in that raw ore—too much work. There's an old cellar with a hidey-hole at grandfather's house where we can keep it until we figure out something better. I'm sure my grandfather would be okay with it."

Harry picked up their rented truck, then he and Jimmy spent an hour securing the new steel box in the dump bed. Then they traveled to the mine to spend the night. With the hired hands gone, they could safely retrieve their duffels with their treasure. They put them in the box and bolted its latch.

The following day, with the first shipment loaded and Harry in the lead in their pickup, they headed for Mexico. The trip was uneventful, and after dropping their load at the smelter, they made a stop at Harry's grandfather's hacienda before returning to the mine. Esteban had agreed to store their duffel bags in his cellar until they could find a better arrangement.

They would have to hustle to keep up with the pace of the mine's production. If the vein held up, they would be making two, maybe three shipments per week. The yield so far had been significantly better than they had hoped.

They stayed that night at the mine. Harry said, "I never thought this old mine would ever produce this much ore. I figgered it was gonna be a sideline for a few months to give us cover for our gold exchanges."

"No kidding," Jimmy said. "This has turned into a real business." He paused and stuck another piece of mesquite wood into the fire. The flickering firelight lit their faces and danced on the walls of the old stone house. "In a short time, we are going to have a lot of refined silver on our hands. I suspect the news will travel fast around Caborca. There are many desperate people around that will be looking at that. Even with our hired guards, we need to be cautious."

Jimmy had made a trip to Tucson to meet with an attorney to discuss the best ways to set up and manage the mining business. The attorney recommended an accountant to handle their books and suggested a limited liability partnership, known as an LLC, might be best for them. Jimmy laid it out for Harry, and he agreed it would make it much easier to do business as their mining operation grew. And it had the extra benefit of protecting them from lawsuits or liability issues against either of them personally. Given recent history, that in itself was reason enough to organize that way. They decided to call it J &H Mining LLC.

Jimmy said, "Something else I've been thinking about, Harry. My mother told me a story about some friends in Denver who are struggling to get by in the Depression. They are a family with three kids, and the father is sick. They are barely getting by on welfare. She said she has been giving them part of the money I send her to help them out and that she was grateful I could help with it. But even with the expense and difficulty of my sister's sickness, my mother finds it in her heart to help others."

"So, what are you thinkin'?"

"We are going to make far more money with the mine than either of us imagined. Maybe there's some way we could give back some of the money from the gold to help out people who are hurting so much right now. I feel guilty sometimes about how we came by what we have. It would be good if we could find a way to do some good with it."

"That's an interestin' idea, Jimmy. And, yeah, I feel a little guilty about it too. We came by it accidental, and I wonder if somethin' like what you are talkin' about would be the right thing to do."

Jimmy said, "I'll look into it. And, one more idea—If the mine takes off, we might want to give your dad and uncle a bigger interest in it as part of our new LLC. It would help them since they're out of work. They helped us; we could help them back. We only have to decide on how to split the profits.

"That's a great idea, Jimmy. Let's talk to them about it. Thanks for doin' all this stuff. I think everything's gonna work out great!"

The following two months were a whirlwind of activity to keep up with the mine's production. The partners made three, sometimes four trips per week to the smelter in Caborca and were barely able to stay ahead of their workers at the mine. Jimmy traveled to Tucson every two weeks to meet with their accountant and attorney.

CHAPTER 25

WEDDING BELLS

October arrived with clear skies and cooler days. Jimmy wished somedays he was at the mine with nothing to listen to but coyotes. He was tired of hearing all the details for his wedding with Joann; rehearsals and planning seemed endless.

Joann and Jimmy asked for and received marriage permission from the Catholic bishop in Tucson. As Joann predicted, her mother became an unstoppable whirlwind planning every day of the wedding.

Finally, the date had arrived. All Maria's planning and preparations paid off, and the ceremony and reception come off with no problems. Joann was stunning in her white wedding gown. Jimmy couldn't take his eyes off her. She took his mind off the discomfort of the tuxedo Joann's mother insisted he wear.

The church had an adjoining hall overflowing with people Jimmy had never seen. They all wanted to shake his hand and wish the couple well. He couldn't wait for it to be over.

Harry insisted Jimmy invite the banker and his family. He wanted an opportunity to introduce his new girlfriend to his family and everyone he knew. He had dated *Angélica* several times, and their relationship was quickly becoming serious. She was radiant in the crowd. Her bright red sleeveless dress stood out, and her eyes had a mischievous sparkle.

Most of the men in the room watched her furtively. Harry could tell she enjoyed the attention and was quite experienced with social gatherings. He was a little jealous, but he also felt pretty awesome about having a gorgeous new girlfriend. The women were gossiping and speculating about another wedding, maybe not too far in the future.

Harry and Jimmy used profits from the mine to cover the reception and honeymoon costs. Harry said to consider his part a wedding present from him. The couple were going to honeymoon in Tucson. Harry told Jimmy he had made reservations for them at the El Conquistador Hotel, the best place in town. He said they deserved the best, and he wanted them to enjoy their time together.

The new couple left in the partners' truck and headed out of town. A loud clattering of cans tied to the bumper chased them down the street. Jimmy stopped and untied them as soon as they were out of town. Joann snuggled up against him, and they headed for Tucson.

The sun was setting behind them as they pulled into the El Conquistador Hotel's parking area. Their pickup truck looked conspicuously out of place among the Cadillacs, Chryslers, and a glistening Rolls Royce.

They were awed by the hotel's sixty-five-foot-high bell tower, topped with a copper dome. Then they entered the resort's equally impressive main room—a cavernous and magnificently decorated space. It was nearly as wide as the length of a football field across the front. Neither of them had ever seen anything remotely like it.

The desk clerk eyed them suspiciously. They didn't have the look or the air of the hotels' typical guests. Jimmy didn't care how hoity-toity the help was. He had the most beautiful bride in the world, and his money was as good as anyone's. Harry had made all the arrangements for their stay. The clerk continued looking down his nose at them as he summoned a bellman to show them to their cottage. Harry's father had coached Jimmy on the art of tipping; he handed the man what he hoped was an adequate amount. The bellman thanked him, gave him a big smile, and left.

Their room was as sumptuously decorated as the main hall had been. Intricately ornamented furniture and expensive paintings gave it an aura of wealth and refinement. The quarters included a private dining room with gold plated utensils and beautiful china, a private terrace with a view of the mountains, and an oversized bed that looked like they could get lost in its blankets. It was a perfect place for their honeymoon: Something so far out of the ordinary as to be beyond their wildest fantasies.

The resort had riding stables, and Jimmy arranged for them to hire a couple of horses with a guide. Joann said she had ridden horses on her grandfather's ranch when she was a child. Harry had never been on one. The guide gave them a quick lesson in horse etiquette and control, and they were off into the desert surrounding the resort. The Catalina Mountain range loomed in front of them. Its forested peaks lay hidden in a morning mist.

Jimmy said, "This is amazing. I always dreamed of doing this. I've stayed awake nights thinking about you and me riding horses like these on our own ranch, looking over a herd of cattle in the hills. I want to make that happen, Joann."

"You know I will follow where you lead, Jimmy. You have already made my life more than I could have ever hoped for." She laughed and said, "We can learn to be ranchers together!"

"You never told me your grandfather had a ranch. I thought he just had the farm. Where is the ranch?"

"It's a long way east of his farm in Caborca, near the town of Cananea. Grandfather spent a lot of time there years ago, but I think he has concentrated more on his farm since he's gotten older. I haven't been to the ranch since I was a young girl. I don't know if he still has it. I haven't heard him say anything about it in years."

They spent five days there, exploring Tucson, riding horses, enjoying fabulous meals in the hotel's dining room, and luxuriating in a life of endless pleasures. A hotel bellman helped them load their luggage in their pickup as they were leaving. He said," I'm sad to say you folks will be some of our last guests. They're closing this hotel shortly." It was another victim of the Depression.

The newlyweds had found a two-bedroom furnished house to rent on the edge of Ajo. It was one of the few non-company-owned places available. It was plain and sparsely furnished, a far cry from the surroundings they had enjoyed for the past week. But they would be comfortable there until they could find something better.

Joann's mother arranged to place their wedding gifts in their new home before they returned from Tucson. Jimmy marveled at the generosity of people he knew were going through hard times. He felt guilty about having so much.

There was a large envelope tied with a lovely ribbon and bow lying on the kitchen table. It had the couple's names printed on it in a fancy calligraphic style. It was unopened. Joann picked it up and showed it to Jimmy, and they wondered what it might contain. They sat on the couch together, and she opened it.

Inside were some official-looking documents printed in Spanish, and a card from her grandparents, wishing them well and hoping they would enjoy this gift. Joann read through the first page of the documents and caught her breath.

"What is it? It looks important."

Joann was speechless for a minute. She looked at Jimmy and said, "It's a deed. I'm not sure of it yet, but it looks like a significant portion of land and buildings. I will have to talk to grandfather Esteban to see what it means."

"Land and buildings? What do you suppose?

Her hands were shaking as she laid the documents aside. "I can't imagine what it is. But it is something big, I think."

They cleared the gifts away, but the suspense was too great. They had no phone, so they drove to Joann's parents' house to use theirs. Joann asked her mother what she knew about it. She wasn't saying if she knew.

Joann nervously had the operator put her through to her grandfather's residence at Caborca. He answered and asked her if she had a nice honeymoon. Joann said it was wonderful, and she thanked him and her grandmother for coming to the wedding. "But I am confused, Abuelo, by this gift you have left for us. I do not know what it is."

"Well, *nieta*," he began, "it is our gift for you and Jimmy to begin your new life. Your mother told me that Jimmy had dreams of someday becoming a rancher, and I remembered how much you enjoyed riding a horse. I am in a position to make

Jimmy's dream come true for both of you. That deed is for the ranch I have owned for many years. Now it is yours."

She nearly dropped the phone and was speechless for a moment. "*Abuelo*, thank you! I loved being at that ranch. But this is too much!"

"It would be your inheritance, *nieta*. I would rather you have it to enjoy while I am alive to see it. You and Jimmy must plan a trip here soon so I can show it to you."

Joann thanked him and told him they would come as soon as possible. She hung up the phone and collapsed on the couch next to Jimmy.

CHAPTER 26
TREACHERY

Emilio Lopez had worked at the bank for *Señor* Estevez for almost two years. Estevez and Emilio's father had a long history dating back to the revolution's days with Pancho Villa. Estevez was always laughing about old times when his father came into the bank. That relationship was the only reason Emilio had this job. Deep inside, he was resentful that he was dependent on his father's influence. He was an only child, unused to having to work for himself.

Estevez trained Emilio to be a teller, and his job was working at the front counter when customers came in. He was good with numbers but had not done well in school. It made him impatient. The time it took for studies always annoyed him. Moreover, he was unhappy with his job in the bank— he would never be able to make enough money to live the way he wanted. Men like Estevez and others who had made fortunes in their businesses made him envious of their success. The Depression had made it nearly impossible for those like him to become wealthy on their own.

He started thinking of ways to use the information he overheard in Estevez's conversation with the two young gringos. They had discussed exchanging some gold coins. One of them said there might be as much as fifty thousand dollars more to come. There were many possibilities if they had that many gold coins to exchange.

***

El Cuchillo, as everyone called him, was humiliated by his failed attempt at robbing the two *gringos* a few weeks before. Who would have thought they would be well-armed and react the way they did? It wasn't right. He wanted revenge—needed revenge. He couldn't let something like that go unchallenged; it would cause his men to lose faith in him. Worse, it would ruin his reputation as an outlaw to be feared. Those two would feel the bite of his knife, his *cuchillo*.

At the smelter, his contact assured him the gringos would be returning with even more ore to refine and a more considerable amount of silver for the taking. He would be prepared the next time. He would take the truck, too.

***

Harry's grandmother was excited about her granddaughter's marriage to the young *norteamericano*. She loved describing the wedding to her friends and gushed about what a wonderful couple they made.

She stopped off at the bank to chat with her life-long friend Esperanza, the other clerk working there. Esperanza said she had seen Yolanda's granddaughter's new husband in the bank. She gushed about what a fine-looking young man he was. The two women chatted about the couple's plans for the future. Yolanda said she was thankful her granddaughter was marrying a man with such excellent prospects.

***

Emilio heard the two women's exchange, and it gave him an idea—an idea for a daring plan to make him rich. It could give him the foundation he craved to be successful. He knew a man who worked for his father who might have the connections he needed to make the plan work. The man had been in jail for robbery and was known to have links with some lawless men around the area. He made arrangements to meet with him and put his plan in motion.

***

Jimmy went back to work hauling ore from the mine to the Mexico smelter after their honeymoon. Joann was resentful of his time away but knew he was building the business for them. She hoped he would be home for Halloween the following week. It was one of her favorite holidays. She loved seeing the children in their costumes and couldn't wait for the day she would have children of her own.

Joann was walking home from the Phelps Dodge Mercantile store in Ajo with a few packages of hard candies for the trick-or-treaters. She hadn't noticed a car that had followed her when she left the store. It was just one more old black Ford sedan like dozens of others around town. She left the plaza and turned up her street, lost in a daydream about her future children and Halloween. The car sped around the corner and came to a screeching stop beside her. Two men jumped out and grabbed her. One clamped a hand over her mouth, and they shoved her roughly into the car. The old Ford raced away headed south, out of town toward Mexico.

Rough hands bound her hands and leg. One of her captors stuffed a filthy handkerchief in her mouth as a gag. He said in a gravelly voice, "You be still on the floor, *señora*, make no noise. Maybe you live, eh?" The car's backseat floor was filthy and smelled of rotting garbage, making her choke against her gag. The old Ford continued, rattling over the rough pavement.

Joann couldn't judge how far they traveled, but it seemed like about an hour when the car began slowing. She felt it stop and could hear a conversation in Spanish with someone outside the vehicle. Then the old car continued over even rougher and uneven pavement. It felt like it had no springs and made every bone in her body rattle against another. Then, in a short while, she felt and heard a change in the road. It sounded like they had left the pavement and were on a washboard dirt road.

They continued for a few minutes, and the car came to a stop. She heard her captors outside the vehicle, having a conversation. The car door opened suddenly. The men jerked her from the car, wrapped a handkerchief around her head as a blindfold, and carried her bodily inside a building. She was tossed unceremoniously onto a bed and left there—bound, gagged, and blindfolded. She heard a door close and could hear muffled voices from another part of the house.

***

Early the following morning, Harry's grandfather found a note that someone slipped under the *hacienda's* front door during the night. He was stunned by what it said and had to find a chair to sit down. He called his wife and read the hand-scrawled note to her:

> *We have your granddaughter. Tell your grandson's friend it will cost fifty thousand dollars in gold to get her back. Put the gold coins in a bag. We will tell you what to do with it three days from now.*
>
> *No gold, she dies.*

Yolanda started sobbing and collapsed against a wall. Both of them sat in horrified silence. Finally, Esteban said, "We must call Maria in Ajo to see if this is true. Then we will decide what to do."

When Maria answered the phone, she was almost in hysterics. "Joann disappeared after shopping yesterday. I've been to her house and searched all over town and can't find her. The men are at the mine. There's no way to reach them. Oh, Papa, I don't know what to do!"

Esteban said, "Try to stay calm. We received a ransom note last night. She has been kidnapped." Maria broke down in uncontrolled sobbing into the phone.

Esteban waited for her to calm herself. "Maria, can you get to the mine?" he asked.

"I was only there once, but I think I can find it."

"You need to go there as quickly as you can. Tell Harry and Jimmy to come here as soon as possible. Tell them to come armed. And tell your husband and his brother to stay close to a phone in case we need them here. Is there someone who can be with you?"

"Rita, Fred's wife, is home. I'll get her to go with me."

"Go quickly but be safe driving. Don't tell anyone else about this. We will work out a way to handle it when the others arrive." He hung up the phone and looked at his wife, shaking his head. "This is going to be very difficult, but we will get through it."

Yolanda said, "I just want our granddaughter back unharmed. Do whatever you have to do." She broke into sobs again.

Harry's mother got to the mine as Jimmy and Harry were preparing to take a load of ore to the smelter. She told them what had happened. They jumped in their pickup truck and drove to Caborca as fast as they dared. It was noon when they arrived at Harry's grandfather's house.

They parked and raced to the door, bursting into the living room. Harry shouted, "Abuelo! Is it true? Tell us what happened!" Jimmy said nothing. His face was a picture of rage and determination.

Esteban said, "Right now, all we know is what this note says and the fact my granddaughter is missing. We need to figure out who is doing this, and quickly!"

Jimmy studied the note and spoke for the first time. "This seems very suspicious to me. First, few know anything about us having gold. But the most telling clue is that they want fifty thousand dollars in gold coins. That happens to be the number I gave Mr. Estevez at the bank. We've never used that number anywhere else. So, I believe that's where this is coming from."

Esteban was thoughtful. "I've known Pablo Estevez almost my entire life. We rode together with Villa. I don't believe he would do something like this, especially not to my family. Who else knows about that number?"

Harry said, "There's a young man who works at the teller counter and an older lady who sits behind him doing paperwork."

Harry's grandmother spoke up. "That woman working there is my old friend, Esperanza Perez. I don't believe she would do this to our family."

Jimmy said, "Well, that leaves the teller. What do you know about him?"

"I believe he is the son of Miguel Lopez. He has a farm near ours," Yolanda said. "I don't know much about the boy. I think he has been at the bank a year or two."

Jimmy and Harry looked at each other. Jimmy said, " I think that's where we start. We need to talk to him, and not in a nice way."

Esteban cautioned them to be careful. "We don't want to make a mistake. But here's something else. A man who works on the Lopez farm has a bad past and has been in jail for robbery. I have heard that he may hang out with an outlaw gang. They may be the same ones who tried to rob you before."

Harry said, "That might be a connection that Lopez's son could use to find some people to help him do the kidnapping. I doubt he could do it alone."

"Let's catch him today when he comes out after the bank closes," Jimmy said. "Would it be okay if we bring him here for a talk?" Esteban nodded. "But," Jimmy continued, "there's one more thing bothering me. How did they know about Joann and me?"

Yolanda covered her mouth, sobbed, and said, "I was in the bank a while back, and I told Esperanza about your wedding. The Lopez boy was standing right in front of us at the teller counter. I'm sure he heard every word!" She sat with tears running down her cheeks. "I'm sorry! I'm so sorry! I only wanted to share the good news."

Harry stood and put his arms around her. "It's all right, Abuela. You had no way to know."

"Let's get ready for Lopez," Jimmy said.

***

Jimmy and Harry were waiting on either side of the bank's door when Emilio walked out at five o'clock. They grabbed him and tossed him into the seat of their truck, which was parked on the street. Jimmy pulled the menacing .357 revolver, stuck it in Emilio's ribs, and said, "Sit still and be quiet. We're going for a short ride."

"Wait! You can't do this!" Lopez spluttered. "My father will have you in jail for this!" Jimmy backhanded him in the mouth, drawing blood. "I told you to keep quiet!" He poked the pistol's barrel harder in his side.

They tied him to a post in one of the *hacienda's* barns. He was struggling and crying, shouting about his father, the police, and his friends. Jimmy hit him in the mouth with his fist. "We think you have answers to some questions we're going to ask you. If we think you're lying or don't answer, I will hit you again. And again," Jimmy said. "If I get tired, my partner Harry will take over. He's a lot stronger than I am."

299

Lopez looked from one to the other. "I don't know anything! I don't know what you are talking about." Jimmy hit him in the ear.

"Where's my wife, Joann? Talk!"

"I…I don't" was all Lopez got out before Jimmy hit him in the other ear.

"You're likely to go deaf if you keep this up," he said.

"*El Cuchillo! El Cuchillo's* got her! It was all his idea!"

"Got her where? Here, in Caborca?"

"I don't know for sure. I don't think it's here." Emilio was crying now. "He'll kill me if he finds out I told you he did it. It was all his idea!" Jimmy hit him again, breaking his nose. His blood splattered down the front of his white shirt.

Jimmy's face was a mask of black rage. "I'll kill you if you don't come clean," he growled. Harry had never seen him like this. "She's my wife. I won't hesitate to kill you if that's what it takes." He shoved the barrel of his pistol up under Emilio's chin and said, "Talk!"

Lopez wet himself and started shaking uncontrollably. "They said they had a house in Sonoyta where they could hide her. I don't know exactly where."

Jimmy pressed, "Whose house?"

"El Cuchillo said something about his cousin's house. That's all I know."

“What’s his cousin’s name?”

“I don’t know. Please, I don’t know anything else!”

“Who set you up with *El Cuchillo*? I don’t think you would hang around with people like that. Who’d you talk to?”

They finally got the name of the man who worked for Lopez’s father. Jimmy and Harry looked at each other.

Harry spoke for the first time. “You are an idiot. They will simply keep the gold, then kill you and my sister! How did you think you could avoid that?”

Emilio spat out a mouthful of blood and said, “We were going to split it 50-50 because I knew how to handle the gold.”

Harry laughed in his face. “You are an even bigger fool than I thought. Let’s tie him up better, Jimmy. I’ll stuff somethin’ in his mouth, so we don’t have to hear any more lies from him.” He shoved a dirty rag in his mouth while Jimmy tied him more securely to the post. They left him standing, bloody and unable to move, as they went off to talk to Harry’s grandfather.

“I’ve heard rumors about this man called *El Cuchillo*,” Esteban said. “They say he has killed many men with a knife. But I don’t know his real name. I think he was the one who tried to rob you. Let’s see what we can find out about this cousin of his.”

He picked up his phone and called Lopez’s father. “Miguel, Esteban. I need a favor. You have a man who works for you who was in prison a few years ago. I need to speak to him." He listened for a moment. "Only two days. Do you know where he went?" More listening. "Yes, it is extremely important, but I can't tell you why right now." They talked another minute, and Esteban said, *"Muchas gracias, amigo,"* and hung up the phone.

Esteban smiled for the first time. "I believe *El Cuchillo* is a cousin of Lopez's employee— and he is from Sonoyta.

Jimmy jumped up and said, "Let's go! We have to find Joann now!"

"It is seven o'clock, Jimmy, and it will be almost nine by the time we could reach Sonoyta," Esteban cautioned. "We need more information about the kidnappers and where they are holding Joann. That would be difficult to get that late at night, in the dark. We need a good plan if we hope to rescue her safely. Let me make a call."

Jimmy reluctantly agreed and paced the room while Esteban phoned Roberto Sanchez, the Chief of Police in Sonoyta, at home.

"Esteban, old friend! We have not talked in a long time. Surely you have not called me at home to discuss old times!"

"Roberto, I am sorry it has been so long. You know how it is as we get older. But I need a favor from you which must only be between us. I need to find a man who lives in your town. It is a matter of great urgency for my family."

"Of course, Esteban. Who is this man you seek?" Esteban gave him the name. "Yes, I know this man. He is not a good man, I might add. What is wrong, my friend? How can I help you?"

"I would like to talk to you in person early tomorrow morning if that is possible," Esteban said. "I will explain it all in detail. But, as I said, it is an extremely urgent matter. And, I would rather meet you at your home than at the police station."

They agreed on a time, and Esteban hung up. He told Harry and Jimmy, "This is another man I can trust. He, too, has benefitted from our activities during the revolution. I'm sure he will be of great help to us."

They made plans to leave for Sonoyta before dawn the following day. Jimmy had a sleepless night, thinking and worrying about Joann. He badly wanted to jump in their truck and burn up the road to Sonoyta to free her—but Esteban was right. It would be a dangerous mistake to attempt it without a sound plan.

Already one of the three days the kidnappers had given them had passed. Tomorrow they had to find and save her. If these men harmed her in any way, he would make them pay. He turned possible scenarios over in his mind until it was time to leave.

CHAPTER 27

JOANN

Joann lay unmoving on the bed, listening to her captors in the next room. She could tell the night had passed by the dim, filtered light through her blindfold. The sheets on the bed smelled dirty and musty. She shuddered at the thought of who might have previously used them. The air in the room was musty, close, and still. She was sweating despite the fall morning's chill.

She could tell they were discussing her and the gold she would bring them. They didn't know she had learned Spanish from her mother at an early age and understood all they said. They had kidnapped her as a way to get the gold from Jimmy and Harry. She didn't know how they knew about that or her relationship with Jimmy, but it was clear they knew enough.

They had given her some food and water the previous night and allowed her to use the bathroom. There were always two guards when they unbound her. She heard one of them say it was better to let her use the bathroom than to have to clean up a soiled bed. They both laughed and bound her again. She was left blindfolded and lying on the bed overnight. She knew she would have to escape if possible. There was no telling what abuse and, possibly death, might await her at the hands of these men. Sleep was impossible; possible scenarios scrolled through her mind all night.

Then, she heard the door open and heavy footsteps approaching the bed. Rough hands removed her blindfold. The bright light of day momentarily blinded her. As her vision cleared, she saw a large Mexican man standing over her. He examined her like a piece of meat in a butcher's shop. He wore dirty denim jeans and a faded red western shirt. The shirt was missing several white snaps, and his ample belly protruded through the shirt's gap. He had an evil smile with tobacco-stained teeth and was missing two of them in front. She could smell his sour breath, a mixture of stale beer and garlic, as he drew closer.

"Buenos dias, señora! You like our hospitality? Is nice, yes?" Joann glared at the man and said nothing. "They call me *El Cuchillo*. Maybe you hear of me, yes?" Again, she said nothing. "Well, is okay. You no have talk. I tink maybe you change you mind soon, yes?" He took a large switchblade knife from his pocket and snapped the blade open in front of her face. "Is why they call me *El Cuchillo*, see? The Knife. I love good sharp knife, like this one." He stroked the side of her face with the blade. "Maybe I teach you all about it when we done with you husband. Maybe we start tonight, eh! What you tink of that?" He laughed in her face. Joann gagged at the smell of his fetid breath. Then he walked out of the room.

The two men from the night before came in and unbound her to use the bathroom. She rolled off the bed and hit the floor. Shoving the nearest guard aside, she dashed for the door. But the other guard was too quick and grabbed her before she could get out. She fought and scratched at him. But the other man joined in, and they managed to wrestle her back to the bed. They laughed as she struggled against them and tied her hands and feet. When she was still, one of her captors said, "No breakfast for you now. You bad girl. You try get away again we hurt you." He replaced her blindfold.

***

The men traveled in two pickup trucks from Caborca. They figured the kidnappers would not recognize Esteban's truck; they would use it to reconnoiter when they arrived in Sonoyta. They would need both vehicles when they rescued Joann. Harry drove with Esteban, and Jimmy was alone on the road with his thoughts: *What if the treasure is a curse causing bad things to happen? Was it his fault for not being more careful? It was his fault Joann was involved; would he have met her without the treasure?* The worry and guilt ate at his insides through the long drive to Sonoyta.

They arrived at the police chief's house at seven o'clock in the morning, the second day of Joann's kidnapping. Esteban introduced Harry and Jimmy, and Sanchez poured them each a cup of freshly made coffee. He and Esteban reminisced a few minutes about old times, and he said, "You didn't come all the way up here to gossip like old men. What can I do to help you?"

Esteban said, "My friend, I must ask you for your complete confidence in this matter. My granddaughter's life is at stake."

Sanchez sat forward. "Tell me. Anything for you and your family, Esteban!"

Esteban showed him the ransom note. "Jimmy and Harry have, in fact, come into some gold. Never mind how. We know how the kidnappers got their information about the gold and my granddaughter's marriage to Jimmy. We know who two of them are." He told him what they knew about the kidnappers and how they found out they were in Sonoyta.

The Chief said, "I believe I know the house where they may have her. We would have to be extremely careful to get your granddaughter out without harm. What do you propose?"

Esteban said, "I believe the best way would be to capture this *El Cuchillo*. The others would be easier to deal with without their leader. If we can watch the house, perhaps he will leave. Then, we could capture him at gunpoint."

"It is a dangerous plan, my friend. This man is vicious and ruthless. We suspect that he has killed several people he has robbed with a knife. He will not be an easy one to catch."

Jimmy said, "Harry and I have already had a run-in with him. He tried to rob us near Caborca after we collected some silver at the smelter. We beat him then, and we are not afraid of him."

Sanchez studied them carefully. "You are brave but lucky; this man doesn't make many mistakes. You must use extreme caution with this."

Jimmy looked the Chief in the eyes and said, "We don't have time to be cautious."

Sanchez said he had a trusted deputy he would have help. They needed to start watching the house quickly and outlined their plans. Esteban, Jimmy, and Harry left to have a look at the place where they were keeping Joann.

They parked the partners' truck at the police station and took Esteban's pickup to check out the house. Harry drove, and they went past the house at an average speed. They could see two cars parked in front and two men outside smoking. Neither of them was familiar. The two men watched them pass but didn't seem particularly concerned. Harry drove down the street a couple of blocks, turned off on another road, and parked. They waited for about ten minutes, then went back past the house again. No one was outside this time. Harry slowed so they could study the place in more detail.

The adobe house looked to be a basic square four-room "shotgun" style layout, with a living room and kitchen on one side and probably two bedrooms on the other side. They typically had the kitchen in the back, with a back door. The men agreed Joann would likely be in one of the bedrooms.

The house looked like all the other houses on the street, the only difference being brightly colored paint on a few of them. But it had been many years since this house had seen a paintbrush. The places were close together, which could afford some cover for an approach. The lots mainly were barren dirt with no fences and a few scattered mesquite and palo verde trees. There were other similar houses behind it, facing another street.

The police deputy set up a station to watch traffic. There was only one way in and out on the street the kidnappers' house faced. Jimmy and Harry would take turns relieving him in their vehicle so the surveillance wouldn't be too obvious.

Chief Sanchez said *El Cuchillo* was known to hang out in a *cantina* outside of town. He would most likely go there if he did show up. It might be the only opportunity to capture him away from the house.

Nothing happened all day. The wait was agonizing for the rescuers. There had only been a couple of cars with families coming and going. Jimmy was growing nervous and edgy. Surely the bandit would come out soon; he was too much of a braggart and show-off to stay cooped up in a tiny house.

A car came out of the street around sundown, with only the driver. Jimmy and Harry were watching and said at the same time, "That's him!" They watched him head out of town and followed at a discreet distance. He turned in at a rundown, decrepit *cantina* with neon signs in the windows advertising Tecate and Modelo *cerveza*. There were two other cars in the dirt parking lot.

They raced back to the Chief's house in town to alert the others, and they all went back to the *cantina. El Cuchillo's* car hadn't moved. The Chief pulled his car up close behind to block it. The sun had gone down, and the only light in the parking lot was the glow of the neon beer signs.

Harry looked through a filthy flyspecked window and could see *El Cuchillo* sitting at a table talking to another man. He was facing the door to avoid being caught off guard. Jimmy found the back door unlocked. They decided to come in from the front and back simultaneously: Jimmy and Harry through the back, the Chief and Esteban through the front.

They agreed on slamming a car door as a signal, and they would all rush the table with guns drawn. Esteban had his vicious-looking double-barreled 10-gauge shotgun, which was intimidating all by itself.

Esteban slammed the door on his truck, and they all rushed in. *El Cuchillo* saw the two men coming at him from the front. He started to rise and pull a gun from his waistband, but he didn't see the other two come from behind. The bartender yelled, "*Cuidado detras, Cuchillo*!" But the warning was too late, and Jimmy hit him in the back of the head with his heavy revolver. He went down in a heap; Harry grabbed his gun and fished the switchblade out of his pocket. The man he had been sitting with started to run out the door. The Chief stopped him and handcuffed him to a steel post. A thorough search of *El Cuchillo* yielded another knife in one boot and a double-barreled derringer pistol in the other. He started to come to, and they handcuffed him before hauling him out to the Chief's police car and locking him in the back.

Chief Sanchez called his deputy to come and take their prisoner back to the station and lock him up. *El Cuchillo* was still groggy and unsteady from Jimmy's blow to his head when they transferred him to the deputy's car. "Be very careful with this one, Jose," the Chief told his deputy. "He's mean and tricky. Take no chances with him."

The deputy said he understood and left with their prisoner locked in the back of his car. He watched *El Cuchillo* in his rearview mirror. "So, you finally got yourself caught! We will enjoy having you visit in our jail," he laughed. *El Cuchillo* glared back at him like a cougar trapped in a cage.

They arrived at the police station, and the deputy said, "Enjoy the car's seat. It's a lot more comfortable than the cot in your jail cell!" He laughed as he went inside to get the cell ready for his prisoner.

There were only two iron-barred holding cells in the small station. The town drunk currently occupied one, snoring comfortably. "I have some company for you, *amigo!*" the deputy laughed and went out to his car to fetch *El Cuchillo*.

He drew his revolver and opened the back door of his patrol car. He said, "Nice and easy now, *señor.* Stand up and face the building; make no quick moves. I'd like nothing better than to shoot you." He nudged his prisoner in the back with his revolver. *El Cuchillo* took a step, then, quick as a rattlesnake, spun on his heel, knocking the pistol out of the deputy's hand with his body. Then he head-butted him, knocking him to the ground. He kicked him in the head several times until there was no movement. *El Cuchillo* dropped to the pavement next to the inert deputy and fished in his pocket for the handcuff keys. He cursed, dropping them twice before he finally fumbled them into the cuff's lock. He stood up, gave the deputy another vicious kick, and jumped in the car. Smiling to himself, he roared off back to the house where Joann was held. He had the deputy's pistol and ammo belt along with a sawed-off 12-gauge pump-action shotgun in a holder beside the seat. He would soon put a stop to the gringo's rescue attempt.

***

The men crept up to the house and looked through cracks in the curtains. They saw three men playing cards at the kitchen

312

table. The kitchen and living area appeared to be one open space.

Jimmy looked through the front bedroom window and said, "There doesn't look to be any other kidnappers in the house. I'm guessing they have Joann in the back bedroom. Harry and I will go through the back. If you kick in the front door, we'll surprise them by coming in the back door. I'll find Joann and Harry can give covering fire from the back. I'll try to get her out when the gunfire stops."

"A good plan," the Chief said. "However, what if you find the back door locked? If you have to break it in, it will take away the surprise."

Harry said, "From the look of it, I doubt anyone locks their doors around here. It's a chance we'll have to take. We'll wait for a gunshot from the front, and go through the door, one way or another."

They took up their positions. Esteban held his shotgun at the ready, and if that wasn't enough, he had a .38 revolver tucked in his waistband. Chief Sanchez drew his pistol and whispered, "*Listo*, Esteban, my old friend? It's been many years since we had this much excitement. It makes me forget I am an old man!"

"*Sí*, Roberto. It brings back many memories. But remember, when the shooting starts, it only matters to get my granddaughter out safely."

They took up positions on either side of the front door. "*Listo?*" the Chief whispered. "*Listo!*" came the reply. The Chief stood back and kicked the door as hard as he could.

The men at the table were startled and jumped up. They knocked over the table and scattered cards and money across the floor. They grabbed for their weapons, but Esteban fired both

barrels of the shotgun. Two of the kidnappers went down. The other took cover behind the overturned table. He started firing wildly toward the front with his pistol.

Jimmy and Harry rushed in from the unlocked back door. Jimmy ran into the bedroom in the back to find Joann. Harry fired two shots at the kidnapper shooting from behind the table. One bullet hit him in the neck, and he collapsed with blood pulsing from the wound.

The shooting was over in seconds. All the kidnappers were down.

Jimmy rushed to Joann, removed her gag and blindfold, and untied her arms and legs. She threw her arms around his neck and buried her face on his chest, sobbing. Jimmy stroked her hair and said, "It's alright now, sweetheart—it's over! Are you hurt?" She shook her head no. She was weak and shaky as he led her out of the bedroom. He said, "Try not to look, Joann," as he walked her to the front door. There was blood everywhere around the table where the kidnappers had been shot. The men lay in tangled heaps on the floor. Esteban had been wounded in the leg by one of the kidnapper's wild shots. Harry tore up a sheet from a bedroom and put a tourniquet on his leg while the Chief went out to get his first aid kit.

A shot rang as Jimmy and Joann stepped out the front door. They froze. Jimmy saw the chief lying on the ground beside his car. The deputy's car was parked behind it. It was like a scene from a gangster movie in slow motion, but it was instantly clear to him what had happened. *El Cuchillo* had escaped!

Jimmy moved by blind instinct, roughly shoving Joann to the ground beside one of the other cars. A shotgun blast roared, and the pellets hit the front of the vehicle with a sound like a thousand hailstones hammering metal. A few of them hit him in the back as he dove behind the car with Joann.

"Hey, *gringo*!" It was a raspy voice Jimmy would recognize anywhere. *El Cuchillo* yelled, "How you like my lil' surprise, eh? What you do now, eh?" More gunshots, this time directed at the house. "You kill all my men, eh? Now I kill all you!"

Jimmy whispered, "Slide under this car, Joann, and don't come out for anything!" He crawled toward the back of the car; a bullet ricocheted off the trunk when he chanced a look. He saw the outlaw had a well-defended position between two parked cars. There was more exchange of gunfire with the house. *El Cuchillo* taunted, "Hey, you aim no better than baby girl! You shoot like old woman!"

Jimmy hoped Harry wouldn't waste his ammunition responding to the taunts. It would be nearly impossible to hit the outlaw in the dark in his position between the cars.

Jimmy hatched a risky plan— the only way he could think of to break the stalemate. He started a slow belly crawl under the car they were behind, made it to the next.

El Cuchillo hunkered down on the car's opposite side. "Hey, *gringo*!" he yelled. "I trade you that tender young wife you got for you gold! I can tell how sweet she is! What you say to that, eh, *gringo*?"

Jimmy had slipped under the car while the bandit was shouting taunts, and he could now see his boots on the other side. A couple of feet further, and he would have a shot. He could see the outlaw's feet shuffling around, no doubt trying to watch all sides at once.

"Where you at, *gringo*? The sun come up, I find you sure. Better take deal I make you!"

Jimmy slid closer while the man was shouting and took careful aim. He fired one shot, hitting *El Cuchillo* in the middle of his shin. The heavy magnum round shattered the bone; *El Cuchillo* screamed and started firing wildly under the car. As soon as he fired, Jimmy rolled out, and the outlaw's bullets ricocheted harmlessly under the vehicle.

He moved quickly to the back of the car as the outlaw stumbled to turn around and began to raise the shotgun toward him. Jimmy aimed his revolver at the center of the outlaw's body and fired the pistol's five remaining rounds. He kept pulling the trigger when the cylinder was empty. The click and snap of the revolver's mechanism and hammer echoed in the dark, eerie silence. *El Cuchillo* lay in a spreading pool of blood between the cars. Jimmy approached cautiously and grabbed the shotgun to cover him, just in case he was still alive.

"Come on out, Harry. I got him," Jimmy called. He was shaking uncontrollably. The oil and gasoline from the undersides of the cars smeared his clothes and gave off an eye-watering odor. Barely able to speak, he helped Joann out from under the vehicle where she hid. "You're safe now, sweetheart. Are you okay?" She shook her head, yes, and he helped her lie down on the car's front seat. He found Chief Sanchez lying dead beside his patrol car. There was a single bullet hole in his forehead.

Harry said, "We have to get my grandfather to a hospital. They wounded him in the leg, and I don't know how much longer I can control the bleeding." They went inside to get him, and Esteban said, "There is no hospital here. But there is a doctor. Try to find out where he is."

Some people had come out of their houses when the gunfire stopped. Harry ran up to the closest woman and asked her in Spanish where he could find a doctor. She gave him instructions, and they hurried to get Esteban to him.

The doctor removed the slug from Esteban's wound and bandaged it up. He said he should be okay but to check with his doctor back in Caborca. Next, he examined Joann and said she was in shock. He gave her some pills to help her relax and said she would be okay.

The deputy was still alive. He lay in front of the police station with a small pool of blood slowly spreading from his scalp wounds. They got him to the doctor, who bandaged his head and put him on a cot in his office. The doctor said he thought he would be okay, too.

They roused the other town deputy, who was not on duty, and had him meet them back at the house. About a dozen bystanders gathered around, all asking questions at the same time. The deputy moved them back. He was speechless at the scene before him.

His Chief lay dead at his feet, *El Cuchillo* lay lifeless close by, and there were three more bodies in the house. He had never expected to deal with a catastrophe like this in his quiet town.

One of the kidnappers in the house was still alive. Esteban's shotgun blast had done terrible damage to his stomach area, but he had not taken the full blast directly. It had not been so kind to the other man. He had died almost instantly from the barrage of pellets.

The town doctor was also the coroner. He showed up to take care of the wounded man and begin the other bodies' formal processing. He shook his head and said he had only seen something worse during the revolution so many years ago.

***

Jimmy left with Joann as the sun was coming up. She lay with her head on his lap and slept most of the way back to Ajo. Harry and Esteban went back to Caborca.

Joann's parents rushed out when they pulled up in their driveway. Her mother, sobbing and her eyes bloodshot from lack of sleep, showed the strain on her face; the stress aged her beyond her years. John and Jimmy each took one of Joann's arms and helped her into the house.

Joann lay on the couch and smiled at Jimmy. "I don't know how you found me. I thought I was going to die."

"It's a pretty long story," Jimmy said. "Maybe you should wait until you are more rested."

"Tell me now. I need to know. What you and Harry and Grandfather Esteban did was a miracle."

"Harry and I could tell from the ransom note that the kidnappers had inside information. The only place it could have come from was the bank. It didn't take long to figure out who it was. Harry and I persuaded him to tell us who his contact was."

"Persuaded?"

"Let's say we gave him strong encouragement. From there, the rest of it was all your grandfather. Once we had a name, he used his connections to figure out you were in Sonoyta. He is an amazing and brave man." Jimmy paused and said," What matters now is that you are safe. I don't know what I would've done if anything happened to you."

"You saved my life, Jimmy. *El Cuchillo* would have killed me— after he had some fun with me. I don't think I would have survived another night. Thank God he is dead."

Jimmy said, "A good man died to save you, too. We could not have done it without help from the police chief. He was another one of your grandfather's old revolution buddies. The rest of the dead were scumbags and deserved what they got."

"*El Cuchillo* acted as if he knew you, Jimmy. How can that be?" Joann asked.

"He and his gang were the ones who tried to rob Harry and me at the smelter a few weeks ago. I think he wanted revenge as much as money because we embarrassed him in front of his men."

Joann smiled at him and drifted back into sleep.

Harry made his grandfather comfortable back at the *hacienda* and returned to Ajo when he was sure he would be alright. A week later, when all the excitement had died down, he and Jimmy loaded up the rented dump truck and left for the border. They used the same strategy as before, with Harry in the lead to deal with the border guards. They arrived at the smelter without incident.

Jimmy noticed a face he had not seen before as the smelter workers were preparing to offload the truck. He looked vaguely familiar to him, but Jimmy couldn't quite put his finger on the connection. He thought no more about it and went on with dumping the ore into the smelter's receiving area.

He stood at the front of the truck with the door open, operating the controls for dumping its load. He heard the last of it go out with a hissing and rattling sound and dropped the dump bin back into place. That done, he had one foot on the truck's running board and was preparing to enter the cab and leave when a strong arm grabbed him around the chest. He felt the cold, sharp blade of a knife at his throat.

"I know who you are, *gringo*," the man rasped in Jimmy's ear. "Now, you will know who I am before you die!" Jimmy's foot on the running board kept him too off-balance to try breaking away.

The knife pressed harder against Jimmy's throat. He began to feel a warm trickle of blood oozing down his chest. There was little time to act before the blade would bite deeper. It would likely sever an artery, and he would quickly bleed to death.

"You remember the man you shoot all those bullets into in Sonoyta, *Señor*? Sure, you do. That man was my brother, *El Cuchillo*. He was only family I have left, and you take him away. Now you will pay with your life!"

Jimmy took a deep breath, braced his foot against the truck's running board, and shoved as hard as he could. The sudden motion threw both men off-balance, and they fell to the ground. Jimmy rolled away and jumped up. His attacker was on his feet quick as a cat and came at him with a vicious stabbing thrust. Jimmy was able to step back and out of the way of the lunge, but his attacker immediately came at him again.

Harry wondered why it was taking so long with the dump truck. He had been at the office talking with the owner and walked up behind the truck, looking for Jimmy. Then he noticed two of the workers standing off a way, staring toward the front of the dump truck with their mouths hanging open, a look of shock on their faces. Harry sensed something was wrong and slowly looked around the dump bin's corner. He saw a large man thrusting a nasty-looking knife at Jimmy as he was trying to spin away. The whole scene seemed to play out in slow motion in Harry's vision.

He instinctively grabbed the .38 Smith and Wesson from his waistband. Stepping out from behind the truck and into a shooter's stance, he pointed the gun at Jimmy's attacker's left chest. He carefully squeezed the trigger and shot him through the heart. Then he fired three more rapid shots at the center of the attacker's chest. A look of confusion creased the assailant's features as if that couldn't be happening to him. Then he collapsed in a heap on the ground.

Jimmy had barely sidestepped the attacker's lunge. The man pivoted for another attack but stopped dead in his tracks—a spreading blossom of blood had appeared on his chest. Jimmy was confused, too; he hadn't even heard the first shot. But he heard the three shots that followed. His assailant staggered several steps backward, then collapsed on the ground.

For an instant, no one moved. The only sound was the insistent slapping of the smelter's conveyor belt.

Harry ran up and grabbed Jimmy, holding him in a long hug, checking him for wounds. All he found was a bleeding but shallow gash across his throat. One of the workers ran to the office to get the owner. Arredondo came rushing to the scene carrying a first aid kit, a look of shock and disbelief on his face.

"*Amigos, amigos*! What has happened? Why did this man attack you?

Jimmy said, "He was *El Cuchillo's* brother. He wanted revenge on me for killing him."

"I am so sorry!" Arredondo exclaimed. "I had no idea. I had to replace the man who had been a problem before. I made a huge mistake! I had never seen this man until he came asking for a job a few days ago. I took him on, and he seemed like a good worker." He stood and wrung his hands. "I don't know how I can ever make up for my mistake. I am only glad you are alive, *Señor* Baker!"

They put a bandage on Jimmy's wound while waiting for the police chief to arrive. "It seems trouble follows you around, *Señors*!" Chief Gomez said.

Harry told him what his father had said—that trouble has a way of finding you in Mexico.

The Chief chuckled. "Your father is a very wise man. But, *Señor* Baker, you are fortunate to be alive. This man had an evil reputation—he was a wanted outlaw in Chihuahua for years, known to have murdered several people."

The police chief looked at Arredondo and said, "Humberto, maybe you check with me next time before you hire somebody you know nothing about, eh?" Arredondo looked at his feet and nodded.

The Chief said he didn't need them for anything else since several witnesses saw what happened. He told Harry he had done another service for their community.

***

The partners headed to Harry's grandfather's hacienda. Jimmy was exhausted. Dirt covered his clothes, his shirt was bloody, and he was visibly shaken.

Esteban met them at the door. He took a look at Jimmy and exclaimed, "My sons! What has happened? Jimmy, are you injured? What happened?" He called his wife to help clean him up and redress the shallow wound on his neck. Jimmy went to change clothes and bathe, then rested until Harry called him for dinner.

Harry had explained it all to his disbelieving grandparents. Esteban said he hoped it was finally over. "I thank the saints you are both safe. But, in my life, I have found that money has a way of attracting trouble. And we can never know what form it might take—or where it might strike."

They had a quiet dinner, and Esteban motioned Harry and Jimmy to follow him to his study. He poured each a glass of his fine tequila and trimmed up a Cuban cigar for each of them. They sat quietly for a few minutes, enjoying the warmth of the tequila spreading through their bodies. The smoke added to the calming and relaxation of the drinks. Jimmy could feel the stress of his close brush with death finally starting to ebb.

Esteban said, "Jimmy, you are now one of my family. I think of you as my own blood, and I will treat you as I treat Harry. You

and Harry are the future of my family." He looked at each man in turn and said, "I need to tell you both some important things which will affect your futures."

He poured them each another three fingers of the smooth but fiery tequila and continued, "I have lived a long and good life. Through great good fortune, I have become a wealthy man. It has long been my plan to pass on that good fortune to my grandchildren before I die. Jimmy, this is why I gave the ranch to you and Joann. I knew you wanted to become a rancher. I have no further use for mine."

He paused, savoring his fine cigar, his gaze drifting out the window for a moment, then he brought his focus back to the room. "Harry, when you marry, I will give you this hacienda and the lands that go with it. I hope you will make it your home."

He sipped the tequila and studied both men through the light haze of cigar smoke in the room. "I will transfer the land in Harry's and Joann's names because they are both natural-born citizens of Mexico. Jimmy, this will save you many headaches with paperwork and Mexican laws governing land ownership. It will also save you a lot of money on taxes. Of course, you can change it in the future if you wish, but I would advise you to keep both names on any formal documents."

Jimmy and Harry looked from Esteban to each other, too overwhelmed to say anything.

Esteban continued, "Neither of you has experience in farming or ranching, but I have good people to help you learn. I will be here as long as I can to guide you. I hope you both have many children and raise them on these lands I have worked to keep for you."

Jimmy found his voice and said, "Grandfather, thank you. This gift is beyond any of my dreams. I will do my best to live up to your confidence in me. I can't wait to see the ranch.

Harry said, "Abuelo, I had never dreamed of anything like this, either. I don't know what to say."

Esteban chuckled and said, "Perhaps you should move your romance along with that beautiful daughter of Pablo's. I am not getting younger, and I want many great-grandchildren while I can enjoy them!"

Harry blushed brightly and grinned. "I'll do my best, Abuelo!"

***

Harry and *Angélica* married in the Catholic church in Caborca in December. Her father said if he was going to pay for it, he wanted it there so friends and family could attend. Harry hadn't minded. Besides his parents and aunt and uncle, there was no one else in Ajo he felt strongly about being there

Jimmy was the best man, looking as uncomfortable as Harry in the rented tuxedoes *Angélica's* mother insisted they wear. Jimmy wondered why women were so taken with tuxedoes; they seemed a terrible waste of good fabric.

There was a grand reception that night. *Angélica* was dazzling in a brilliant white wedding gown with a long train, and Harry rightly figured nobody would be looking at him with her beside him. The following day the couple headed to Mazatlán for a week-long honeymoon. They would be moving into the main *hacienda* house Harry's grandparents had given them. Esteban and Yolanda moved into a smaller guest house on the property.

***

Jimmy and Joann moved to the ranch and started their new life together. Jimmy learned to handle a horse, rope, brand calves, turn a bull into a steer, and all the other chores required to operate the ranch. He no longer needed the gentlest pony in their remuda.

He made a special trip back to Caborca after he and Harry had both settled into their new lives. The partners had tequila and cigars in Esteban's old den.

Jimmy sipped the tequila and said, "I have a proposal concerning our remaining gold." Harry waited expectantly, and he continued, "Let's divide it equally. That way, we will have it if either of us needs it in the future."

"I've thought about that, too, Jimmy. With the mining income, my farm, and your ranch, we don't have any pressing need to cash it in."

"That's right. Here's my suggestion—keep it in a safe place, and never use it unless you have an emergency. That's what I plan on doing, anyway. Gold holds its value better than any paper money. And it's great insurance for the future. Maybe it's something we can leave our children, assuming we both have some," Jimmy said with a mischievous grin.

They brought the remaining gold up from the hacienda's basement hiding place and spread it out on the desk in the den. Their nearly unbelievable good fortune never ceased to amaze them. They sat in silence for a few minutes, reflecting on how they had come by such wealth. Finally, Jimmy said, "I could never have imagined anything like this when I left Denver: riches beyond belief, a great friend for life, a beautiful wife, a ranch. Sometimes I have to pinch myself to realize it's not a dream. None of it would have happened without you, my friend."

"I feel the same way, Jimmy. We made it happen for each other. We can thank the CCC and that dirty ol' cave for showin' us the way." He tossed back the rest of his tequila and said,

"Let's get this done"

The court sentenced Emilio Lopez to life in prison for his part in Joann's kidnapping; his pleas for innocence overwhelmed by the evidence against him. But most people believed his father's influence would likely shorten his time behind bars. Jimmy and Harry were reluctant local heroes and were relieved when the commotion died down. Esteban recovered from the gunshot wound in his leg but would always walk with a slight limp.

***

The mine proved successful beyond anyone's dreams. Harry's dad became the general manager, freeing Harry and Jimmy to pursue their new farm and ranch businesses. The LLC Jimmy had wisely set up served everyone well. Harry's father and Uncle Fred no longer worked for the Phelps Dodge Company. They both built homes outside of town and moved out of the company-owned housing.

***

Jimmy and Harry cashed in some of their gold to set up a charitable foundation in Tucson to help people in need of food and shelter. They had their attorney design it to conceal their names and select a board of directors from the community. The charity attracted donations from many businesses and wealthy people, eventually helping hundreds of people trying to recover from the hardships of the Great Depression and beyond. The partners preferred to remain anonymous.

***

Jimmy's sister, Sarah, lost her battle with polio. Jimmy was devastated by the news and couldn't help feeling that he should have done more for her. Joann reminded him that his financial help had given her a few months more of life, and there was nothing else he could have done for her. His brother Michael joined the Army during the war, and his mother had no reason to remain in Denver. Jimmy invited her to live with them on the ranch, and she readily accepted. She was a great help with the children.

***

The years passed quickly. The Great Depression gave way to World War II, Japan and Germany surrendered, and finally, life seemed normal again. Jimmy had become a naturalized Mexican citizen, learned to speak Spanish, and made the ranch even more successful with the help of Esteban's long-time foreman. Joann bore them two sons and a daughter.

***

Jimmy took his family on a long-planned trip to Tucson. The children had been to Douglas, Arizona, a few times, but this would be the first time they and his mother had been to Tucson. It was a much larger city, filling the children with wonder at the big city sights.

332

On their first night, Jimmy and Joann left their children in their grandmother's care at the hotel. They met Harry and *Angélica* at the Starlight Bar and Grill; Harry's dream come true. He bought a restaurant that had gone out of business, completely remodeled it, and hired his cousin Bill to manage it for him. It was one of the nicest places in town. It had posh red leather booths, a large dance floor, a bandstand, and a menu that featured fresh seafood brought in on ice daily from Puerto Peñasco, Mexico.

Harry spent time there whenever he came to town on business. He told Jimmy it didn't make much money, but it made him feel good to have a bar of his own. The couples enjoyed a fun night dancing, catching up on all their adventures, and comparing notes on their children. Harry and *Angélica* had two daughters, and Harry said he hoped a son would soon join them; *Angélica* was four months along.

Jimmy's main goal for the trip was to revisit the cave. He had not been back there since his time with the CCC. He wanted his children and his mother to see what he was talking about when he told them stories of his time there. They stayed at the Westward Look Resort on Tucson's northwest side, a place frequented by movie stars like John Wayne and other famous people. The children were much more excited by the large swimming pool than the prospect of seeing some famous person.

They relaxed at the hotel and toured around the city for a couple of days. Then, one evening Jimmy took them to the train depot to see the Sunset Limited arrive. They were excited to see a train up close and impressed he had ridden it to Tucson all those years ago.

The children were anxious to see the cave where their father had worked. Jimmy told them more stories about his time there while they drove out of Tucson to the cave. Steps from the parking area led down to a visitor's center with a store in the old headquarters building and a small café next door. A sign said, "Welcome To Colossal Cave Park."

They stopped at an overlook outside the store's entry. Jimmy pointed out the ranch headquarters down the valley where the camp had been. It was as if a giant hand had reached out and erased all the tents from the landscape, but the scene was vivid in Jimmy's memory. They admired the *Posta Quemada* Creek valley and the distant silhouette of the *Santa Rita* mountains in the distance to the south. Jimmy said he never tired of the view when he came out of the cave.

A metal gate barred the cave's entrance. "Is it closed, dad?" his oldest son asked. "Will they let us in?" Jimmy explained they would have to join a tour group to guide them through it. "Couldn't you do that, Dad?" his son persisted.

"I could, but it's not how they do it here now." He led them inside the store and through the displays of souvenirs and postcards.

"Jimmy! Jimmy! Is that you?" a voice behind the counter called as soon as he entered the building. "Hell's sakes! It is! I ain't seen you in years!" The voice belonged to the old man Jimmy knew as "One-eyed Charlie." He hadn't changed much, looked as bedraggled as when Jimmy had last seen him.

"Hey, Charlie! What are you doing here? You were slinging hash in a mess tent last time I saw you."

"I manage this place now. They couldn't find anyone else to do it, so I volunteered," Charlie said with a wink. "Is that your family?"

Jimmy introduced him to his wife, children, and mother. He told them Charlie had been a good friend when he worked here.

"Jimmy was the best," Charlie said to the family. "We hated to see him leave here when his time was done. Whatever happened to your buddy Harry?"

Jimmy gave his old friend a brief history of what he and Harry had done.

"So you boys did have a mine! Scuttlebutt floated around here for years that you guys were coverin' up for something else. Like lost gold, for example. Wouldn't know anything about that, would you?" he said with a raspy laugh.

"Charlie, far as I know, people are still looking for treasure in that black hole. Harry and I simply got lucky with our business venture. Sell me some tickets so my family and I can join the tour."

Joann smiled at how smoothly Jimmy had evaded the question about the treasure.

"I ain't sellin' you nothin'," Charlie said," but I'll arrange a special tour for you and your family. Hang on a few minutes."

A pretty young girl found them in about 10 minutes and said she would be their guide in the cave. She opened the gate and motioned them in.

Jimmy tuned out the girl's voice and was almost overwhelmed by his memories when he stepped into the cave mouth's twilight darkness: The pungent odor of bat guano, the leathery fluttering of hundreds of bats' wings, his chill from coming out of desert heat into the 70-degree coolness of the cave, and the mysterious but alluring sense of complete darkness ahead. It all felt very real to him. He could hear the gruff but kindly voice of Big Al on his first day on the job and feel his first fright by coatimundis scurrying past his feet in the darkness. Finally, in his mind's eye, he saw himself nearly falling into a rock wall illusion and finding the secret behind it.

Their guide told them to follow along, and Joann nudged his arm to jolt him out of his reverie. The lights were pretty much as they were when he helped install them and explained his role in laying them out. The guide had not been told of Jimmy's work there and was embarrassed about being so elementary in her cave description. Jimmy said she was doing great, and he wanted his family to learn all about it.

They moved on, following the path, occasionally stopping for their guide to point out one of the many unusual features. They passed through the "Crystal Forest" before coming to the 'Drapery Room." Jimmy told them how he had been the first of the workers to see it and how he told the others it looked like a room in a fancy home filled with drapes. The Park shortened the name, and the Drapery Room became the official designation of the unusual formations.

Their guide told the story of the train robbers and how they supposedly hid out in the cave. The children's eyes widened when she recounted the legend of how they had hidden their treasure somewhere in the cave, never to be found.

"Wow, Dad!" Jimmy's youngest son said. "Did you see any robbers?"

Jimmy laughed and said they were long gone before he got there.

"Did you see any of that gold and stuff they stole from the trains?"

"Well, son, this cave had been searched from one end to the

other by many men looking for that treasure before I got here. I've never heard of any of them finding it." Joann smiled to herself again at Jimmy's careful circumvention of the truth.

"Maybe we'll find it today! I'm gonna look real hard!"

Jimmy and the guide laughed. "You do that, son. But don't get too close to the drops and crevices. Pay attention to what our guide tells us."

They came to a passage with solid rock walls on either side before some steps that led up a level. Jimmy took Joann by the arm and told the guide and family he would follow shortly. He led her to a spot that looked like the rest of the wall, but, to her amazement, he seemed to step into the solid rock. She followed him in, and with the beam of a flashlight he had borrowed, Jimmy showed her where he had found the bags of gold and silver from Wells Fargo. He moved a few rocks from a pile and was surprised to find tattered fragments of the old bags used in the robbery.

Joann was speechless. It was one thing to hear Jimmy tell of finding the treasure; the reality of seeing its hiding place was almost overwhelming. Jimmy showed her the bag's remains, and she shook her head in disbelief. He carefully replaced the stones, concealing any trace of the old mailbags.

They went on and joined the others. The kids wanted to know where they had been, and Jimmy said he had only wanted to give their mother a kiss in the cave. They made retching sounds and asked no more about it. However, he didn't so easily fool their guide or Jimmy's mother. He knew he would face many questions later from his mother. The guide looked at Jimmy with an appraising eye but said nothing.

As they continued, Jimmy asked the guide about the second entrance. "Oh, we don't take groups there. It hasn't been made safe; we're afraid someone would be hurt." She went on to talk about how important it was for ventilation in the cave. Jimmy told her he had been in and out of it many times during his work there. She again looked at him appraisingly, silently questioning why he would have done that. Jimmy changed the subject to talk about bats and coatimundis, which generated a barrage of questions from his children and kept the guide occupied.

They went on, occasionally stopping for their guide to point out significant features. Finally, the tour's circle ended at a steep rise with steps. The light from the cave's opening shined like an inviting lantern at the top. When they came out, Jimmy pointed out the spot a rattlesnake had nearly bitten him; it would have if not for their uncle Harry. The children's eyes got wide, and they gave every bush a wide berth after that. Jimmy thanked their guide and gave her a large tip.

Before they left, Jimmy went back to the store to say goodbye to Ol' Charlie. They chatted a few minutes about old times, and Charlie said again how good it was to see him doing well.

Jimmy said, "I see the old rumors about hidden treasure are alive and well in the stories the guide tells. Of course, you wouldn't have anything to do with that, would you, Charlie?"

Charlie laughed. "I only tell stories that people want to hear. I don't tell 'em about the mountain lion killing one of our men, or the man who drowned in a summer flood, or about the man who tried to kill you because he thought you had the treasure. Better to let folks just go away thinking they might find that robbers' loot themselves someday."

Jimmy drove the family down the valley to the *Posta Quemada* Ranch headquarters, which had become part of the county park. They crossed the beautiful little creek, its stream running enough to nourish the cottonwoods and sycamores along its banks. They walked around with Jimmy pointing out where the camp's tents had been and the features of the ranch's headquarters. When he told them about the antics of Payday, the camp's pet dog, the children immediately set up a chorus of wanting a dog just like that. Jimmy laughed, winked at Joann, and said, "We'll see."

They stopped at the old ranch house. Jimmy told them how he and Harry had started a rumor that sent Reuben and his buddies on a wild goose chase, digging up the grounds around the area, looking for clues to the treasure's hiding place. They had a good laugh. But Jimmy didn't tell them about Reuben's knife attack on him later, his close brush with death, or Reuben's horrible fate in jail.

They ate a picnic lunch packed by the hotel. The tent encampment was gone with no trace. Then, Jimmy explained what it was like living there. His younger son thought it would have been great fun to live in a tent. Jimmy laughed and told him occasionally it was, but other times not so much in the heat of summer or a winter blizzard.

They headed back up the road leading out of the valley. Jimmy stopped for a last look up at the buildings on the rugged and rocky hillside in front of them that held the cave's entrance. The stone buildings his CCC coworkers had built were lasting monuments to the hard work it took to construct them and develop the cave as it now was. The tall saguaros looked on in silence.

He silently gave thanks for the good fortune and friends he had found there and marveled at how it had shaped his life. The Great Depression had brought him here, and despite the hardships so many had suffered, it had been a godsend for him.

He loaded up his family and drove back toward Tucson. His children, finally exhausted and out of questions, slept and dreamed dreams of lost treasure.

##

AUTHOR'S NOTES

This is a work of historical fiction. Except as noted here, any resemblance or connection to other persons living or dead is purely coincidental.

Geographic settings and features are accurate as much as possible, with the exception of the old Spanish silver mine; it is a composite of several old mines in various locations. Esteban's hacienda, farm, and ranch in Mexico are all fictional but appropriate to the described areas.

Pancho Villa was rumored to have briefly invaded a bar near the border in Douglas, Arizona, during a siege across the border in the town of Agua Prieta. The rumor is popular but unsubstantiated.

The robberies of the Southern Pacific's Sunset Express are as described in historical accounts. The robbers identified by name, posse members identified by name, the robbers' use of the cave as a hideout, and Kid Smith's death in an attempted third robbery are part of the historical record.

The cave has a long history of treasure seekers looking for the robbers' loot. To date, there is no evidence any has been found. The historical estimates of the actual value of Wells Fargo's losses in the robberies vary widely; the company has never provided an accurate accounting of it. My descriptions of the amount of stolen Wells Fargo property, where it was hidden, and its discovery are all fiction.

Descriptions of the Civilian Conservation Corps training at Ft, Huachuca, the work camp near Tucson, and its operations at the cave are generally accurate. Captain Yoder and Lieutenant Godwin were the actual military personnel in charge of the camp. Payday was, in fact, the name of the camp's pet dog,

Many conditions during the Great Depression of the 1930s were as described. President Franklin Roosevelt imposed restrictions on American citizens holding gold in 1933 to stop the drain on the nation's gold reserves. President Gerald Ford rescinded them in 1974.

I have used occasional common Spanish words to add color in dialogue with Spanish-speaking people along the border and in Mexico. For ease of reading, I have kept most of the conversations in English. *La Mordida*, 'the bite," or bribe, was and still is a way of life in Mexico.

Colossal Cave County Park is now a major regional attraction near Tucson. A typical CCC worker's statue stands in front of the gift shop, overlooking the valley where the work camp had been. The *Posta Quemada* ranch and buildings are now part of the park; the ranch house is a museum.

Tucson, Arizona

July, 2021

9 781737 402923